DEDICATION

This novel is dedicated to

my great-great-great grandfather, Wyllys Hill,

and those like him, who brought the plough

to Nebraska Territory and transformed the wild prairies

and rolling hills into the farms that now

supply much of the world with its daily bread.

ACKNOWLEDGMENTS

I thank my wife, Sylvie Shires, for her enthusiastic support and for reading through my final draft and making thoughtful suggestions to improve the manuscript. I also extend my gratitude to my granddaughter, Kaliantha Shires, for meticulously reading through the rough draft and identifying unclear passages and grammatical mishaps.

This book is a work of fiction. Names, characters, places, and incidents are the product of the author's imagination or are used fictitiously. Any resemblance to actual events, locales, or persons, living or dead, is coincidental.

SAVED BY THE BULLET

NEBRASKA MYSTERY SERIES

PRESTON SHIRES

Copyright 2019, Preston Shires. All Rights Reserved

Cover designed by Julius Broqueza

www.prestonshires.com

"
Having the last word is one of the tokens of victory.
"

Catharine Maria Sedgwick
Hope Leslie

Chapter 1

Summer of 1857

eing on the receiving end of a bullet makes one think about a lot of things. About the brevity of life for one, but that's just a thought in passing. Thinking about who sent the bullet, that's a more enduring one. I pondered this well and came up with a solution that has not humored everyone.

For you to understand my conclusion, of course, I must begin at the beginning, shortly after I found my heart entwined in the embrace of Mr. Cameron Davenport, my beau. Although he's not tall, dark, and handsome, he is tall enough, fair in hair and eye, and increasingly handsome.

His profession is known to few, but assuming my future grandchildren to be my readers, I doubt that it produce much harm to announce it in these pages. He is an engineer of sorts, working on a railroad that moves sable passengers from the deep South northward, up into the free air of Canada.

I understood that if his employ became known to others, it

would mean danger not only for him but for his loved ones as well. And he professed his devotion to me as unsurpassed; so, I sensed my life would not be without peril.

The adventure that led to the bullet began innocently enough, out on the porch of the Nebraska House, the nearest thing we, in the nascent frontier town of Brownville, have that resembles a hotel. It was the seventeenth of June, a warm and pleasant Wednesday, and I sat there, alternately enjoying the flow of the wide and muddy Missouri, with its steady current transporting the occasional tree trunk, and the story of Hope Leslie in my lap—she's a fictional character of Puritan pedigree whose sister weds among the Indians. Fiction the story may be to others, but for me, whose Aunt Adeline, my namesake who shares my red flowing tresses, lives no doubt beyond the pale of civilization as an honored squaw, it is relevant, and therefore full of truth. She was kidnapped in her youth, and I dedicate myself, when time allows, to discovering my Aunt Adeline's whereabouts, and I feel that out here in Nebraska Territory, I draw closer and closer to her.

But then, as I had sunk back into the tale of Hope Leslie, there arose a whinny that startled me and caused me to lift my eyes toward the street before the wharf. Little Dermot Brightly, who couldn't have been more than a year over ten, led a pony toward Main Street. The druggist, a Mr. Thomas Whitt, who fancied the little boy's elder sister, but not elder by many years in my estimation, stopped him and enquired about the horse.

"Oh, he ain't mine, sir," Dermot explained. "He don't belong to nobody. He be estrayed."

The conversation grabbed my attention, which made me

study the horse in some detail. It was a strawberry roan, with a star on its forehead, and a roached mane. I guessed it to be younger than the boy by about three years. Little did I know at the time that this pony would help me unravel the mystery surrounding my would-be assassin. And how could I have known? The attempt on my life had not yet been essayed.

"How'd you come about to have him?" asked Mr. Whitt.

"Sheriff Coleman gave him to me to take up to the livery stable. He's gonna hold him there 'till the owner shows up to claim him."

As I was in earshot, I called out to Mr. Whitt. "Well that's mighty nice of the Sheriff to offer his livery stable to keep the lost soul."

"Isn't it, though," said Mr. Whitt as he quickly abandoned the boy and stepped in my direction.

"Of course, the Sheriff will have to charge boarding fees if the owner wish to reclaim his animal."

"Nothing gets past you, does it, Miss Furlough?" he asked rhetorically upon reaching the porch and doffing his hat.

"Or close to me, I would hope."

"Not with that beau of yours keeping you from enjoying your youth and fine looks."

I really could not stomach the druggist's manners; they were as distasteful as his medicines. So, I suggested, as I noted the pony yanking back on the rope attached to the halter, he help the boy out lest the horse become the leader of the pair.

"Oh, Dermot can handle a pony, Miss. I was wondering...."

I cut his wonderings by saying, "I suppose he'll manage, especially with his sister coming down the street to help."

At this pronouncement, our town druggist turned sharply in the direction of the pony. "I reckon I oughta lend a hand," he said stiffly, as if his mind were disconnected from his vocal cords, "that little pony's got a will of its own." And with that said, he jaunted off to the rescue.

I concluded Mr. Whitt's own willpower was very weak when confronted with a feminine presence. It is one of the duties of womanhood to rebuff male weaknesses and educate men that they might live useful and purposeful lives. It does seem, does it not, that too few women take their God-given role seriously enough.

As journalist, editor, and owner of a promising newspaper, the *Brownville Beacon*, I felt I had a platform from which I could harangue the masses and create a polite order out of a frontier chaos.

Imagining my well-written prose for my upcoming first edition, I espied on the wharf Sammy and his crew unloading cargo from the *Alonzo Child*. The items that caught my eye were a red-cushioned side chair and a sizeable and well-sculpted side table, perhaps of cherrywood. These seemed to be necessary articles of business for a female editor.

From the corner of my eye I caught the approach of a familiar face, my brother Teddy, whose practical nature is balanced out by a tendency to take cross cuts, usually inspired by a desire to finish a job before it starts: What some people might refer to as laziness. But as he is generally my only resource, I depend on him, and under my guiding spirit, I do believe he progresses in the right direction.

He noticed what attracted my attention, and his hazel eyes

fell on me as he said, "You've got your mind on furniture, Sis."

"I can't imagine writing my stories on anything less becoming than a side table like that one."

"You'll have to be quick, then," he said running his fingers through his curly hair, which never did decide to be either quite red or quite brown. "Those things are headed up to Mr. Muir's abode. Should be safe there, seeing how he's now in the business of selling fire insurance."

"Is he now? I thought he ran the Nebraska Settlement Company."

"Well, nearly everybody who's anybody is a shareholder in the Nebraska Settlement Company. That doesn't keep Mr. Furnas from being the editor of the *Nebraska Advertiser*, or Reverend Wood from being a doctor of both body and soul."

My friend, Katherine Sturwell, or Kitty, who does up rooms and minds meals at the Nebraska House, and who stayed with me at my house until the hotel offered her a small room free of charge, came out on the porch to greet Teddy.

Kitty is one of those rare beauties whose dark hair and eyes, that might make a stolid woman appear severe, are sharpened into gaiety by her natural vivacity. Imagine the true and faithful Athena filled with the joy of a playful Greek nymph. Kitty and Teddy are very dear friends, but each has another's heartbeat. Teddy is partial to Mary Turner, the milliner, and Kitty to Mr. Stewart Winslow, entrepreneur.

"What exactly does the Nebraska Settlement Company do?" asked Kitty, unconsciously twirling a loose strand of her brunette hair around her index.

"They invent towns," I informed her, "and then charge

people to live in them."

Teddy looked at Kitty with one of those soft smiles that betrays a thought. I knew what amused him. How could Kitty be so pretty on the one hand, with her brunette hair highlighted against her ivory skin and her beaming dark eyes, and so clueless on the other. It wasn't a mocking smile, because Kitty was not dull witted. Rather she just didn't pay attention to the things that interested her least and wasn't afraid to admit her ignorance.

"You do know that Stewart hopes to buy shares in the company," Teddy finally said.

"I suppose so, he does so like owning land."

"Yes," I agreed, "but only until another man comes along who likes owning land twice as much and is willing to pay the difference."

Kitty gave me a knowing look. She knew she had perhaps the best catch along the banks of the Missouri. Stewart was a proper man. No need for an etiquette book to train him. Like some of the clothing you now find in stores, he came ready-made.

Speaking of Stewart Winslow sufficed to bring out the man in person. He appeared in the doorway and acknowledged me with a kindly nod. "Miss Sturwell has finished her duties, I understand." He came beside her and she slipped her arm under his elbow. "Why don't we all retire to my . . . " he paused. "I would say home, but I don't know if my little cabin qualifies as such, and not just because it is deficient in pillars and lawn, but because it lacks a mistress as of yet." He said this with a kind and suffused gaze that he bestowed upon his beloved.

Mr. Winslow's cabin was a temporary structure put together last week. Behind it, he was leveling out the lot and hoped to have a regular house standing tall by fall. No one wants to face a Nebraska winter in a windswept cabin.

The anticipated marriage would take place back in Saint Louis in mid-August, both hailed from the city, but the couple insisted on making their home on the frontier, where profits are as great as the risks.

We all made it up to Stewart's cabin and settled down around a lone table, and as Kitty discovered there were coals yet alive in the stove in the summer kitchen, an enclosed back porch to be more precise, she offered to boil up some coffee.

Stewart began our conversation. "So, when is the debut for your newspaper, Miss Furlough?"

"Soon, maybe in a week or two. As you know, my original idea was to have a story about Mr. Davenport's doings, but I've dropped that notion."

"I don't doubt it, seeing that you two seem to have buried the hatchet and extended the hand of friendship, a most cozy one by all observances."

"Yes, well, it's hard to confess one's error of judgment, but we Christians must. And I believe I was of the wrong opinion about him formerly. He's not the criminal I imagined. Quite the contrary."

"Still is a mysterious figure."

Teddy, who knew Cameron's business, began to defend my beau, but when he saw my eyebrow raised, he desisted.

"Well," said Kitty, putting saucers and cups on the table, "I think you should publish a lady's gazette rather than a newspaper like what Mr. Furnas puts out. Really, there's hardly room for two such papers, and his, as would be yours, is so full of boredom. The whole first page is but the doings of foreign powers and the like. There's nothing much for the ladies, and I believe we need our own news."

Stewart looked up at his beloved a bit surprised. "You know Addy is determined to stand shoulder to shoulder with Mr. Furnas. I hardly think she would, well, would want to leave the field to the likes of him."

Some time passed before I realized everyone was looking at me. Kitty had touched a nerve. I hadn't any deep-seated ambition to compete with Mr. Furnas. To put out a single edition and tease him by challenging some of his wayward views, yes; but to carry on such an enterprise week after week, no. I was not one of those Seneca women calling out for equality with men. I am not a man. And for the first time I realized the flaw in my newspaper enterprise. Kitty spoke truly. I needed a woman's magazine so that I might encourage those of my kind to take on their responsibilities in the reformation of society.

"Sis?" Teddy said studying my face. "I can see your mind's at work, but I can't see what the work is."

I turned to Kitty. "You're perfectly right."

"Well, I never." I heard this from Stewart's side of the table.

"Yes," I insisted. "I can still call it the *Brownville Beacon*, but it will be a gazette for the ladies. Once a month."

Stewart repeated another "Well, I never."

"Nonetheless," I informed them, "I shall still have an investigatory article squeezed in between those of instruction and edification."

Kitty looked confused. "You mean like that murder story you've been going on about?"

"Which one's that?" asked Stewart.

"You know," Kitty explained on my behalf, "the Friend murders that happened a year ago. Just down on the bottom. Mother, father, son, two children, infant, and a seventeen-year-old maiden. All massacred in their cabin, then set afire. They say a Mormon was in on it."

"I can't see the interest in that," remarked Stewart. "They caught the villains and gave them their due."

"I don't think that's the whole story," I said in a whisper.

Teddy cocked his head, then looked around. "Why are you whispering?"

I hadn't the faintest idea why I was whispering, but I continued in the same tone, "Like I told Kitty, a reverend and his wife told me about a week ago there was more to the murder than meets the eye. Those where his very words. He said the Sheriff rounded up the suspects quickly, got a confession out of them, and then, just as quickly, a sentencing by the judge."

Teddy objected. "Why just because something's done quickly doesn't mean it isn't done right."

"I would expect you to say something of the sort," I retorted.

Stewart sat back in his chair pleasantly, as if surveying a plantation in the deep South, his cravat well starched and the chain of his pocket watch visible on his vest. He asked, "Where did you meet this reverend and his missus?"

"I met Reverend Cannon on the stage, coming back from Bellevue."

"What were you doing up there?"

"Gathering information about our aunt," I said looking at Teddy, "from the Indian mission there. I think she might be among the Pawnee."

Stewart kept to the subject of the Friend murders. He knew how to remain focused, and I appreciated this simple quality given to men. Of course, no one could run a household with such a limitation.

"Now," he suggested diplomatically, "I wouldn't want to discourage you from doing what you will, but I wouldn't want you wasting your time either. But really, the word of a reverend is of consequence coming from the pulpit, but coming from a stagecoach? He was just making conversation, no doubt. Simple as that, I wouldn't bother my head about it."

I felt that silence was the best defense, and I performed it well with my lips tightly drawn in against each other for as long as I could hold my breath. "That's just like a man!" I exploded. That's generally what going silent results in. "Trying to keep things simple just so he doesn't have to think. Well I'm no man, and justice must be served. The whole plate."

Kitty gave me a sidelong glance, the way she does when she actually puts her mind to work, and invariably with result. "I know what's got you ticking like a seven-day clock. It's because that Judge Kinney who was riding with you in the stage told you to leave the story alone. That's what's got you wound up."

"I applaud you, Addy," said Mr. Winslow, conceding with a chuckle. "You just let us know how we can serve you in this noble endeavor, and we'll be at your side." Kitty did oblige him by clapping and uttering further words of encouragement.

I judge this is how you separate true friends from the fair-weather variety. True friends, perhaps like Phaedra's nurse in Seneca's play, come over to your side, whether they agree with you or not, when they see you're committed.

I knew I had Teddy's support, whether he wanted to give it or not. Such is family.

* * *

On Thursday morning, the eighteenth of June, I was awakened by the hammering going on in town. *At the rate they're pounding away*, I thought, *we'll have another fifty homes and businesses built before the year's out.* The carpenters' zeal kept the birds flittering and chirping about, continually surprised by the novel activities going on in their ancient riverside paradise. Nature was obligated to give way to our Manifest Destiny.

I sat up in bed, placing my pillow behind my back and lifting the Bible from my nightstand. There is a ritual to facing the new sun, and though I am not superstitious, it is best to follow it. A dutiful reading from the Good Book and a heartfelt prayer are necessary preludes to a successful day. Mind you, it doesn't mean you'll achieve your earthly goals, for God has the power of veto, but if you exclude him from your mind, you will have no progress at all, here or hereafter.

The next ritual is more mundane: make my bed. This done, I possess a sense of accomplishment, and have the day under control, at least for the moment.

After these matinal proceedings, I stirred my woodstove into action, rewarmed yesterday's biscuit and coffee and carried plate, jam, and cup over to the gueridon by the window to enjoy my home and its view.

My house is of consequence in Brownville, however inconsequential it might be anywhere eastward of the Missouri. I had it built of three oversized Cincinnati houses, which are ready-framed structures, twenty feet by twenty, and delivered to the frontier on a Saint Louis steamer. Each structure hoped to be its own solitary home, something a squatter might erect on a piece of soil he hopes to pre-empt. However, I, being a devoted Trinitarian, had the ingenuity to meld three into one.

This frontier palace possesses a parlor, followed by dining room and bedroom, side by side, and behind these, and again abreast, a kitchen and bathroom. If the parlor is small, these other rooms are miniscule, but each has its purpose.

Finally, Teddy, a carpenter by profession, built a tall hutch for the dining room to hold dishes in its upper shelves and table clothes and linen down below. He also put up shelves in the kitchen as well as a bookshelf in the parlor. Outside he tacked on two porches, one in front, the other in back. Stretching away from the back porch is my garden, tended by John Carr, an old French laborer, and beyond it, the privy. Water must be drawn from the town well, I haven't one of my own, and Monsieur Carr helpfully attends to this task as well.

The view from my parlor window looks eastward down Water Street, a broad pathway more than a proper street. It fronts my home, and wanders toward the river, which is obscured by a hill, a scattering of Brownville homes, shacks, a few lonely trees silhouetted by the morning sun, beneath which stretch patches of brambles alternating in thickness. On that morning, the birds had retreated to an orphaned mulberry tree, not too distant, that had so far survived the pioneer's axe. They pecked at its purple fruit hanging among the upper branches. Some boys had already cleared its lower limbs.

While studying this idyllic picture, framed by my window, the Friend murders came to mind. How the doomed family must have awakened to a similar morning, unconscious of the fact that by the next sunrise they would lay dead and blackened among the ashes of their cabin. Yes, the murderers had been caught, but why so quickly hanged?

I finished my breakfast, washed and stowed cup and plate, then fitted myself for town in a sage-green dress, while topping my red hair with a dark green bonnet and its veil. Winning a complimentary nod from my looking glass, I set off in the direction of Mr. Winslow's cabin.

In the distance I could hear some commotion. Men hollering and whooping. The uproar seemed to be descending Main Street and flowing toward the river. Mixed in with cries of "Go Jerod!" and "Go Harry!"

The ejaculations reminded me of jubilant exclamations I'd heard more than once in my childhood. Usually they occurred on a Sunday afternoon when we observed the Sabbath as best we could. Jerome, assisted by my other brothers and a smattering of neighbor boys, would bring out Hezekiah, my favorite pony, and Jerome would be so attentive as to saddle up my steed and put on the bridle. I hated putting on the bridle because, when inserting the bit, it seemed Hezekiah repeatedly mistook my fingers for carrots. Then Jerome, strong and gallant, would lift me up by the waist and drop me down into the saddle. I always beamed atop a horse, even a pony. One has a command of one's surroundings. Confidence. You can't help but sharing the emotions of Wellington overlooking Waterloo when Blucher finally arrives. And then I would hear Jerome's words of encouragement: "On your way!" Which, without fail, caused me to look over my left shoulder with eyes grand as an owl's as I saw the flat of his hand slap down on the rear of Hezekiah. Shrieks of laughter were followed with words of encouragement: "Go Addy, go!"

So, putting two and two together, I divined what all the stir was about in Brownville: A horse race kicking up dust and confusion and no doubt emptying the pockets of more than one gambler. One more thing to warn against in my gazette. I love a fast horse, who doesn't, otherwise we'd all be riding donkeys. But to see a man lose his week's wages in a matter of minutes was heartbreaking, especially if he had a wife in tears at his elbow.

I hadn't yet reached Stewart's door, when I found the successful entrepreneur already in the street, marching purposefully in the direction of Cyrus Wheeler's headquarters. Cyrus, with whom Stewart does much business, is the town's most popular architect.

"Good day, Miss Furlough," he greeted me as chipper as a bird on a well-endowed mulberry tree.

"Good day to you, Mr. Winslow." I paused my stride and he obligingly approached. I went right to the point as it's unwise to beat around the bush with pleasantries about the weather and so on when engaging a businessman. "I'm beginning my enquiry into the Friend murders," I said, "and as you offered advice, I freely seek it."

"Well," he said ponderingly as he took me by the elbow and

maneuvered me to the side of the broad but uneven trail, "you might best ask dapper Mr. Whitt about the affair."

My heart sunk; the druggist was the last person I wanted to question. However, I also knew that every path seems to be of little value unless it be encumbered by thorns sown by the Enemy.

"Why him?"

"Oh, I think he may now own the land where the Friend family met its demise."

Normally I'm wary of land agents, but there is an advantage to having a friend in the business, so I thanked Stewart. He offered me his arm and accompanied me to the druggist's door. I think he knew that his presence would have a sobering influence on Mr. Whitt's doubtful behavior around women.

Stewart pushed the door open with the back of his hand to let me pass. Mr. Whitt was removing bottles from a crate and putting them on a shelf. When the door shut, he turned and smiled graciously. "Miss Furlough," he said with a nod that ignored Stewart. "What can I help you with? I should say that I've just received some of the finest French perfumes. Nothing more refreshing and inspiring for a young lady than a sprinkle of heaven in the morning." He walked over to a shelf, removed a bottle from it, opened it and waved it before my nose as if to mesmerize me. "Enticing, isn't it?"

The mesmerizing fell flat. I noticed the label said "Parisian Perfume," but nothing of its pungently sweet odor indicated its provenance from a famed French manufactory.

"For a certain type of woman, I'm sure," I responded.

Mr. Whitt finally acknowledged my companion. "Mr.

Winslow, though, I suspect knows just the lady. I'm sure Miss Sturwell would appreciate a gift of quality. Nothing better than knowing how to please a woman." He finished his phrase with a glance in my direction.

Stewart moved between us. "Miss Furlough has come to inquire of the Friend murders. She's looking into them because we believe there might have been more malice done than thought." He said this rather gruffly, and I appreciated the performance.

Mr. Whitt dropped his smile and took a step back, turning in a circle as he did. "Whatever do you mean? More malice than the slaughter of seven innocent people?"

At this moment my brother Teddy passed through the door. "Hi, Sis. I thought I saw you coming in here. Everything all right? Not like you to be seeking out medicines."

"We're talking about the Friend murders," I said, "and I'm curious as to why the culprits were judged so quickly."

"Because they were guilty," said Mr. Whitt, looking straight into the eyes of Teddy, as if my brother would be a favorable arbiter of our discussion. Given that Teddy was working on Mr. Whitt's house and putting up shelves in his store, he was right.

"You've got a good point, Mr. Whitt."

"But why not question them further," I asked, "and find out what inspired such a group of men to murder not only the men folk but also the women and children?"

Mr. Whitt lost all his charm and said as gruffly as Stewart had spoken, "Because the settlement wanted to show that we were a community of law and order. You don't want news getting out that murderers don't get caught and punished in a new town.

Nobody would want to live in such a place."

After he said this, I couldn't help asking myself, *What if they were not guilty, what if the town fathers had just rounded up a gang of ne'er-do-wells and hanged them before anybody would know if they were guilty or not? In that case, the real murderer or murderers could be alive and well, and possibly amongst us.*

"Did they confess their crimes in public?" I asked.

Mr. Whitt looked increasingly irritated. "I don't know. I doubt it. That's not the way of things. After the justices questioned them, they let 'em all go but one. So, the townsfolk, sensing that they ought not be let go, rounded 'em back up and they gave their confession."

"Voluntarily?" I asked. "No coercion? Knowing the outcome would be the noose?" No wonder Reverend Cannon thought something askew.

Stewart and I were eyeing each other. I knew what he was thinking: exactly the same thing I was thinking. The people wanted the scandal over with and hurried it along to its conclusion without a care for justice.

As we silently exchanged our thoughts, the door opened and another person entered. He had the airs of a doctor and carried a well-worn leather medical bag.

It seemed Mr. Whitt could read our judgement. "Now look here," he said, paying no attention to the new customer, "their ringleader, who was George Lincoln and not the Mormon in the end, said they were told that Jacob Friend kept a lump of money or a cache of jewels or something valuable in the floor of his cabin, and that's what they were after."

"So why did they kill them?" asked my advocate, Stewart.

"Why not wait until the family was in town to break into their cabin?"

"Now that part I do remember," answered Mr. Whitt. "According to those who were questioning them, George Lincoln said, 'I was told that if there ain't no witnesses, there ain't no criminals.' Now that part stuck in my ear like tar."

I rolled this around in my mind a bit and understood why the phrase impressed our druggist. "It is filled with ambiguity, isn't it Stewart?" I said with some excitement, "You don't know if this George Lincoln meant that this was just a saying of his youth, one that he had always abided by and applied to all situations, or if someone in particular had told it to him for this specific crime. And that's significant!"

"Yes, because if it's the latter," suggested Stewart, energized by my enthusiasm, "then someone put him and the others up to it!"

"'Some smug man who thought he knew it all,'" came a voice from across the room. It issued from the newly arrived gentleman. He had his back to us and was running his fingers across the titles of books standing shoulder-to-shoulder on a shelf. "Yes, yes," he continued, but following another train of thought, "you're missing *The Illustrated Self-Instructor in Phrenology* by the Fowler brothers. No purpose in dispensing medicines if one doesn't understand the mind and its relationship to the body."

He turned to us with a professorial air and lectured. "Although medicinals can alleviate certain malaises, heredity is the ticket. Infinitely more potential in the parental disposition than all education and circumstances of life can import." He continued in the same vein, reciting by memory chapter titles and contents of the missing book.

The classroom audience stared blankly at this peroration, and I believe my jaw and those on either side of me, lowered a bit, Teddy's dropping more than Stewart's, Mr. Whitt's and mine put together.

Arriving at the conclusion, the gentleman picked up his medical bag, advanced to our position, and extended his hand to Stewart, because Mr. Winslow, with his jaw a little less ajar, looked to be the class leader. "Allow me to introduce myself," he said. "Christopher Martin, phrenologist."

CHAPTER 2

he phrenologist, Mr. Martin, had the bearing of an aristocrat, standing straight and erect with his high forehead, ample moustaches and goatee. If we had been in France, I'm sure we would have addressed him as "Your Imperial Highness." Stewart, however, realizing we were on the American frontier, was somewhat less formal in extending the hand. "Uh, Stewart Winslow, land agent, and this is Miss Adeline Furlough, hmm, gazette owner, Mr. Theodore Furlough, carpenter, and, of course, Mr. Whitt, druggist."

We politely exchanged how-do-you-dos, and then the emperor said patronizingly, "Miss Furlough is no doubt a devotee of Charlotte Wells, your colleague in the print business."

"I'm a devotee of my Lord God, but none other whom I can think of."

"Tsk, tsk," he uttered. "Mrs. Wells is proprietor, with her husband, and prime editor of Fowler and Wells, arguably the most productive publishing house of New York City, and the New World to boot."

"Unknown in these parts, however. So neither Fowler nor Wells can capture my interest, but what does interest me is your comment," said I, punctuating my declaration with a brief silence. He lifted his chin and I continued, "What did you mean when you spoke of a 'smug man'?"

He peered down upon me over the length of his aquiline nose. "A curious mind, you possess. And a fair shape of head and face that betray it."

"That isn't the half of it, Sir," said Teddy, always so proud of his sister. "She packs a punch too, so beware."

I knew he meant well, but somehow I felt my womanhood diminishing.

"Thank you, Teddy," I said with a tone that added the codicil, "That will be enough out of you." Teddy did acquiesce, but he fixed Mr. Martin in the eyes and bobbed his head up and down quickly to let the man know he spoke truth.

There was a silence that Mr. Martin broke by saying, "I suspected you were speaking of the Friend murders."

"Indeed," I said.

"As it happens, I was in Brownville at the time, although you wouldn't know it as such if I described what the place resembled back then, just a year ago. An invaded wilderness. A dozen or so shacks among riverine trees as I recall. Anyway, I have made human temperament my life's study, and at that time I was on my way to visit the savages, following up on Mr. Samuel Morton's research on the Aboriginal Race of America. You know the title?"

"No, but I fear you do. Could you not stick to the order of business?"

"Yes, certainly, although you must read Morton's slim volume. In any case, the Pawnee are of particular interest to me. I was anxious to move westward to further my investigation, but when I landed here, the town was astir over a massacre, the Friend murders. I saw the group of thugs they brought in and charged for the crime, including that Mormon, Amos Davis, and I dare say I was not surprised to see them convicted and hanged. Taking the best parts of all their skulls and assembling them together into a single head, you could not have constructed one better than Quasimodo."

"And the 'smug man'?"

He gave a light cough in his handkerchief as if to clear his throat for another public performance. "The 'smug man' reference comes from the gang leader himself, Mr. Lincoln. He said this on the scaffold. I don't think he intended to be there so quickly, but apparently the citizens had other things to do that day and expedited the process. Once face to face with the noose, he decided it was time to start talking. He said it wasn't his idea, and someone in the crowd yelled out 'Then whose idea was it? Your mother's?' Mr. Lincoln took offense at this on behalf of his mother, then said it was...." Mr. Martin paused and opened his medical bag to extract a bound journal. He flipped through the pages until satisfied. "Yes, yes, here it is, the quotation exactly: 'Some smug man gave me the means, and if you don't know him a medley...'" He then closed the book.

"A medley?" I asked.

"That's as far as he got in his defense. As soon as he finished the word 'medley,' the floor went out from under him. I suppose the hangman was anxious for his dinner, or, not having much experience yet, accidentally tripped the lever. But I wrote Lincoln's words down in my journal, as I thought the incident, after seeing the party of malefactors assembled, a study in itself. They fit the emerson classification of men, as defined by Fowler in his book."

"Poets?" I asked.

"No, no, certainly not, though Ralph Emerson is partial to phrenology. It's simply a categorization. You really need to get the book and you'll see the sketch. The man with the pronounced eyebrows but whose forehead slopes away, whose chin sinks, and whose nose is deflated."

"And Mr. Lincoln, like the others, matched this textbook sketch?"

"Better than any other."

"Sounds awfully suspicious to me," remarked Stewart. "The hangman 'anxious for dinner,' I doubt it. What was the real reason for not hearing the poor man out?"

"Because he was attempting to shift the blame, prolong his imprisonment, stay the execution if you will, but being a brute, it never occurred to him that he incriminated himself further. It did not help his case that his thickish skull could not invent a name to stick to the 'smug man'. If he'd uttered the name of just any old John Doe, they would have heard him out."

Stewart and I looked at each other in amazement. Our suspicion had become fact. Our town founders wanted the affair over and done with, whether or not the right men died.

Mr. Whitt set the bottle of "Parisian" perfume down on the counter and turned his head slowly in my direction, perhaps so Mr. Martin could get the full measure of his skull. "Miss Furlough," he said, laying a hand softly upon the counter, his thumb flicking at the edge of it at a measured pace, "why all this interest in the Friend murders?"

"For starters because I think Mr. Lincoln had a point: someone put him up to the crime, someone who has gone unpunished and needs a reckoning. I aim, Lord willing, to see justice come to pass."

"Uh-hum," intervened Stewart. "Well at least as an intellectual exercise, no doubt."

I knew what Mr. Winslow was up to. He didn't want me to put myself in any danger in case the man ultimately responsible for these murders discovered my purpose. Any man who would commission the murder of a mother with an infant at her breast and a daughter in the bloom of life would not refrain from doing me harm.

I humored Stewart by saying, "Of course, I'm not a sheriff or judge or marshal, much less a hangman. I am but a weak woman, and violence doesn't befit our sex."

Teddy guffawed at this and received a sharp elbow in his ribs to tighten him up. "However," I continued, "I do think it important to get the measure of the culprits; Mr. Lincoln to begin with. I don't imagine he had any worse upbringing than any other, but he made choices that set him down the path of perdition. In my gazette, I believe that if I can demonstrate the importance of making the right choices, and of mothers in particular in encouraging those choices, then I might be a benefit to society."

I heard a snort from the phrenologist. "My dear woman, how innocent, how naïve, how unmodern, how unscientific, how typical of your sex. Now you take the Reverend Henry Beecher, brother of Catharine Beecher and Mrs. Stowe, he understands, in spite of his religious position, the scientific certainty of phrenology and how a man's behavior is dictated by his physical characteristics."

"Reverend Beecher may be a grand abolitionist, and I laud him for that, but he's not my brother, and it seems to me like he's found a way to blame a man's sins on the Creator's way of fashioning his skull. Sounds like that gives license to Reverend Beecher to act as he will without regard to his conscience."

Mr. Martin turned his attention to the one who actually is my brother. "Now Mr. Furlough, you're a bright and attractive gentleman, would you care for me to take the measure of your head. I think you have potential, given the outline I see."

Taking a good look at my brother's skull, I could just see the water wheel beginning to turn inside. "Now don't you take any notes from him," I warned Teddy. "And as for you, Mr. Martin, keep your calipers in your pocket."

"All I have here," he began to say as he tapped his pocket, "is...." He dipped his hand into his pocket and then searched the others. "By gad, I've misplaced my pipe. It's a one of a kind, porcelain." He then went into a lengthy account concerning his prior movements during the day to establish when and where his smoking device could have fallen from his pocket. He did prove himself to have a good memory, and to a fault.

I decided it was time to drop the curtain and bid all an *au revoir*. But as I reached for the door, I did announce to Mr. Whitt that I understood he now owned the old Friend property, and I would be obliged if he were to show it to me some day.

"There's nothing out there to see," he said coolly.

"And that's why it won't be a bother for you to show it to me," I said as I exited.

CHAPTER 3

n the evening, I revisited my gueridon under the window. It was fine for a cup of coffee or tea, and might even manage a teapot if one had no appetite for a plate of biscuits, but it was inconvenient as a medium for writing. I could lodge a sheet of paper on it, but if I decided to lay aside my pen, put my elbow down, rest my chin on the points of two fingers and a thumb and ponder romantically about my next well-chosen word, I would have to reach to the floor to collect my pen in order to proceed. I definitely needed that side table on the wharf.

Nevertheless, I managed to compose a dozen messages to friends and family in the States. In each I entreated the addressee to dote me with a little feminine news or bit of wisdom that I might include in my gazette. Pioneer readers are always anxious to read a word from their home state, or even just something from the East.

The next day, Friday morning to be more precise, I gathered up my letters, put them in my basket, and set off toward the Post Office via Mary Turner's millinery. Her shop sells much more than hats and bonnets, she deals in all sorts of articles and notions, basically anything to do with cloth.

Along the way, beside a building where Water Street and First Street join, I espied a small cloud of smoke, underneath which sat a cluster of young boys huddling together and passing around a pipe. The aroma of tobacco disgraced the morning air by wafting to my nostrils. While one of the boys puffed away, I could hear as I approached, another youngster recounting a ribald story sprinkled with descriptives drawn from a dubious lexicon.

The conniving band, rehearsing vices they intended to expand upon as adults, had no knowledge of my presence until I had grabbed the largest ear of the group. The owner, whose gingered head, freckled face and protruding teeth no doubt found their likenesses in Fowler's taxonomy, squealed noticeably. Increasing the pinch, I demanded to know the names of their parents. The boy with the ear was immediately abandoned by his fair-weather friends, their little feet kicking up puffs of dust as they disappeared around the corner. My only prisoner squealed out "Mr. and Mrs. Smith," which earned him bail and I released him. He proved as quick a magician in disappearing as had his comrades.

I picked up what I at first assumed to be Mr. Smith's pipe. It was singular, though. I had never before beheld a white porcelain pipe with a colorful escutcheon upon it, with the letter 'J' in a gothic hand emblazoned in the middle. I tapped out the tobacco, and deposited it in my reticule. I wasn't going to promenade about town with pipe in hand like a backwoods matriarch, nor was I to leave the instrument behind for the children to recuperate. I had an inkling as to whom the pipe belonged, but I thought to keep it to myself for the moment.

I reached Mary's shop in a cheerful mood. Mary's a dear childhood friend and sweetheart of Teddy. She welcomed me with an embrace.

"What brings you my way?" she asked.

"Mrs. Annie Medford."

"Did she now? She's such a lovely woman. You know her husband and Teddy are putting up a house for Mr. Whitt on Atlantic Street."

One thing I do have to credit Teddy with is his carpentry skills. His tendency to take short cuts seems to serve him well in his profession. If you want a house built in a jiffy, Teddy's your man.

"Yes, she is lovely," I said. "At church she invited me to come quilting this coming Monday. Her excuse is to have a quilt ready before her baby's due, but I think she enjoys company as well."

"Oh, yes, I know exactly what she's up to and what you might need."

As Mary gathered items for me, I saw a copy of our local *Nebraska Advertiser* on the chair. In its columns, there was a long list of citizens who owed taxes. I rapidly glanced down the names to make sure I had not earned a place in print. I wondered if our wholesale man Mr. McPherson would be obliged to pay his since they misspelled his name so horribly.

Underneath the paper I discovered a booklet entitled, *Now Rapidly Approaching, Will It Strike the Earth?* "What's this about?" I asked.

Mary, arms full, glanced at the book. "Oh, nothing to worry about. A comet was expected to land upon us. Went right by, apparently."

"Yes," I observed, "it does seem that every so many years we humans demand a catastrophic event of our God. And now, thanks to Mr. Newton, we have more ways than one to doom ourselves."

"I imagine someday God will humor us," said Mary, spreading out her accoutrements.

I picked out what I needed, paid for the items, and then stowed them in my basket.

"Addy," Mary said as she returned my change, "I have it from Teddy that you're to put out a lady's gazette. If you do, I would like to support the cause. Could I place an advertisement?"

"Certainly, and up front for you!"

"A mutual help, I'm sure. But your monthly, if that's what it's to be, will have wholesome stories to encourage women in their work and leisure?"

"Yes," I said, "and what better work and leisure than to sew and the like. But," I warned her, "it won't be simply about the economies of a household, nor a collection of moralizing pieces of literature like something Miss Straightlace would write."

Mary burst out laughing remembering Miss Straightlace, otherwise known as Miss Prudence Withers. "She even followed you to Oberlin didn't she? And that brother of hers. He was so charming with you, always bending your ear after church."

"Remind me not."

"But," insisted Mary, "he was the most handsome and intelligent of God's creatures, and so knowledgeable."

"You must have got that from him, not God."

"In so many words, yes," confessed Mary. "But I wonder

what became of him?"

"When I left the county for Oberlin, I don't believe I saw him again, not that I complain."

How those two came packaged together, Prudence and Jonathan Withers, I mean, I could not decipher. She was the most prim, moralistic, judgmental, restricting, and controlling personality born since the inventor of the automaton. Her ban on strong drink I support, as it alters personalities and transforms dutiful husbands into brutes and miscreants. However, her scowling at music, dance, and certain novels written or performed by clearheaded and gay souls, I cannot abide. Of course, her greatest fault is her devotion to her obnoxious know-it-all of a brother. It's strange how men who think the world of themselves are constantly trying to prove themselves to the world.

"I will tell you Mary, in my gazette there shall be words of wisdom and etiquette and stories to edify the faltering heart, but I shall include a column about other serious matters. Abolitionism will make it into my pages, and so will the Friend murders."

Having said this, a thought came to mind. I searched into my reticule and produced the fine porcelain pipe I'd recently acquired. "Funny," I said. "Just look at this pipe I requisitioned from some naughty boys. It's got a 'J' emblazoned upon it, like the first initial of Mr. Friend's first name...Jacob."

Mary took a look at the pipe. "Probably stands for Jaeger, they're a company that manufactures such things."

"Jaeger?"

"Yes, made in Germany."

I returned the pipe to my reticule thoughtfully, and as I directed my steps toward the Post Office, I thought, even if the initial on the pipe indicated Jaeger, it still could be connected to the Friend family.

* * *

I returned to my house for my noon repast. Soon after I'd cleared, washed, and stored away my dishes, I received a welcome caller on my front porch, Mr. Cameron Davenport. He said he had actually arrived earlier aboard McCary's stagecoach. He had seen me down the street walking away from the Post Office, but didn't have the courage to topple the coachman to get to the reins and stop the stage.

"I didn't know you were afraid of coachmen," I remarked.

"Well, there was also the matter of getting my money's worth for the fare. We still had another fifty yards to go."

"True, you mustn't let businessmen take advantage of you. Besides, I'm sure you were dusty and unfit to embrace a lady."

"Truly stated. And so I've shaved, washed up, put on dapper clothes, and I've been all over town looking for a lady."

"Then step into my parlor and I'll see if I can find you one."

With the door closed to the outside world, my beau kissed me ever so gently on the cheek. "You know," he said, "the artists have it all wrong in their celestial inspirations. They don't know that a true angel has hair as red as love."

"And freckles?" I asked hopefully.

"Only as many as yours."

Then he looked down at *Hope Leslie*, the novel I held in my hand. I felt obliged to explain the story and how touching it was that the author herself had an ancestor taken up by the Indians and found happiness in marrying a brave.

"I hoped," he said with a note of concern in his voice, "that I might convince you, before you slipped out onto the plains to become a squaw to a lucky warrior, that you might join me in an afternoon promenade into the countryside."

"Let me get my buckskin and feathers," I said, ducking into my bedroom before reemerging with my bonnet, basket, and parasol.

We stopped by Mary's and I invited her to join us, so as to stump the gossips. As business was slow, or so she said, she willingly came along to play the role of chaperon.

We took up a small trail paralleling the embankment of the Missouri. It was narrow and Cameron let me pass before him, mentioning something to Mary about it being good policy to let an Indian guide take the lead. I, for my part, felt protected having a proven frontiersman commanding the rear guard.

Mary, who trailed immediately behind me with her basket, surprised me with a question. "Do you think Teddy happy?"

I must admit I cannot picture Teddy unhappy, but I sensed what she was getting at. "Do you mean you think he could be happier?"

"That's a way to put it. I just wonder what you once said to me, that I might be better paired with a businessman. Don't get me wrong, I love Teddy dearly, but I think he…" Mary was at a loss for words, so I supplied them.

"…fears you like a sister?"

"I see you know what I mean. He's attracted to women who know what they want and know how to get it. However, I fear it's because he's afraid of making choices and prefers to have another do the task. I don't believe it a benefit to him. Now Stewart, on the other hand, knows what he wants and always carries sound advice. He's someone even a strong-willed woman might lean on in time of need. With Teddy, well, when adversity strikes of a certain nature, as in business, I'm afraid I'm on my own. But I wouldn't want to offend Kitty, she's become your dear friend and hence is becoming mine. It's all so confusing."

I could sense Cameron losing ground on us, no doubt wondering if his guide hadn't led him into an ambush of feminine conversation.

"What do you think, Addy?" Mary asked.

I am ashamed to say I had nothing substantive to offer. I equivocated by asking weakly, "Perhaps Teddy shall harden into a man of iron will? I simply didn't know what to suggest.

The trail finally branched out into a tiny meadow rising slightly to the west against a hillside. We stood breathing in the salubrious air, as if we'd finally reached Paradise, and Cameron rejoined us. Mary, noticing some black-eyed susans, turned toward the river to pick them. Cameron took me by the elbow and directed me up the gentle slope.

"I don't know why I can't give Mary a straight answer," I confided. "Goodness knows, you'd think I possess enough opinions to spare a few."

"Because, whether you fully realize it or not, you see Teddy better suited to Kitty, and therein lies the dilemma, she's spoken for."

It's not that Mr. Davenport sees through me, but rather that we see together. "And how do you come to this conclusion, concerning my subconscious quandaries?"

"Because we're looking at the same landscape, from atop the same hillock," he said as we turned and glanced down toward the Missouri. His eyes followed the course of the river, and having looped my arm in his, I held it tightly, I knew what he was about to say.

"Tomorrow, this time, I intend to be down to Saint Jo. I'm expecting a delivery." He looked down upon me with his smiling blue eyes. "I'd much rather spend tomorrow here, with my Indian maiden."

"You won't let anything happen to my warrior, will you?"

"I'll keep," he said. "It's those around me that fall away." A certain sadness clouded over his eyes, and now it was I who looked out to the disappearing river.

"When I remember," he said poetically, "all the friends, so link'd together, I've seen around me fall, like leaves in wintry weather; I feel like one who treads alone…" He paused, took my chin in his hand, and approaching my lips to his, said, "finding you, to all replace."

"I don't remember that last line the way you do," I confessed, "but I like it much better."

Mary appeared with a basketful of black-eyed susans. "I think these ought to brighten up the shop."

I looked at her bounty, but must admit I thought more about a black-eyed Mary than anything else. She was such a conscientious chaperon.

I surveyed the meadow and the deer track leading across it which we had followed. "It's rather peaceful out here, and lonely. The Friend farm lay beyond a bit farther, I suppose. Strange."

"Whatever do you mean?" asked Mary.

"How many people have we crossed paths with?"

"None."

"That's just it, strange."

Cameron turned to Mary. "I think Addy's trying to say that because the farm was so isolated, even more so then than now, that it's strange the murders were discovered so quickly."

"Just so," I said.

We began our trek back to Brownville, and I couldn't help but notice Mary humming the tune of "Oft in the Stilly Night," and remembering Cameron's rendition of it.

* * *

At home on Saturday morning, I did my accounting. Father had supplied me with the wherewithal to come west and establish myself. Teddy, being a man with a vocation, did not receive the same financial backing. Besides, I was on a mission for father, locating Aunt Adeline.

Though Father was generous, his contributions did not account for the full expenses of setting up my business or building three houses in one. The printing press alone emptied much of my purse, and I'm afraid I lifted my little bag before my eyes and surveyed it in the same way the town drunk contemplates a diminishing bottle of rum.

Considering my resources, I remembered I still owed Mr. McPherson for furniture. My father's stipend would cover this, but it was late in coming. I was also in arrears in regards to the monthly rent for my Atlantic Street office, a standalone cabin that shelters my printing press and my print man, Teddy. My landlord, J.D. Thompson, being both land agent and attorney, was not someone to let a criminal act slip by unnoticed.

Then there was my French gardener, Monsieur Carr, who would want his *monnaie de poche*. Thinking of the garden brought to mind another expense in the offing. I desired a pair of those unusual shoes made of rubber, so that I might walk around like a lady of the manor, directing the plantation of petunias and pansies. And, I confess, I planned to have an appropriate dress for the July Fourth celebration, something sharp and smart to honor our Republic by. Cloth suited to the occasion hung upon the wall at Mary's shop. Having intimated my fancy for the color to Mary, my friend took my measurements and set aside the necessary yardage. And who can do without a new book every fortnight? I'll tell you: the woman who manages to buy a new one every week. I soon realized I was a master of expenses; what I needed was income.

If I could get a client to pay his advertising fee in my gazette ahead of time, I would survive, but, in order to secure advertisements, I promised my three first clients they would see proof in print before they paid. It didn't feel right asking my latest and fourth client, Mary, to be an exception, it would be taking advantage of a friendship. No, this had to be done businesslike. So, I creased my brow appropriately, like Washington looking over his bursar's books at Valley Forge, and tried inventing stratagems for getting early payments.

I hadn't gotten very far in generating a plan when a knock on the door blotted out whatever foggy idea was coalescing in my shapely skull.

It was Teddy. He apparently had been doing some accounting

of his own, and it led him to the conclusion that I had more money than he. Considering this, he suggested a donative in his direction, which earned him a frown from me. If not a donative, he then proffered, perhaps a loan, which earned him my doubting Thomas look. He, not being Christ, was unable to shake my skepticism. Finally, he assumed the voice of a businessman and encouraged me to consider a loan with interest.

"Aren't you getting paid for that house you're putting up on Atlantic Street? Mr. Whitt's?"

"Yes, I'll be paid tomorrow."

"That's what you said three days ago."

"Because that's what I was told three days ago. And I'll probably be told the same thing tomorrow. It's going to be a hefty sum whenever 'tomorrow' arrives, so that's why I'm willing to pay interest. It's just for ten dollars."

"Ten dollars? That's five times my monthly rent and nearly all I have left!"

He sat down opposite me, shaking his head slowly and rubbing his forehead with the palm of his hand. The spirit of the businessman had left him, and he had resolved back into the form of my little brother.

I put a hand on his knee. "What's the money for, Teddy?"

"It's to pay for some tools. I'm down fifteen dollars at McPherson's, but ten should keep him at bay." He looked up at me much like a catfish out of water, just blinking at me with nowhere to go.

I lifted my waistband and dug into the bottom of my watch pocket, where I kept a little reserve, and satisfied him. "Thanks, Addy," he said, jumping up. "Who knows, maybe I'll get paid this afternoon."

Teddy is ultimately an optimist, and I knew Mr. Whitt took advantage of this character flaw by delaying payment.

* * *

On my way to the *Brownville Beacon* office, as I walked out into Main Street, I could see down on the wharf more offloaded furniture. Among the articles were another side-table and lady's chair. Surely Mr. Muir didn't need two sets. I would have to inquire, but presently I had other business to attend to.

I reached Mr. Whitt's drugstore, hoping to find him at his cash register. I fancied myself a collection agent for Teddy. It would be awkward haranguing the druggist in his place of business, especially with customers present, but Teddy needed an advocate, and Mr. Whitt deserved a lesson. Unfortunately, Mr. Whitt's shop was closed, though I did observe a notice stuck to the door reminding the citizens of Brownville that there would be an organizational meeting tonight at six p.m. to prepare for the Fourth of July celebration.

I knocked a few times on the door without result. I resumed my march toward my office, however, turning off Main Street and toward Atlantic, I spied Mr. Whitt advancing toward me; he had a wad of money in his hands and a cigar protruding from his lips. I observed his tailored suit and imagined the expense it must have incurred. So well outfitted he was, and yet soulless in a way, wholly absorbed in this world's fancies, his own pleasures. If he were to marry, I would pity his mate.

Mr. Whitt's attention was presently so absorbed in counting his bundle of bills that he bumped right into me. I snatched the wad from his hand. He snapped to attention while stepping back a pace, his eyes fixed on me like a Britisher cresting Bunker Hill. I, on the other hand, felt like a Pawnee, who, upon coming home from the hunt without a rabbit to show for his efforts, finds a buffalo all cooked up and waiting for him at the wigwam.

"Oh, Ho!" I exclaimed with a war whoop. "My dear Mr. Whitt, what have I found here? When I think that my poor brother, and I say this not as a figurative of speech, has just borrowed ten dollars, maybe at interest, while you owe him a week's worth of work. *That*, by the way, is more work than I can get out of him in a month."

"Miss," remonstrated Mr. Whitt out of the side of his mouth, while clenching his cigar between his teeth and delicately wriggling his fingers in the direction of my loot, "that's not your money." Of a sudden he attempted to retrieve his treasure, but my hand was quicker than his.

"I know, this actually belongs to Teddy," I explained, "so I'll keep fifteen dollars." I handed back the balance, which was as much. "You can thank God I'm a Christian, for, as you know, I'm reasonable, leaving you half." Although, if Teddy had been wise enough to inform me of the total amount owed, I would have taken the difference.

"Mr. Whitt," I continued, "'thou shalt not muzzle the ox that treadeth out the corn', for 'the workman is worthy of his meat'." I think I had confused myself a bit, wondering whether that meant an ox would eat meat or not, but I didn't let this stifle me for long. "You should be ashamed of yourself for not paying what is due, when you demand it of your customers."

The old nature quickly got the better of Mr. Whitt. "Well,"

he said warmly, "for a pretty young lady, nothing's too costly." He attempted to brush my cheek with his hand, but there again I was quicker than he and avoided him.

"Miss Furlough, I assure you at your next visit, you shall have that perfume on my account." He tipped his hat in my direction, stepped around me and headed toward Main Street.

I glared at the back of his fashionable suit for a minute before resuming my jaunt. Consumed by my anger, I could not fix my thoughts, which caused me to stumble blindly ahead, right into Mr. Thompson.

"Pardon me, Miss," he said, "I was distracted."

I gathered he was, for he too had a sum of money in his hands. I supposed he and Mr. Whitt were headed down to invest in Mr. Brown's new bank. It's attracting interest because he's putting up a building for it on Main Street.

"No, I'm sure I'm at fault," I said.

"Good," he said looking at the fifteen dollars in my hand, "business is well, I see, and I see you have the money for the rent."

With all my necessary expenditures approaching, I could hardly part with the fifteen dollars. "Oh, yes, well..." I stuttered, "this is spoken for. It actually belongs to my brother, Teddy. I'll pay you as soon as possible."

"You know," he said with both eyebrows raised suspiciously, just like Mother used to do when Father offered to do the dishes. "I have an offer to sell the shop," he continued, lowering one eyebrow while raising the other higher yet, which Mother had never been able to do, "at seventy-five dollars. So, I hope you're not too attached to it."

I was stunned, and I believe my eyebrows now surpassed his. "Whatever do you mean? We have a deal, we shook on it, Mr. Thompson." He looked at me indifferently, as might a horse who's been offered hay, when he has a bucket of oats before him.

Finally, Mr. Thompson conceded that we did have a deal, but he also pointed out that he was a lawyer, a good one, if that can be said of a lawyer, and nothing in the handshake said he could not sell the cabin. The handshake only confirmed he would rent to me on a month-to-month basis. "But," he ventured magnanimously, "Nothing forbids me from selling it to you."

"Well," said I, which is always how I begin a sentence when I'm buying time. "Well," I repeated three more times, "mightn't I rent from the new owner?"

"As I understand it, he needs the space."

I shook my head disapprovingly. "I can't believe you'd put me, and all my workers," which consisted of Teddy and myself, though Teddy was only part time, "out in the street."

"Like all," he explained, pulling from his pocket a gold watch worth more than the land upon which my office sat, "I'm in need of cash. I shan't want to gain publicity by having my name entered into the rolls of those owing the city's tax."

I proceeded to my next question. "Who wants to buy the property?"

He studied his watch for a moment, looked satisfied with the results, and told me, "I'm not at liberty to pronounce his name, but I believe you were in conversation with him but a moment ago."

Mr. Whitt, I should have reckoned as much. He was probably just trying to stir me up so I would come talk to him. He would do anything to attract the attention of a single woman, but hadn't a clue as to how to do it properly. He needed a wife and baby to preoccupy him, but it wouldn't be me or mine. I looked down the street for sight of his suit, but the spectacle had disappeared. What a sapless, sinewless, hopeless, selfish man, I thought.

"For what possible business reason," I asked Mr. Thompson, "should Mr. Whitt want that property?"

"Like I said, I suppose he wishes to expand?"

"Expand into a little out of the way shack where he'll get no business?"

Mr. Thompson said nothing.

"Well," I concluded, "you'll have to give me time. I can't come up with fifty dollars out of thin air. Good-day, Mr. Thompson."

"And good-day to you, Miss Furlough," he said pocketing his watch. "You've got a week or two to think about it. Mr. Whitt has yet to put any purchase money down on it. Mind you it's seventy-five dollars, as you well know, but I'll let you have it for fifty, if you allow me space for an advertisement in your publication equal to the difference. Some good work about my own person in regards to electing a justice of the peace."

One always speaks of conniving females, but I suppose whoever came up with that observation had never met a lawyer.

CHAPTER 4

he head-quarters of the *Brownville Beacon* consisted of one shabby room and a side kitchen, complete now with stove, chair, and gueridon, set on a sharply sloping hillside. The printing press stood in the left half of the room as one entered from the north door, with Teddy's trunk behind it, within which I commanded him to dispose of all of his belongings each morning, and my desk with chair occupied the other half. The chair, hard and rough, was a perfect match for my desk. I sat down, put a sheet before my eyes, and dipped my quill in ink.

In my first edition, I hoped to provide advice, entertainment, and news. I began with advice:

To bachelors: Is there one that supposes he was created for the purpose of using up woolen manufactures, cigars, and tailors? If he does, he is soulless, and when he dies, will he simply be annihilated, rot in dust, and turn up in time as a part of the terra firma of a cabbage orchard? Man's destiny is to govern—to rule—to command… every great man has, in the midst of his greatness, a part of his time devoted to the culture of a wife and to the tending of babies. So, ye bachelors, ye that have not withered into sapless, sinewless, hopeless selfishness, brush up the charms of mind and person, that are wasting and fading, and make one grand attempt for blissful days, comfortable nights, posterity, and an honest future.

My inspiration was broken by hollering and cheering down below on Main Street. Looking out the kitchen window, I could see dust rising in the west, and it was traveling down toward the Missouri. I knew it had nothing to do with the Pawnee, because I could guess what was going on simply by interpreting the mostly impious ejaculations: It was a gang of young men riding fast horses through our town, driving men and women off the street, and putting the lives of our children in peril. However in the world were we to become a civilized city, and a beacon for proper folk, I knew not...unless we brought an end to raucous and juvenile behavior.

I returned to my desk and drew forth another clean sheet and penned an open letter to the *Nebraska Advertiser*, calling for ordinances. A twenty-five dollar fine for horse racing, just like for rioting, and another fine for the use of vulgar language in public, to be levied on the parents of disrespectful children. I finished with a flurry: *Fathers of Brownville, hear the remonstrations of womanhood, or you will be left to yourselves, and 'be a story and a by-word through the world,' to be shunned by every emigrant who calls herself a lady.*

I set my first epistle in a box labeled For Print on the table. Teddy would take care of them in due course. He had improved as a pressman since the first attempt at an edition, when the end result was a newspaper with bold enticing titles followed by words written backwards. Since that day, he had reclaimed himself by punctually delivering newspapers from the steamers:

The *Saint Joseph Gazette*, the *Kansas Herald*, the *Saint Louis Republican*, just to name a few. I had to admit that I'd come to depend on him.

I sat back looking at the box satisfied. My thoughts then turned toward the Friend murders, and I recapitulated what I knew: *A family, all women and children but two, killed in cold blood, then their home set aflame over their bodies to hide the deed. Someone came upon their charred corpses the next day. The coroner deduced they had been murdered. Suspects immediately rounded up, released, but quickly rounded up again, judged, and hanged. All within a fortnight. The chief of the gang, George Lincoln, claimed that some smug man gave him the idea by saying there were no lawmen of any account in Nebraska Territory and that "where there's no witnesses, there's no crime."* I paused for a moment and sat up straight, pondering Lincoln's other comment: *"He gave me the means to do it."*

Whatever could this mean? Did he pay him? Did he give him a firearm?

I mulled this over a while, staring blankly at the door. I couldn't have looked too different from Bessy back home, ruminating on some choice grass while studying the motionless horizon. But unlike Bessy, my ruminating resulted in an inspiration: *I can understand the motive of the gang. They expected to find money, lots of it; but what was the motive of the instigator? Nothing indicated that George Lincoln and his cohorts were going to share the loot with anyone.*

This called for yet another sheet of paper, upon which I jotted down two words: *Instigator, Motive*.

I then realized it was nearly six pm, and there was a meeting to attend. I took up my second missive to the *Nebraska Advertiser* and made an envelope for it.

I arrived at the July Fourth planning meeting in good order, though narrowly. A certain William Ruth had blocked my way unintentionally as he enjoyed an altercation, with an Andrew Kountze, over the question as to who had the most legitimate claim to a particular quarter section of land. Each seemed to have established some sort of squatter's rights. Words, however, failed to resolve the issue, and Mr. Kountze found it more effective to send Mr. Ruth in my direction with a shove. As a gesture, which I thought at the moment to be in favor of Mr. Ruth, I shoved Mr. Ruth's body back from whence it came. This apparently caught Mr. Ruth by surprise as he made no attempt to counter Mr. Kountze's next maneuver, which came in the form of a fist to Mr. Ruth's smallish nose. I had the presence of mind to save Mr. Ruth from any further blow by stepping aside as his body returned once again to me. His fall was cushioned by his spine. He looked up at me and I observed his smallish nose growing considerably in size and color. I stepped away, and the last thing I heard was Mr. Kountze saying something pedagogical. "And let that be a lesson to you," to be exact.

* * *

The meeting was held in the cabin currently serving as Brownville's foremost schoolhouse and church. As I entered, I spotted Mr. Furnas, who caught sight of me at the same moment. It's a blessing to be born without the ability to read lips, because as he mumbled something to Sheriff Coleman, the lawman quickly turned his head in my direction like a weather vane slapped by a gust from the frozen north. I rallied my dignity and made a beeline toward the pair, that is, as best a bee can do without wings. There were chairs and benches to circumnavigate but I reached the hive. The two drones smiled politely, although the Sheriff did so anemically. I stretched out my gloved hand that held the envelope. Mr. Furnas graciously took it.

"An invitation to your wedding, perhaps?" offered the sheriff.

He was forever hoping some man would take me in charge, but I think he had in mind a taskmaster like they cultivate in the cotton fields of the South rather than the gracious Mr. Davenport.

"How could you think I would offer such an invitation to Mr. Furnas without equally addressing you, Sheriff? Although, upon consideration, I think the letter will be of interest to you both, if you deign to do your duty as I'm sure you do."

Mr. Furnas turned the envelope over once or twice, as if trying to find which end to tear open. Satisfied that any side or end would serve the purpose, he extracted its contents and perused them. I saw a small curl taking shape on the left side of his mouth. It was in the same shape of a curl often seen on Teddy's face whenever he finds a solution to some conundrum that's been badgering his mind for a day or two.

He folded up the letter, turned to Sheriff Coleman, and with a nod in my direction murmured mysteriously, "I'm now more certain than before that our little issue has been resolved."

Sheriff Coleman's eyes darted in my direction. "You really think it wise?"

"I think it genius," came the reply.

Having said this, the pair departed before I could inquire as to what was wise and ingenious. At the same time people began populating our little public venue and Stewart Winslow courteously placed himself beside me.

"Have you seen Teddy about?" I asked, looking around as I did.

"I saw him at the wharf two hours ago looking over merchandise, perhaps he's expecting something?"

I couldn't think of anything.

Our newspaper editor, with his friend the sheriff at his side, called the meeting to order. Once discussion ensued, many ideas for food and entertainment came forth. I volunteered to help organize a dance and suggested a choir be formed to encourage us with patriotic hymns.

We finally came to the issue of speakers, and Mr. Furnas noted that we had a full bill of male orators, but that he had heard that the settlement on the Big Blue River expected to have a female Cicero harangue the plebs. It seemed like a fine exercise to him and one that might encourage women to settle among us if we had a lady equal to the task. "What we need," he orated, "is someone of an educated mind, someone who has an opinion other women might identify with, and who is no coward." He paused and looked out upon the audience as if soliciting a volunteer. I followed his eyes across the sea of faces and discovered only moustaches and goatees. As my gaze circled back to his, I discovered his eyes had fallen on me.

"Miss Furlough," he announced, "would be more than gracious to honor us with her encouraging and patriotic thoughts. Do I hear any who might object?"

I was stunned into silence, and I thought I heard a disapproving murmur arising from the rear, but it was hard to determine because Mr. Furnas let pass but half a breath, before his fist slammed down on the table before him as he declared, "Motion passed! Seeing that Sheriff Coleman seconds it, right James?"

"It's your idea," replied the lawman skeptically.

Stewart smiled and chuckled and patted me on the hand. "A right good choice," he said encouragingly.

I was still dumbfounded at meeting's end and sought out Mr. Furnas. I believe he was avoiding me, so I placed myself next to the only door, and he had no choice but to cross my path.

"I thank you for your community spirit," he said in an effort to slip past me.

I was in no mood to be brushed aside so easily. "Why would you want me speaking at the celebration?" I asked as I grabbed ahold of his sleeve. "You and I hardly see eye to eye on the weighty issues of the day."

"I want you to be just as provocative and as objectionable to me as possible. Don't you worry about whom you're pleasing or displeasing, my good lady," he said while placing his reassuring hand upon my mine.

"Whatever can be your motive?"

"Why, publicity my dear friend. I run the *Advertiser*. We want our community known throughout the States. And I can think of no better way of being heard than letting a single-minded woman vent her thoughts."

Having explained this, he passed on.

Somehow, I didn't know quite how to feel. Was I being

used? Certainly. But was this not also an opportunity given me by God to make a difference, to help shape our world? No doubt it was that as well. The Athenians prompted the Apostle to speak his foreign message from their pulpit, why shouldn't I avail myself of Mr. Furnas's?

With each step homeward bound, my spirits lifted. I crowded my mind with the well-turned phrases I would use to advance abolitionism and the duty of men to serve their wives, and of wives to edify their husbands.

As I crossed the home porch, my front door swung open with Teddy occupying its frame.

"I've got a surprise for you in the house, Addy!" he said gleefully. "I found 'em down at the wharf!"

Looking at him with wonder I could but note how much I approved of the new and sensible Teddy. It's true that he always sought to please, but traditionally he had been always off the mark. But, as he had become more responsible in his own private life, as when he picked up his clothes and placed them in the trunk at the office, he had come to understand the needs of others better.

"And look," he said, reaching into a pocket, "I got my pay as well! Here's your ten dollars back, and counting up the other times I've borrowed, or eaten off your plate, I figure I owe you a good forty more as well." He extended his hand and I instinctively refused, but he would not accept my refusal and pressed the money into my hand.

Teddy had been right, it appeared. This "tomorrow," which Mr. Whitt had repeatedly alluded to, finally came, and it had a lot of yesterdays bound up into it. What a windfall. In my hands was not money, but a wonderful and patriotic dress for the Fourth and rubber boots for my garden. And to think he bought me that red cushioned chair and a sizeable and well-sculpted side table as well. I threw my arms around him and hugged him with all my might.

Looking over his shoulders, though, I did not see the table and chair I sought. I saw instead my dining room chairs in my parlor forming a half circle facing me, but what disturbed me is what Teddy had put in two of them. In one sat Miss Straightlace, and in the other, Jonathan Withers, her brother.

* * *

Jonathan Withers stood up. He gave a curt bow and extended his hand to receive mine. I don't know if you have a fear of spiders, but I believe I inherited this trait from Eve herself. I think the only reason the Bible speaks of Lucifer as a snake is that if he had been a spider, no woman would have read the Bible.

In any case, I remembered my elder brother Jerome bringing me an oblong box, a handspan wide and a foot in length. He asked me if I wanted a cookie. My other brothers rubbed their tummies telling me how good they were. Being a little girl, I could think of nothing better to put in a box, so I reached in. When I hit bottom with my fingers, I felt a tickling rushing up my hand, along my forearm, and onto my shoulder. It was the biggest, hairiest arachnid a brother could find. I screamed, slapped at my shoulder, hopped up and down, and sprinted for my life, and all at the same time.

Well, in seeing Jonathan's extended hand, I felt like I was

reaching back into that box.

"What a surprise," I managed. As Jonathan lightly kissed my hand, I couldn't help but look away as if I were undergoing a bloodletting.

"I imagine it has become lonely here in the Territory," he said. "We've come to keep you company. I can't imagine the dullness of conversation amidst these ploughmen."

I noticed my hand still captive and I tugged at it as if I wished to shake hands with Miss Straightlace.

"So amazing," I said to her, "to think you made it out all this way."

"Yes, but Jonathan is ever a comfort, always seeing to my every need." She paused, scanned the walls and ceiling, then resumed, "What an adequate little hovel, so much the frontier."

"To really experience our life," I said suggestively, "a house of sod, or perhaps of log is really the ticket."

"I can't imagine, nor need I. Your father has been most generous in encouraging me to come, and explaining what a hostess you are, dear Addy."

"Now isn't that sweet of Father," I said.

"Your father has done so well by himself. To think, nearly one-hundred and forty dollars per share on the Illinois Central, I hear. How many shares does he have? It must be substantial, as he's kindly paid my way out."

"Apparently too many," I said.

Miss Straightlace cocked her head wonderingly at me. Then I remembered she was ever at a loss for understanding my comments. She was like those disciples that followed our Lord about, never understanding his parables. The only difference is that Jesus finally took them aside and conked them on the head so that they understood. I planned on doing no such thing.

Jonathan never paid much mind to what I said, or anybody else. He was too engrossed in furthering his personal objectives, which usually consisted of making others think he was the brightest star in the sky since the latest comet, and just as breathtaking.

"Oh," said Miss Straightlace finally. "You are so cagey. I suppose it is none of my business. In any case, he is a fine man, and so rightly concerned about your welfare. When I suggested I would love to travel west he immediately inquired if I meant to grace you with a visit, and if I'd be generous enough to deliver your stipend to you. I understood immediately he wished me to do so, and replied in the affirmative. He insisted I bring brother Jonathan as a companion."

"How thoughtful," I said on the same tone I'd spoken of my father's stocks.

My father is not a mean man. He and I share much in common, especially in temperament. Indeed, I think my mother regrets that she and I don't share in conversation as much as father and I. However, there is something wickedly teasing in Father, and he can read a personality in one glance more accurately than can a palmist read a hand in a day. He knows I loathe Prudence Withers, and that any self-respecting woman would rather reach into a box of cookies offered by Jerome than spend a minute with Jonathan.

Teddy knew of the Withers, since they lived in our neck of the woods back in Ohio, but did not know them as I knew them. Teddy was much younger and had not borne the hair-shirt of attending Oberlin College with Prudence.

In this ignorance, Teddy asked them how long they would be staying with us.

While Jonathan advanced to the looking glass to adjust his cravat, Prudence informed us she would be staying but a month to lend moral support, and she was expected to return to Ohio to report back to my father on how Teddy and I were getting along.

I think it was the word "month" mixed in with the image of "bloodletting" that got the better of me. The world around me became shadows and I felt my body sway. Then nothing more do I recollect.

CHAPTER 5

onathan, with his airs of nobility, refused to share Teddy's quarters at the office, explaining that if Teddy were not present each day, he himself could not be expected to stoop to making his own meals. He went on to the Nebraska House, where Kitty later told me she understood why he could never be a cook: He hadn't the patience. He expected his food to magically appear before him on the table within thirty seconds of pronouncing the words "I'm famished."

Jonathan's sister made space for herself in my bedroom. While I was recovering from my swoon, she rearranged my furniture to her liking, which enabled her to pull my spare mattress up close to mine that we might chat into the wee hours of the morn. I feigned to have another bout of apoplexy, which preserved me until sunrise.

I always am prepared to attend church on Sabbath morn, but on this particular Sunday I was doubly anxious to get going and escape my new family. Having donned a particularly cheerful dress to match my spirits, I set out. Prudence, however, had detected my movement and prevented my evasion. Requiring me to wait a moment while she dressed, she soon joined me.

On our way, she kept stride with me, taking me by the arm and again gushing about how wonderful it was to be among friends. She went on at length about her dress, asking me to guess where she bought it. A funeral parlor I suggested.

"Oh, no, dear Addy," she said. "They don't sell clothing there, except for those poor souls who haven't the means to own anything becoming in life. I made this dress myself, so suited for church and any occasion, though I do keep a light yellow one, but only for picnics on hot summer days. I should hope I could make you one as I wear now. I looked at your wardrobe and it's most unsatisfactory for a Christian lady."

Miss Straightlace delivered a rather lengthy discourse on the proper style and purpose of vestments. I nearly pitied her. She was plain in appearance, a nose too small for her face, a lower lip too large. But she could be improved upon with a little care. She did have attractive eyes and petite ears that could be enhanced by earrings. Not that I'm one to endorse fancies, but one must look one's best without playing the part of an actress.

Soon, her conversation moved on to other topics. She didn't want to impose on me, she said, but she understood that Mr. Furlough, (my father), graciously underwrote their trip but also indicated that his daughter would see to their lodgings.

I knew where she was headed with this preamble. "Prudence," I said, "I offered Jonathan a room of sorts at my office. Besides, I understand, he has been making his way in the world of business, so I'm rather astounded he wouldn't expect to supply himself with lodgings."

"Oh, yes, dear. You're perfectly right. He is most adept at business. He's been everywhere successful. I know you can't but admire his achievement, but he's told me half his money is tied up in stocks and the other half he has lent out at a profitable interest."

If I didn't pay for his room, I could foresee Jonathan's next move...right into my house, where I would be expected to serve him hand and foot. "Yes, I'm sure he's grand at what he does," I said. "And I understand that he doesn't have ready access to his funds. So let me pay his room and board there. But won't he be lonely? Don't you think you might want to share a room next to his?"

"Oh, no, Addy. I wouldn't do that to you. Jonathan does well on his own, among people. He's very popular, always finds someone to talk to. And I do think you'll come to appreciate him more and more, if that can be imagined, but it is also so nice to be just the two of us. There's nothing like a friendship nurtured in youth, where souls grow up side by side, learning the ropes of life together. We know each other as well as sisters."

"Yes, I do know you well."

Prudence's conversation now diverged yet again. She had all sorts of ideas for rearranging the other rooms of my house, but I warned her not to fatigue herself overmuch, considering her lengthy journey and that she must store up energy for the return trip.

* * *

Waiting for Reverend Wood to commence the service, I introduced Prudence and her brother, who appeared with Teddy at his side, to friends and neighbors. Kitty and Stewart were in attendance. The usual chit-chat ensued concerning the weather and the condition of crops, but it also included things proper to the frontier, such as the birth of a new township located twenty miles south, far below our nearest southern neighbor, Nemaha City, but on the route to Pawnee City. They shamefully named it Breckenridge, after our vice-president who hasn't a care in the world for the enslaved.

The thought of Pawnee City brought to mind my dear lost aunt, wandering about the hills as part of the rear guard of a hunting party, I suspected. I awaited autumn with impatience: the Pawnee would all be at a rendezvous with the government, as I understood it, to negotiate a treaty. No doubt someone amongst them would have heard of "Hair on Fire". That's my aunt's Indian name. Perhaps she would be there herself?

I pondered this in my heart as we took our seats, Jonathan placing his back squarely in front of me. Suddenly Reverend Wood's voice interrupted my contemplation about Hair on Fire. "Shall we be as savages," he called out, "condemned to the eternal flames? Let us hold on to God, our Savior, and in song."

The thrill of singing out our faith in unison can only be likened to General Washington's troops stepping out toward Yorktown, knowing that the decisive hour had come to bring down tyranny. I hoped they marched in unison better than we sang, for it seemed that in our frontier church each squatter sang to his own melody.

When we ran out of song and ritual, we came to the sermon. "How do we hold on to God?" asked the minister. "By letting go of the world. By letting go of our worldly desires. By letting go of our passions for the things of this world! Be it money, be it fame, be it dance!" He held his breath for a moment, but I believe his eyes wandered in our direction, but I slunk down on my school bench, now appreciative of Jonathan for having placed his broad shoulders so squarely in front of me. While I hid, I heard Miss Straightlace utter an "amen" of approval.

Disappointed in not finding the object of his search, Reverend Wood lifted his chin and declaimed, "Dance.... This unreasoned emotionalism, this carrying on of the body, guided only by the brute passions of the old nature, cannot be of the Lord. Did not the Sermon on the Mount warn us against our lusts? When the last trumpet sounds, there will be no dance." He scanned the audience anew, just as my schoolmaster used to do, looking down upon the classroom, trying to identify which little girl had been whispering to her neighbor; then, not having found his target, the reverend concluded with "But there will be Judgment!"

After the service, Prudence presented herself to the minister, congratulating him on his sermon. I kept my distance, but could nonetheless hear her. "It's the duty of us all," she lectured, "to keep people focused on things spiritual. And that extends to the way one dresses as well. Somber colors keep the spirit from the gaiety that leads to so many a misadventure. I do hope you have a chance," she concluded discreetly, yet not discreet enough for my inquisitive ears, "to impart these verities privately to Miss Furlough."

He nodded approval while rubbing his eye thoughtfully, no doubt reminiscing about the only dance I ever sponsored in Brownville. It was to celebrate the building of my house. Unfortunately, at the end, the cotillion got rather out of hand and the men folk, whose footwork was questionable, began adding fists and elbows. In the general melee, Reverend Wood failed to keep in time and received a ball of knuckles to the eye he presently massaged. I imagine it was this little incident that inspired the day's sermon.

Now as for his comments on spirituality, I want to establish clearly that I'm not at all opposed to spirituality, but God gave us a body along with our spirit, and in concert, both can enjoy the wonders of this world he happily placed under our dominion. Think about it, it is God who created us so sensitively that our hearts leap and our bosoms fill with joy as we step to a tune. What Miss Straightlace and her new-found Demosthenes have done is to divide the world in twain: spiritual actions and physical actions. According to their recipe, all we have to do is avoid physical actions and we'll be spiritual, and therefore blessed of God.

I argue that these are not only pointless efforts but also impediments to living life in full measure. Someone once said, and I cannot agree more, "I am come that they might have life, and that they might have it more abundantly." And that Someone got rid of all the restrictive religious laws the priests and rabbis imposed upon an overburdened people. Why should we go back to those former days?

Now, don't get me wrong, there are necessary rules of society, as these guarantee respect and liberty between citizens, and it is to women, who understand biblical principles of morality, to mould and shape these to the exigencies of the present. Men, for example, need direction in their manners so that they forgo selfishness and attend to the needs of others, and in particular to those of the weaker sex. As I've said as much before, imagine the man who disregards his duty to wife and child by gambling away his earnings.

I had half a mind to deliver my own lecture to Reverend Wood when Mr. Thompson appeared and patted Teddy on the shoulder, exclaiming, "You've got horse sense my boy! You outsmarted all of us. The odds were against you eleven to one. How did you know that flea-bitten grey had it in her?"

* * *

I don't know if you've ever sat on a wasp, but I had the look of having sat on a full nest of them. An "Ahh!" escaped me at greater intensity and velocity than steam through a ship's whistle, and the sound was its equal.

Mr. Thompson looked at me bemused, but horror filled the countenance of my little brother, and rightfully so. He had been caught *in flagrante delicto*. I grabbed him by the elbow, and he was lucky I only had five fingernails on my right hand, because all of them made an impression upon him.

I escorted him out of our makeshift church at a quick pace and took him to a secluded corner of the building. "I can't believe you have betrayed me like this," I scolded. "Your honor is attached to mine, how could you have gone gambling on horses, and in full view of the town?"

"Now, wait, Sis," he said nervously. He exuded a wincing, agonizing demeanor, while wriggling his arm a bit. I let go. "You see," he continued while massaging his arm, "if I hadn't got involved, well that money would have gone to someone who would have spent it on alcohol, or to someone like Mr. Thompson who has too much money to begin with. That I lose ten dollars in such a cause was of no account to me."

"Those were my ten dollars!" I pointed out.

"And I returned them to you, and at interest. If you wish, I could take them back and hand them over to Fred Travis who had his eye on Mr. Davis's liquor sale. He even told me, and this is in the strictest of confidences, Addy, that if the bay won the race, he'd have a mind to share a bottle of the winnings with me. I couldn't let that happen."

I hesitated. Fred Travis needed no alcohol circulating aimlessly about his brain. He was a nice enough fellow, and had once taken me and Missus, an elderly lady, on a wagon ride to go out and look over some property; however, from what I have heard, he had no ambition in life but to satisfy his immediate passions, and these were kept under control only by sobriety.

"All right," I heard Teddy say, "I think I know where Fred's at. I can go find him and give him his money back so he can feed his habits."

"Hold on," I said. This was a quandary.

Teddy looked at me admiratively. "While you're thinking about this, I just want to say how proud I am of you."

"For what?"

"Well, I've heard you've accepted to speak to the community on the Fourth of July. I mean, in front of all them folks, half of which you don't know. I couldn't do it. First off they wouldn't take me seriously 'cause I don't have your education. And then I kind of look the part of a bumpkin too. Shucks, I don't know how to wear a fine suit of clothes like Mr. Whitt."

The quandary just got bigger. How was I to outfit myself for the speech if I gave up the windfall?

"No need to be proud of me Teddy," I said, "the speech is not yet given. But as for your ill-gotten gains, we'll keep them, but at the same time, those who lost their wager, ought to be informed as to their folly. I plan on writing an article about this episode in my gazette, and I hope to have the effect of discouraging such behavior in the future. I don't want you participating in these goings on anymore. Don't tempt God twice." I'm far from being Catholic, but I judged this *bonne oeuvre* would compensate for any unintentional sin.

Teddy had donned his serious face, as if he had learned a lesson. "Fair enough, Addy. I promise to do my best."

That's about as good a deal as one can expect from Teddy, so I let the matter rest while we walked back to rejoin those who lingered after church.

CHAPTER 6

I found Mr. Thompson loitering about the church door, much like I would imagine a merchant of the temple. He inspired me, and I approached him with forty dollars in hand. Merchants of the temple don't have to be of the male variety. He, being perspicacious, knew I was making an offer for his shack on Atlantic Street, the present headquarters of the *Brownville Beacon*.

"I believe I said seventy-five dollars," he said in a pious, Christian-like tone.

"And then you said fifty, and now I'm saying thirty but offering you forty. So, unless you're going to continue the trend and offer to sell at twenty tomorrow, I'd take the forty if I were you."

"You know," he said, letting out a puff of air accompanied with a grin, "just to save myself from arguing with you, I'll accept your offer."

"At twenty?"

"Don't push your luck, Miss Furlough," he said extracting the forty dollars from my hand.

"You'll still make a fine justice of the peace," I reassured him, before I went in search of my friends.

At the edge of the road running alongside our church, or schoolhouse, I found Jonathan engaged in conversation with Kitty and Stewart. He was asking Stewart if he'd traveled about much back east. Listening to the back and forth, I concluded that either Jonathan had already visited every place Stewart had been through, or he had visited another place twice the size and twice the interest. Jonathan apparently knew even Saint Louis better than Stewart, who had grown up there.

As for Saint Joseph, Jonathan clearly had the advantage, which surprised me. Saint Jo, as we refer to the city, was a long way from Ohio and I didn't realize Jonathan wandered off so far. It is true he's a few years older than I, and we were not the closest of neighbors, so I wouldn't have been privy to all his goings about. Still, it troubled me, and an air of perplexity descended across my countenance.

"Why Addy," asked Kitty, "what's wrong? You look to have unpleasant thoughts."

"No, not more than one at a time. I see you've been chatting with Mr. Withers."

"Yes, a well-traveled man."

Jonathan took this as a cue. He reminded me of Zachariah Thrumbrill. Zach was the boy I was in love with at our country school. He showed me all sorts of attention, yanking on my braids and the like.

I remember the day Zach impressed us all. The schoolmaster caught him whittling his initials into the bench and obliged him to stand up in front of us all and recite the day's assignment: the introduction to the Declaration of Independence. He had this smug, confident look about him as he marched up to the front of the class. He presented himself with a stately deportment and as near a senatorial voice as an adolescent boy with a modulating tenor could achieve. "When in the course of human events," he said, then slowly wiping his brow with his hand, "it becomes necessary...." He performed admirably and much to the amazement of our pedagogue. As you may have guessed, I had been less intrigued by his verbal recital than by the number of times he wiped his brow, and in fixating upon his hands as he sat back down my eyes detected a stain of ink in the form of the introduction to the Declaration of Independence upon them.

"Yes, Miss Furlough," said Jonathan, with that mix of confidence and contrivance that had marked Zach's face, "I doubt anyone has traveled as much as I have in as short of time to make as much honest profit."

"And you must have made quite a trade with my father, if he funds your present itinerary."

"I'll tell you, Miss Furlough, I've carried out commissions for some of the most important personalities of Ohio. Why, I superintended a load of furniture worth well over one thousand dollars for Mr. Mordecai Malcom."

I heard a gasp from Kitty.

"You see," said Jonathan turning to Kitty. "I may be relatively young, but ingenuity and talent compensate for age." He stated this as fact while tapping his temple with the end of his forefinger.

"Mordecai Malcom of Ohio?" asked Kitty.

"Yes, Ma'am. You've heard of him, I see."

"Why yes, he's my grandfather."

Suddenly, Jonathan changed subjects, and discoursed upon the merits of another man of wealth from Saint Jo.

* * *

Behind the exchange of Kitty and Jonathan, I observed Mrs. Wood dragging her husband away from Prudence, which freed up the latter to join us.

"Oh, my," she said in approaching me, "I see you're at liberty." She gave her brother a knowing look and nodded in my direction. "Jonathan," she continued, "has become quite the accomplished man of business."

"So I understand."

She placed a loving hand on her brother's arm while looking up at his dark eyes, eyes superscripted with arching, rather gothic, eyebrows. "I hope I don't cause you embarrassment in saying so?"

Jonathan was unmoved, except I sensed he would have preferred to continue discoursing with Stewart's fiancée, whose kind and listening manners had a tendency to attract the attention of the long tongued.

"Oh," said Kitty, looking shiftily from me to Prudence to Jonathan and then back to me and so on. Kitty is sharp at detecting certain things, and I believe she perceived Prudence's efforts to unite the interests of her family with mine. Kitty felt a duty to deliver me. "Uhm, Addy," she said. "You haven't heard of late from Mr. Davenport, have you?"

Before I could answer, Prudence wanted to know who this Mr. Davenport was.

Without thinking I responded, "My suitor."

"Suitor!" Miss Straightlace exclaimed, and then, fixing her eyes upon me and smiling said, "You're such a tease, Addy. Such exaggeration. Your father mentioned nothing of the man. Whatever does this Mr. Davenport do?"

Prudence's inquiry into Cameron's ventures constituted a question I could not answer, at least straightforwardly. "Uhm," I said thoughtfully, pawing my lower lip with my index. "He's traveling on business for the moment."

"Oh," said Prudence doubtfully, followed up with an "I'm sure. What business is he in?"

Kitty joined the forces of darkness at this moment. "It's true, Addy," she said, "you've never explained his business to me. Awful mysterious. Remember the rumors that he had transactions late at night up at the cave? No proof it was he, though."

Prudence looked at me, then back to Kitty. I could tell she was both befuddled and concerned. "Now," she said waving her hand in the air, her eyes switching repeatedly from Kitty to me to Kitty, "you're just having fun at my expense, aren't you two? There is no Mr. Davenport, is there?"

"Oh, he's as real as can be," confirmed Kitty. "You ask anyone. Anyone you please will remember Mr. Davenport at the dance dragging Addy out onto the dance floor." At this Miss Straightlace showed signs of fainting away, but she wanted to hear the rest, and refrained. "Oh yes, everyone saw it, and most came away from the dance with a black eye to remember the whole night by!"

"Goodness," said Prudence turning to me, as if I were a fallen lady. "My dear child, whatever have you gotten yourself into?"

As our conversation had become animated, Mr. Furnas

joined us. "Yes," he said throwing in his two bits, "that Mr. Davenport is an awfully mysterious businessman. Bringing things into town but never selling anything."

I defended my beau by going on the attack. "Right, Mr. Furnas, but no worse than the Nebraska Settlement Company, with you, Reverend Wood, and Mr. Muir. Whatever settlement has your lot established? Awful mysterious as well."

"Give us time," he said, as he changed the subject to those around him that he was unacquainted with. "I haven't had the pleasure," he said, extending a hand to Prudence, whose face now resembled one of those Greek masks reserved for tragedies. She envisioned me, no doubt, as Cassandra, lured in by Apollo, and destined by my suitor to a life of misery that could only end with my murder. Strange she would make the comparison, because unlike Cassandra, I had no inkling of what the future lay in store for me.

To break the heavy silence, I began the introductions. "Miss Straight..." I said, before catching myself. "Miss Withers, I mean, *straight* from Ohio. And her brother Jonathan. Mr. Furnas is editor of our local paper, the most widely distributed in the Territory."

"Oh," said Prudence, finally distracted from contemplating my tragic plight. "Do you promote the Republican cause?"

"My dear lady," responded our anti-abolitionist, "the Republican cause, if it gain in popularity, will be the demise of this nation. Now I'm not an advocate of slavery, but to oppose a way of life is futile, no one will convince he who has grown up in the institution to abandon it. But I might allay your concerns, if you've been polluted by Republican notions, slavery is not economically sustainable and will be abandoned over time."

"Meanwhile, Prudence," I said to complete the picture, "Mr. Furnas will stand idly by and allow his brothers in Adam to be whipped to death, his sisters in Eve to be dishonored by their white masters, and allow both brothers and sisters to have their children torn from their arms and sold downriver."

Prudence now spotted an adversary in Mr. Furnas. "Well, sir, I shan't read a paper that derides abolition. My attentions, like those of all well-schooled women, will go to Addy's gazette. *The Brownville Beacon* will shine a light on the evils of slavery and the wickedness of alcohol. We shall, and you may hold us to it, promote the cause of temperance! And we'll get the women to discourage these pernicious dancing affairs. If the women won't go, the men won't have anyone to carry on with!"

I thought it ironic that her rabid opposition to a cotillion, to gay apparel, and the like, might drive me to drink.

Meanwhile, Jonathan, bored with topics not of his own making or in which he had a role to play, said dismissively to his sister, "With over a thousand distilleries in the nation, with families depending upon the revenue for their daily bread, I'm afraid your objections, dear sister, will hardly matter."

"You object to the dance too, Miss Withers?" asked Mr. Furnas with one eye on me accompanied with a mischievous smile. "Like the good reverend, you see dances as the Devil's entertainment?"

"Oh, my," I interrupted. "Is that not Mrs. Furnas in the distance?"

Mr. Furnas turned to look at his wife who walked up the dusty road with children about her.

"She was signaling you, Mr. Furnas, I believe." Then I called down the street, but not quite loud enough for her to hear. "He'll be coming Mrs. Furnas, we're just leaving."

I thought to myself, if I could just keep Miss Straightlace preoccupied with writing articles for the *Brownville Beacon*, I could keep her in ignorance about my plans for a dance come July Fourth.

Now, it's not that I fear Prudence, or think that, in her reports to papa, she'll distort everything I'm doing to such a point of vice that my father would have me dragged back to Ohio, it's rather that I don't want to hear her delivering heated sermons to me through the month of July: it's already hot enough in Nebraska Territory.

"Prudence," I said as we retraced our steps back home, "I would like so much for you to help me out with my gazette articles. I've got some already planned for the first edition, but I'd like to have a store of them."

She beamed. "I know exactly what you need, and Jonathan could be our muse, letting us in on those needs and interests of men which would be of consequence for the ladies." I looked around for Jonathan and located his silhouette disappearing into town along with those of Stewart and Kitty. "He's so perspicacious, Addy. You'll find his company rewarding. Just think, you and he can chat day long about weighty matters of the soul that you can transcribe into epigrams to inject into our gazette."

"I'm sure we'll have words," I said honestly. "But as for myself, I'm going to focus on a tragedy that occurred here one year ago." I told her of the Friend murders in as much detail as I possessed.

"And," I reiterated, "I want not only to find out who put George Lincoln and his ne'er-do-wells up to the crime, I want to show how, unless repentance make way for God's grace, poor choices made in youth result in worse choices as adults. My plan is to compare George with someone who had an equally rough upbringing, but who turned out profitable for society. Peter Cartwright wouldn't be a bad subject."

"The Arminian? The preacher who claims you can lose your salvation?""

"He has a right to be wrong on some things, but overall, he has overcome his childhood. Like many young men on the frontier."

Just then we heard a gunshot and laughter. In an empty lot not far from my house we espied a group of young men carrying on. One of the group held a pistol in one hand and a bottle in another, obviously trying to steady his wavy arm as it pointed the gun, in a circular fashion, at a cat running for cover underneath a bush.

I intervened, grabbing the man's wrist and forcing him to put the gun down. It was quite heroic of me, considering his breath alone could have intoxicated a dozen temperance women. I approached the bush and kneeled down. I gave the poor wretch my gentlest of smiles and followed this up with a quiet "meow" of my own. Then slowly I reached in. She willingly came into my arms and I nestled her against my bosom. She felt so comfortable and safe that when she caught sight of her persecutors, she didn't hesitate to hiss and chomp down on my hand.

I did reassure her, calmed her back down. We brought her

home and christened her "Gunshy," and offered her a lick of bacon.

Prudence stood over me while I petted Gunshy who dutifully cleaned her plate. "Do you think that's how it happened?" she asked. "A group of young men who just had too much to drink and started taking pot shots at the Friends' cat? Mrs. Friend comes out to save the cat, gets mortally wounded, and then the gang decides they must get rid of everyone? I mean it may not have been a cat, it might have been another animal or even just taking pot shots at Mr. Friend for fun, and then all went wrong."

It seemed odd to me that Prudence offered this rather ridiculous explanation. I picked up Gunshy and looked at Prudence. She looked away, saying, "Just a thought. I wouldn't want you to be wasting your time. You know, there are no witnesses, so it's impossible to know what happened."

She walked to the bedroom door and paused in front of it. "I think I'll lie down a bit, if you don't mind. I'm dreadfully fatigued."

"Pay no mind," I said. But as she shut the door, an eeriness settled over my soul, like when you think you hear another's footsteps in the dark of night, but you're the only one home, and then the lone candle, that's far off in the adjoining room, extinguishes itself.

CHAPTER 7

n Monday morning, the twenty-second of June, I planned to awaken myself before my guest could stir but found Miss Straightlace ahead of schedule, standing over my bed fully armed for the day. She had laid out a dress for me but I had no intention on attending a funeral, so I picked out my own.

I was less successful in walking a direct path to the gazette office, she managed to deviate our course toward the Nebraska House where we retrieved Jonathan. Extricating him from the hotel was an effort, as he wanted to discuss matters with the indulgent chambermaid, Kitty.

In particular, he detained her to describe an illness to which he had fallen victim. It consisted of headache and fever, but nothing consistent with what others experienced. His was grander and higher than anything a man had suffered since the Great Plague, but he bore it without complaint, and he told us this multiple times. And even though he ought to have been hospitalized, he agreed, after Kitty excused herself to attend to another guest, to ignore the pains that a normal mortal could never bear, and accompany us.

As we finally moved forward to the office, Jonathan pestered me with questions about Kitty, and wondered out loud why she cleaned rooms when her grandfather bathed in dollars. "Precisely," I told him, "he's her grandfather, not her father. If we inherited directly only from our grandparents, my father would still be wealthy but I would be a pauper." Deeming this sufficient knowledge for someone really only interested in himself, I didn't bother explaining the whole story concerning Kitty's parents, who had estranged themselves from the grandfather.

After entering the official headquarters of the *Brownville Beacon: A Lady's Gazette*, perhaps like von Steuben entering the barracks of the colonial militia, I found Teddy seated on the table with at least three loafers. One was Christopher Martin, phrenologist. Rising from the lone chair in the room, the scientist placed a newspaper under his elbow and informed me that he had just come from the wharf, where he'd found a copy of the *Wilmington Herald*. He said this while patting the newspaper as if it were an appreciative cat.

I doubted his judgment of time, for when I had traversed the threshold, he was so well ensconced in my chair and so at ease in emitting a flow of words commensurate with a speech of the illustrious Daniel Webster, that I imagined he had been stewing in my office for quite some time. Whilst I was calculating this, Teddy hopped off the table and walked spritely over to the east side of the room, gathered up his strewn effects, and stuffed them into his trunk. The two other gentlemen had obviously arrived after Mr. Martin, as they had no claim on the chair and had accordingly propped themselves up against the wall, or should I say they slouched themselves up against the wall, somewhat like tall sacks of grain that bend in the middle. Neither made a move to greet me or even recognize me. One of them chewed on a burnt-out pipe.

Prudence, unacquainted with Mr. Martin, who did rise to greet her, introduced herself and immediately apprised him of what we were going to do with our gazette.

Martin, knowing my mission aforehand, interrupted her with a scoff, especially mocking abolitionism and temperance by uttering some sort of aphorism he'd contracted from the *Wilmington Herald*: "'What would prove sport to you, would be death to us,' said the frogs when the boys were pelting them with stones." He stood back to judge the effect, but seeing none, he felt obliged to explain. "My dear Miss Withers, temperance is a waste of time, except for those with unshapely heads."

"My dear Mr. Martin," returned Prudence, "alcohol is the fuel of vice."

"You," reposted Mr. Martin, "remind me of the old lady who rushed into the garden in search of her daughter, on being told that the young lady had gone there with a rake."

"Bravo for the mother. A young woman's honor cannot be too well protected!"

I observed this exchange quietly as it brought to mind my schoolmaster telling us that in order to calculate the volume of a cylinder one needed to use pi, and Zach, considering how close it was to noontime, asking which kind of pie. Now Zach, I judged, to be of a clownish disposition. My dear Miss Straightlace, on the other hand, being as high minded as a telegraph pole, and just as chatty, could not have been responding with wit.

I intervened. "If you can accept alcohol, then why not the

Negro?"

The professor of phrenology stared down upon me as if he'd just stepped in something unpleasant in a back alley. "The Negro is born of a different creation. Have you not heard of Professor Agassiz's discovery of the various ice ages that have englobed the earth over the centuries? After each there appeared a new creation of flora and fauna. Though the professor does not say as much, I hold that the Negro was not of our creation. Seriously, I cannot believe that even you could look a man born for slavery in the face and find that face fit to make decisions on its own."

There's a time for reasoned argument and a time for feminine intuition, and the situation clearly called for the latter. Beautiful as he may have thought his skull to be, I looked around for an object with which to rearrange it. My parasol looked up at me invitingly, so, grabbing it by the handle, I raised it against the Canaanite. Observing that Teddy had retreated behind the press, Mr. Martin's stare of snobbery transformed into one of either anger or horror. I couldn't take any chances and tilted the tip of the parasol backwards to get more of a whipping effect if need be.

Mr. Martin came at me ferociously, leaning forward as he did. Some might have thought he was simply retrieving his hat from the table, but like I said, I could take no chances.

"Dare you strike a woman!" I cried, while delivering a well-placed blow upon his well-honed skull. I imagine that if he measured it anew, after my ministration, he would have been even more proud of it, as it no doubt increased a fair inch in girth.

"Good Lord!" he exclaimed, picking up his hat.

"Yes, he is good." I agreed. "And he created us all in his image. And I can think of no fairer face than that of a sable brother or sister. And I am not alone in my thoughts, for our Republican Party is a multitude, and I dare say all of my sisters carry a parasol."

He didn't respond immediately, but seemed preoccupied with rubbing the back of his head. He rather cautiously moved toward the door, deferentially, without turning his back to me as if I were royalty. Once on the threshold, however, he resumed his professorial pose and claimed I was not quite the multitude I thought. He then invited me to listen to what my fellow Republicans of the *Wilmington Herald* had to say about the Negro.

"The editor says," he read. "'Whenever negro suffrage becomes one of the planks of the Republican platform we shall feel free to seek some other political organization, and we think we shall find most of our Republican brethren in the same way.'"

"You'll note he did not speak for the women."

"And why should he? The right to vote is given to you neither by the U.S. Constitution nor by your own mental constitution."

"Yet our efforts, as mothers of the Republic, to guide our nation and right our wrongs shall not be in vain." Having said this, I gave a nod to Teddy, and said succinctly, "On his ear."

I had never before seen a phrenologist shift from a professorial stance to a sprint on such short notice. Even his fellow loafers, the tall sacks of grain propped up against the wall, grew legs and found their way out the door.

* * *

In the early afternoon, Prudence and I put away our writings and I surveyed the office. Jonathan had wandered into town to exercise his lungs amongst a boatload of freshly arrived emigrants, no doubt expounding upon how much more difficult his trip to the frontier had been compared to theirs. Teddy had gone off not long after helping Mr. Martin out the door, to lath and plaster walls in Mr. Whitt's house.

Mr. Whitt, I thought, *what audacity to buy my humble office building out from under me. If my gazette turns profitable, I might just purchase another lot and put up a building of my own. It couldn't be any more spartan than this one.*

Meanwhile, I needed more information on the Friend murders in order to write a story that would attract readers.

Making my way onto Main Street, I crossed paths with Judge Black, newly arrived in town. Mr. Furnas was giving him a tour of our settlement and introduced us. I used the opportunity to ask our new judge about the Friend murders, but he, like Judge Kinney, claimed that their confrere Judge Norton duly settled the question a year ago. Mr. Furnas, always interested in promoting the finer history of our colony, echoed Judge Black.

Prudence and her brother found me in the street. When Mr. Whitt exited his shop, apparently to better judge the figure of a young emigrant woman on the other side of the thoroughfare, I asked them to remain where they were for the moment while I approached him.

"Why, good evening Miss Furlough," he said, looking at me with his head turned as if he thought I might want something but was afraid to ask. Oh, how little he understands women. I kept my silence to see if he could remember his promise about visiting the Friend farm.

Apparently, the promise had retreated into the recesses of his brain as he concentrated on exuding a certain male charm. Smiling, he asked, "Would you give me the pleasure of accompanying me for a walk along the levee? I wouldn't want such a fashionable lady as yourself to hold a grudge against me. Your brother is well worth his wages, I had just overlooked his payment. Besides, my clerk is doing an inventory and I wouldn't want to distract him in his arithmetic." He thrust out his elbow and I took it.

"Certainly," I said, "I do appreciate a man of his word." I gave a discreet nod to Prudence so that she and Jonathan follow on.

"Yes, yes," he repeated a few times. "Yes, the levee, I'm so glad I mentioned it." He was thinking on his feet, trying to come up with something pleasing to say, but as his feet were moving, he had difficulty. Finally, he recited Latin names for plants we saw. Then, sensing we were not alone, he looked over his shoulder. "I see we have the Withers taking up the same promenade as we, only her parasol is straight. Whatever happened to yours?"

"It got in an argument, and won."

"Oh, did it now?" He said this in an interesting tone, somewhat like the doctor, who sees nothing at all problematic about his patient's bedroom, but hears her describe to him monkeys of various colors crawling up the walls. I had a great aunt, of Puritan stock mind you, but unfortunately given to drink, who described just such a setting to her doctor. She was very good at storytelling, but he brought up, what I would have considered the critical point, that monkeys were not native to

Massachusetts. "Oh," she said to him in the very same tone he had used with her, "and so you believe we're in Massachusetts?"

"Yes," I said, "Mr. Martin had been most disagreeable with his contempt for others who do not look like him. I had to shoo him out of my office. Hence the state of my parasol." We walked along a little farther, and I dropped my veil to confound the gnats and mosquitoes. I complimented Mr. Whitt on his scientific knowledge and assured him that he would be a splendid teacher if ever we built a high school. He admitted his interest in teaching and told me the passion was shared between himself and Mr. Martin, who, in spite of his sometimes awkward manners, knew his science. Apparently, Mr. Martin was now traveling about the countryside in search of settlements desiring to establish high schools. We walked a little more to where the end of the levee approached.

"I think we ought to take the trail," I suggested.

"Sure enough, there's a splendid little meadow not far off, and an excellent hillside where we might seek some repose."

"Well," said I, "I doubt we have time to take our leisure. I don't want to return too late from the Friend farm."

The words "Friend farm" brought Mr. Whitt to a halt. I could see by his expression that all had suddenly become clear to him. "The Friend farm? Why it's quite a walk down to it, and there's really nothing to see there. I've yet to till the ground and haven't even finished putting up a structure."

As Prudence and Jonathan joined us, I reminded him of his promise, and that my friends had taken useful time out of their day to accompany me.

My druggist surveyed us one by one, and I would say there

was a mix of desperation and futility in his eyes.

I looked at him gently, as I had at Gunshy when reaching down to pick her up underneath that bush. "We're almost there. It shan't take long. You've no doubt things to attend to any given day of the week, so there's no better time than the present."

Mr. Whitt conceded and we continued our peregrination through the wilderness. Sunlight danced down upon us through the overhead leaves, and the uneven shadowing of the trail created a medieval atmosphere wherein one expected to see a gnome, or some other mythical creature, slip behind the trees, ever out of reach.

Jonathan broke the spell by comparing our gothic trail to the highway back in Ohio. If the men of Brownville had half the pluck of their ancestors, he argued, but mostly to himself, there would already be not only a road but also a railroad through Nebraska. I pointed out that railroads didn't exist in the days of our forebearers and that I rather liked our delicate trails, and, though I hoped the railroad would not tarry in coming, I also trusted there would always be a place for these humble paths in the hearts of our entrepreneurs. He paid no mind to my comment and expanded upon the necessity of a bridge to cover the Missouri, like the one recently built over the Muskingum River in Ohio.

I hadn't really noticed at first, but as Mr. Whitt informed us that we were reaching our destination, I observed that Jonathan was a half-step ahead of us. He reminded me of Raven, an old horse we kept on the farm, who insisted on being leader of the pack whenever we went for a ride, stretching her stride out just enough to stay a nose ahead of whichever young mare was next to her.

Mr. Whitt veered off to the left to show us a claim marker he'd pounded into the ground. Jonathan continued along the trail absent-mindedly.

Mr. Whitt removed his hat and scratched at his scalp. "If memory serves me right, the house site should be just ahead, unless the Missouri came up and washed it away." It's true that the river has little patience for sedentary types, and the Pawnee respect this riverine attitude by moving about.

The vegetation was thick where there were no trees, but we didn't expect to find the charred remains of the log cabin under a leafy canopy, so we wrestled our way through the brush. Mr. Whitt referenced the river two or three times more before abandoning hope.

I began to think. It seemed to me the cabin should not have been far from the trail.

Then Jonathan hollered out, "You lookin' for the remains of a fire?"

We made our way over to him and sure enough, not far from the path, you could see the outlines of a cabin with charred logs spread out here and there. I stared at the remains, thinking of the family that once lay amongst the ashes.

"You can pretty well see how she was constructed," observed Jonathan.

Indeed, the scorched area formed a rectangle, with a particular variety of broadleaf weeds that benefited from the ashen soil. On the edge that was furthest from the river lay a heap of stones, which I judged to have been the fireplace. Naturally, their front door would have been opposite it, facing the river and the rising sun.

"Yep," said Mr. Whitt. "That were it, now I remember." He allowed a little silence to pass before adding, "So I suppose we can start heading back."

Jonathan nodded in agreement, but I interposed. "No, I'd like to take a close look." I studied the ground carefully. "If the fireplace were there," I said pointing to the stones, "and the door behind me, then either side would have had a room or a separation of some sort for sleeping quarters." Walking the perimeter I found, on the north end, melted glass, the remains of a mirror, and hinges, most likely from a trunk. "This end," I said, "must have been where the parents slept."

I took my parasol and began poking around where I thought the bed might have been. Suddenly we all heard the parasol go "thunk," it was a deep and resounding "thunk." I pulled up my dress enough to where I could get on my knees. I looked at my gloves and removed them. I could wash my hands better than my gloves.

"Miss Furlough," said Mr. Whitt, "I really think it's getting late."

"It won't take but a minute, sir," I said. And I pulled up some weeds and pushed the soil to one side. Soon appeared a flat, white stone. I picked up the pace and began digging with my fingernails to scrape off the dirt all around it.

"Whatever's in there is mine," announced Mr. Whitt.

I looked up at him. "Is that why you're claiming the land? You heard there's some sort of treasure buried here somewhere?"

"It wasn't uncommon knowledge at the time that the family had more than enough to pay their preemption. Not a penny of it discovered on Mr. Lincoln or his associates. So finding it would be, of course, a bonus for the claimholder...me!"

"Enough to buy a newspaper office?"

By his galled and surprised look, I could tell my landlord had betrayed a confidence.

"Well, er...I uh, suppose so. It was just business. Nothing personal you see."

"You just wanted to close up my business, didn't you? You had no interest in that measly cabin of mine."

"That's my affair, my dear. I'm sure you would have found some place to operate your press. But let's attend to the task at hand. What's under that stone."

The stone was large, about two by three handspans, but I was able to pull it up on edge and then lay it over to peer inside. Nothing.

I sat back on my haunches. Disappointment overshadowed me. I had felt that there would be some sort of clue here that would lead me somehow to unravel the mystery surrounding the Friend murders.

Mr. Whitt was also disappointed but was gracious enough to help me to my feet. As we left the site Prudence let out a gasp and fell to the ground. Jonathan came to her rescue and put her upright.

I looked down and saw a collection of bottles strewn about, most halfway sunk into the ground. Some were medicinal, others soda or mineral water, but like for so many, it was the whiskey bottle that brought her down.

"Mr. Friend, apparently, was no temperance man," I remarked. "But I suppose that goes without saying for a German."

CHAPTER 8

lthough my soul enjoyed the walk into the countryside and back, my legs protested and seemed determined to take me home and put me to bed. Knowing that my aching muscles would be constantly pestering me, I desired a quiet time at home with just my novel and Gunshy for company. My concern was that Prudence would coax Jonathan along, and Gunshy had a distinctive distaste for males of the human species: I suppose they all had a scent of gunpowder about them. I could share her feelings concerning Jonathan.

Then I remembered Mrs. Medford, and a flash of cerebral lightning illuminated my brain. Today, I remembered, was quilt day.

"Dear Prudence," I said, "I've always admired your needlework."

"Thank you, dear," she said, "My mother was very much a mistress of the art. A true Minerva. She taught me well, and I dare say a woman is incomplete without a knowledge of the skill. But whatever brings this to mind?"

I started to say "Jonathan," but thought better of it and took a different tack. "I had forgotten, but Mrs. Medford is hosting a quilting party today. It's already started I fear, but just, so you can yet make it. I bought the necessaries for quilting so that you might go and share your skills with them. My needlework is irregular and makes a mockery of any quilt."

Prudence's eyes lit up, but decorum required her to first refuse. It was on my third attempt that she graciously accepted to go.

"They'll be so appreciative," I said. "And I suppose Jonathan could escort you there and even linger if he wish."

Jonathan thought that he might be a bother at a quilting bee. I told him that I thought he wouldn't be any more a bother there than elsewhere. Nevertheless, he declined to go and preferred to return to the hotel to see if new emigrants had arrived.

"You're right Jonathan," I said encouragingly. "You'll be appreciated there as anywhere."

* * *

On Tuesday morning, while Prudence went to visit her brother, I made my way to Mary's where Mrs. Fanny Smith, a talented English seamstress, fitted my dress. In the afternoon, I wandered over to the Post Office, after the stage had arrived from Rock Port, Missouri, to see if any letters were addressed to me. I was expecting correspondence, principally from my gossips back East.

The sheriff appeared astride his horse, whom he christened Balaklava, a spirited animal with a nervous condition that should require a full dose of laudanum each morning. The name, I should say, caused some confusion, since the real Balaklava, equine hero of the light brigade's charge, had recently arrived in these United States. Several boys inquired of the lawman if his steed were not the one of Crimean fame, and I do believe he led them on a bit in their delusion.

Mr. Brown, our town's namesake and postmaster, appeared before the Post Office, hat in hand, holding it before him like a collection plate. He did this because he managed to keep all of the day's correspondence in his hat. He lifted out the first letter, as if drawing a winning number for a tombola, and called forth the winner, Dr. J. L. McKee, physician and surgeon dentist. And, if you believed the advertisement about him in the *Advertiser*, he plugged and filled teeth "in the most approved method." According to his professional acquaintances, however, he seemed to be the only one who approved of his method.

As Dr. McKee collected his letter, I noticed a haze above the post office. "Is someone burning brush?" I asked Mr. Brown. He thought there might be someone doing such a deed somewhere, but as he was facing me, he didn't know I was inquiring about a possible conflagration in his immediate vicinity.

The sheriff, always with a nose for trouble, caught sight of the haze, and convinced Balaklava to take him to its source. Balaklava had a good and ready heart for adventure, but when the horse disappeared around the corner of the building with his master and got his nostrils full of smoke, he went into a panic. We could hear Sheriff Coleman call out "Fire! Fire!" but rather than remain on the scene and direct any collective efforts to douse the conflagration, Balaklava decided for him that the best course of action was to high tail it in a direction opposite the fire.

A frenzy of activity commenced, with men out-muscling

each other to get to the fire. Mr. Brown, however, held back, protecting the property in his hat that had been entrusted to his care as postmaster. There were calls for spades, water, and blankets. I stood next to Mr. Muir and our local dentist and together we watched our firemen conquer the flames. Every group of heroes requires an audience.

The dentist shook his head as he estimated the damage. Mr. Muir, for his part, commented that it was a sad reality that too few people thought of fire insurance. I noted that it would only cost the life of a medium-sized cottonwood to replace the lean-to shack, but he somehow diverted the conversation to my own home and the advantages to having a policy with him in case an incendiary might target it. I doubted that a possibility, but he assured me that people with strong opinions ought always to have fire insurance. Before leaving my side, he gave me a quick and relevant history of the violent agitation attached to the issue of slavery going on down in Kansas Territory.

After extinguishing the fire, the crowd reported back to the front of the Post Office where Mr. Brown resumed his distribution. I could hear the sheriff coaxing Balaklava to return to the blackened battlefield. "You ought to be ashamed of yourself. And with the name you've got."

I tarried around the burnt-out shack, wondering how it could have caught on fire. On the far side I found a tiny metal box, marked Bryant, in the grass. I opened it and found a single locofoco, and I asked myself what would a box of matches be doing here? Glancing about the singed grass near the charred remains of the building, I observed two extinguished matches. A little farther out, I found an uncorked whiskey bottle with only a few drops left inside. I picked it up, and I don't know exactly why, but something in my mind told me to sniff it. I did, and it had a strange smell. I've smelled whiskey before. My eldest brother Jerome once stored a bottle in the barn. I think it was a trophy of some sort, because he had it for years and would pull it out only to impress his friends. I'd learned not to use it to play hide and seek with him. He tended to locate it rather quickly by twisting my arm or pulling my hair to get a hint as to where I might have gone with it. In any case, I'd had occasions to smell the poison, and this bottle behind the shack smelled of a different poison. One that was familiar to me.

I stood there looking at the bottle when I heard Mr. Brown call out. "By golly! This one's got the same last name as our murderer and that rabble rouser in Illinois. Maybe these two Lincoln families are related. And the letter is addressed to you Sheriff Coleman."

I dashed back around the building in search of the sheriff. He was walking Balaklava up Main Street toward his livery station. I sidled up next to him.

He looked down at me. "I'm rather surprised at you, Miss Furlough."

It was then that I noticed I still had the whiskey bottle in my hand. "Oh! Yes, well it's not mine. I found it down by the shack that caught fire. Smell of it, Sheriff. What do you think was in it?"

He gave it a whiff. "I'd say turpentine."

"That's what I think. And there were burnt-out matches near it. Whom do you think imbibes in this brand of whiskey?" I asked holding up the bottle.

He and Balaklava stopped in their tracks. "About everybody around here." He looked at me rather sternly, almost like Jerome interrogating me about his whiskey bottle. "Look, Miss Furlough, I know you're planning on publishing that paper of yours."

"A gazette, rather, a lady's gazette."

"Whatever you want to call it, you're planning on putting stories in there that you think are going to be smart; stories about troubles in Brownville and the like. Now, whether they're true or not, there's a lot of people who've invested their life savings in the future of this town. We're not going to take lightly to you tarnishing the town's reputation."

I couldn't help but notice that his "they" had quickly turned into a "we."

He continued, "And I'm not sure what Robert has in mind by having you speak at the Fourth of July celebration, but I would mind my words if I were you."

"Is the Sheriff threatening me?"

"No, Miss Furlough, I'm protecting you. I'm glad to know you found evidence of an incendiary, that's helpful, I'm going to do my darnedest to catch the miscreant, but I don't want you hurt. Like I said, if you broadcast information like this, there's people around here, who have nothing to do with lighting any fires at present, but who just might set your house on fire to get you out of here. Do you understand?"

"All right," I accepted. "I'll stop thinking about this fire. Don't know what the importance of it would be anyway. Couldn't have been for insurance because the building wasn't insured."

"Now how do you know that?"

"It doesn't matter, because I'm not interested in that fire at present; but what's that letter about?" I asked, pointing at the envelope.

"Listen carefully, Miss Furlough, because I think you're a bit hard of hearing. I know you've been going around kicking up dust about these Friend murders. It's old history, been settled, and best forgotten. Brownville needs emigrants."

By this time Dr. McKee joined us, but it didn't stop Sheriff Coleman's scolding. "Even when you're not trying to cause trouble, you somehow manage to create it. Why think of that disastrous dance of yours. We were the laughing stock of the frontier all the way to Saint Joseph."

"Now Sheriff," said Dr. McKee, a true gentleman, "in Miss Furlough's defense, I should say I didn't see the lady throw a single punch."

"Thank you doctor," I said. "Now, if you could get Sheriff Coleman into your chair, I suppose you might be able to extract from him the contents of that letter."

The sheriff, not typically a loquacious man, decided to end my interview by mounting his horse. Up on the saddle, he adopted a more jovial and confident attitude, much like a brave knight ready to launch himself into a joust with the court jester. "I'd rather have Balaklava take my teeth out with one swift kick," he said while Balaklava chomped at the bit, "than sit in that chair and have them drilled and yanked on one by one."

As he trotted off, Dr. McKee let out a "Humph," and went off in his own direction. I looked about for Mr. Brown to see if he had received any letters for me, but he was nowhere in sight. When I asked after him, I was told he'd headed down to the ferry. I decided to go home to get some rest and think things over.

Opening my front door, I discovered Cameron standing in my parlor beside a traveling trunk.

CHAPTER 9

 shut the door behind me by pressing up against it with my back. I couldn't take my eyes off Cameron.

"My dear Cameron, I wasn't expecting you so soon."

"Disappointed?"

"As much as the prodigal's father."

He explained that down at the wharf he saw an old friend, Antoine Barada, who brought him and his luggage up to the house. Toine, as they call the man, is the largest man ever to walk the earth since Goliath. He's half Omaha Indian, half French, and half oak tree. He's the one who convinced me Aunt Adeline might still be alive, because he knew of a redheaded squaw long ago known as Head on Fire. Toine also moved my press from the wharf up to my office because nobody else could lift the thing. If ever Mr. Whitt had succeeded in purchasing my office, I would have needed Toine's help again, or would have had to cede my machine to Mr. Whitt.

But these thoughts came and went like a gust of wind, and I embraced Cameron, holding him tight.

After a heartwarming moment, he took me by the shoulders

and gently backed me away from him a step or two. "I've brought a surprise." Having said this he tapped on the trunk, which sprang open like a jack-in-the-box. Up stood a man, small in stature, and as dark as the night.

"I be Solomon, Miss Addy. I's heard all about you."

He stepped out of his little home to shake hands. Cameron pushed the trunk up against the door, then walked over to the gueridon and picked up *Hope Leslie*. "You're not planning to run off into the wilderness to join your aunt's tribe, are you?"

"I've heard there are vacancies. And I think you would make a satisfactory buffalo hunter."

"Speaking of the hunt, you wouldn't have any game would you. We haven't eaten since yesterday."

"Take a chair in the kitchen, and I'll find you something."

While I removed my bonnet, Cameron picked up his carpet-bag and they passed through the dining room and made their way into the kitchen. He thought he heard a noise outside and he opened the door to the back porch. He abruptly stepped back into the shadows of the kitchen.

"Who's that old man in your garden cleaning off your tools?"

My doors were lined up in such a way that from the parlor I could see clear through to the garden, but I walked to the back door to get a better look. "That would be Monsieur Carr; he's probably getting ready to come in for his *gouter*."

"*Gouter?*"

"Afternoon snack. You two should hide in the dining room while I fix him bread and jam. He only comes into the kitchen."

I shut the door, passed a loaf of bread to my two hungry travelers, cleared the tiny kitchen table of a basket of cherries and set out Monsieur Carr's gouter.

Monsieur Carr soon rapped upon the door; I let him in and he occupied a chair across from mine. As he reached for the jam, I heard another knock, but this time on the front door. Hurrying to the sound, opening and shutting doors as I went, I saw the handle of the front door move and the trunk begin to slide forward. I put my foot up against the trunk to stop its progress.

Unfortunately, the front door had opened wide enough for the postmaster to slip his head through it. "It's Mr. Brown, Miss Furlough. I heard you were looking for me."

I could hear some jingling about in the dining room. It sounded like Cameron had emptied the contents of his carpet bag onto the table.

"Umm, Mr. Brown, if you could wait a minute, I'll just move my trunk." I pulled at the trunk as if it were full of books and slowly moved it off to the side.

Mr. Brown then emerged fully into the parlor. He took off his hat and revealed a handful of envelopes inside it. "I believe two of these are for you."

He handed me the letters and then stood there anxiously, like a schoolboy waiting for the schoolmaster to hand back an assignment he knows he's going to get an A on because his sister did it for him. "Oh," I said to satisfy his curiosity. "This one's from one of my storytellers. And this one is from Papa. He'll probably want to know if I've made progress on locating my Aunt Adeline."

"I wonder what the story's about."

"I'm afraid you'll have to wait until my gazette is published."

"Mon Dieu!" came a cry in French from behind the dining room door. "Un nègre!"

"Is that you, John," called out Mr. Brown, "speaking that heathen tongue?"

"Yes," I said, startled by Monsieur Carr's voice. "He's my help."

"I understand that, Miss Furlough, but what's he saying?"

"I'm not quite sure," I answered less than honestly.

"Un moment, Monsieur Carr," I said, "je viens partager le gouter avec vous."

I thought it might quiet the old Frenchman down if I told him I'd be there in a moment to share in the gouter, but I was wrong.

"Un esclave?" he continued. "Dites moi qu'il ne couche pas chez vous, mademoiselle." I'm glad he decided to keep it in French. He imagined I'd acquired a slave and feared that I allowed him to sleep in the house with me.

I heard some scuffling about, a grunt as if the old man were being pushed back into the kitchen, and then finally the bang of a door closing. There was more rustling about in the dining room, but it didn't sound so much like a struggle as someone rummaging about. Nonetheless, I did hear a few choice but muffled words in French that I shall not repeat. It sounded like Monsieur Carr lodging complaints through a barricaded door.

Suddenly, the dining room door leading into the parlor swung open. Within the doorframe appeared Mr. Davenport. "Don't you worry, sir," he said to Mr. Brown, "I guess Frenchy has never laid eyes on a minstrel."

I must admit that at first, I wasn't quite sure whether it was

Solomon or Cameron, but the taller stature, and perhaps the clear blue eyes gave my beau away. His face was covered with boot polish as black as night, he wore a hat to cover his hair.

"He's practicing for a performance." I improvised. Mr. Brown gave me a sidelong glance of disapproval. I sensed that he wondered what a bachelor might be doing in my house, so I added, "Miss Withers and I are his audience, although for the moment she's, uh...."

I couldn't think what she might be doing but Cameron came to the rescue by stating that she was in the bedroom at the moment working on his costume, sewing patches on trousers.

Mr. Brown seemed mollified by this explanation but asked, "What kind of music do you do?"

"Only the best," affirmed Cameron.

"Well, then, let us hear a tune."

Before I could put a stop to it, Cameron struck up a snappy tune, and about half way through it I thought I heard a humming accompaniment coming from the bottom half of my hutch. Though the melody was predictable, if not familiar, the words were new to me.

"I be a plantin' massa's corn," sang Cameron with his white teeth glistening against the backdrop of his blackened face, "ever since the day he be born. Taint no fun pickin' his ol corn. And de day-long hours makes me frown. 'Cause he be ol Massa Brown."

"Now that's a dandy," cried Massa Brown, slapping a thigh. "You've got them folks down pat."

Meanwhile, I could see behind my minstrel, a Frenchman advancing through the kitchen door, looking suspiciously under the table upon which I observed a pile of linen.

* * *

As Mr. Brown left, I directed my minstrel into the parlor to practice his act and then redirected Monsieur Carr back to our gouter. Having just sat down, I heard the front door open. I thought Cameron was effecting an escape, but then I heard a familiar voice calling for me.

I excused myself and went into the parlor to find Prudence. "Jonathan is busy at the moment entertaining a host of emigrants down at the hotel," she said.

"I'm sure they appreciate helpful frontier information from a man of experience."

"Yes, he's so attentive to the needs of others. Anyway, I've come to collect my handbag from the bedroom as we plan on doing a little shopping. I think we need to hang a picture in the parlor and I hope to find one at McPherson's."

I surveyed my small parlor and saw no evidence of my minstrel. I hadn't seen him in the dining room when I passed through, so he must have escaped into the bedroom. "Why don't I go retrieve your hand bag for you."

"No need, I'll get it."

"You are going into the bedroom?" I asked in a very loud and dramatic tone, as if I were on stage as a minstrel.

Prudence paused and stared at me. "Whatever is the matter with you Addy?"

I didn't have a reply and she opened the bedroom door, grabbed her handbag and exited, looking down at the palm of her hand as she did. It was black as shoe polish.

"Here," I said, offering my handkerchief. "I had some shoe polish on my hand earlier. Didn't realize it had migrated."

"Goodness," she said as she wiped her hand clean.

I eagerly opened the front door for her, but before she stepped through it, she asked, "Do you know anything of a minstrel?"

"A minstrel?" I returned the question with a look of surprise.

"Yes, I saw Mr. Brown on the way up and he said he thought I was with the minstrel."

"Oh, that minstrel. Yes, yes. That was my Cameron. He was showing me and old Monsieur Carr a routine he does. And I'm afraid I shook his hand when he left, which explains how I got the shoe polish on the bedroom door."

The explanation satisfied Prudence, especially if Monsieur Carr, completely harmless, even though French, were at the house. She hurried off to rejoin her brother whilst I finished the gouter with Monsieur Carr, who, when rising to return to the garden, arched his eyebrows while putting his index finger alongside his nose. I think this is French sign language for "I know you're up to something, but I'll say nothing."

No sooner had I closed the back door than I detected yet another rapping at the front door. My patience had worn thin and I imagined a peddler, probably selling pencils and ledger sheets, which could only be of interest to accountants, and I, having always been at war with numbers, was in no mood to be imposed upon. I opened the door with a jerk and saw two hands holding a ledger.

"Not interested, sir," I said.

"Oh?"

Then I looked up from the hands to the face and recognized Mr. Kennedy, Cameron's old friend and fellow abolitionist. His wagon stood out in the street.

"I've been told I could pick up my order here, and I've brought the *proof of purchase* with me." He said "proof of purchase" sarcastically, which told me it was a counterfeit document. A prop for the play, so to speak.

"Yes, do come in, Mr. Kennedy."

I turned around and gave a "Come out, come out, wherever you are" call and heard the lower doors on the hutch open and someone scrambling to get out from underneath a bed. The two appeared in the parlor in short order and I noted that Cameron had wiped most of the polish off of his face. Solomon was squeezed back into his trunk, which was hoisted onto the wagon that Mr. Kennedy, with Cameron at his side, drove back to the Kennedy farmstead.

Rejoining Monsieur Carr in the backyard, I told him I would transform my basket of cherries into three pies tonight, one for the office, one for the home, and one for him.

He invited me into the garden so that I might have a visual understanding of what he had already explained in some detail during his previous visits. So, bonnet set, I followed my help out of doors, and as I did, an idea, totally unrelated to gardening or pies or minstrels, popped into my head. I suppose this is how geniuses, like Ben Franklin, come up with new ideas. Perhaps the inventor cast hook, line, and sinker into a river, snagged a lively trout, and for some reason perceived in the event a string, a kite, and electricity.

Considering my unique idea, I resolved to visit Mr. Brown

on the morrow, first thing.

Meanwhile, Monsieur Carr gave me his horticultural lesson on tomatoes. The lecture lasted some time, and he does believe repetition helps the memory, because I think I had previously heard several excerpts of his oration. He had reached the point about pinching off budding stems when a darkness spread over us. We looked up to the sky and noted the heavy clouds rolling across it, their greenish hue, and the blustery breeze arising.

Jonathan and Prudence, who had earlier noticed the ominous sky, had abandoned their shopping and reached home port, probably during the lecture on squash, and observing us a little later in the backyard, joined us in the garden. Jonathan came equipped with an umbrella. How thoughtful, I presumed, as soon the storm broke. Monsieur Carr, not yet accustomed to the thunderous heavens of the frontier and the torrential downpours, herded us, with outstretched arms, toward the house, and all the while warning us not to take a chill. Considering the thermometer couldn't make it down below ninety degrees, I had a hard time sharing his concern.

When large raindrops began to fall, Jonathan popped up his umbrella, aiming it into the wind, and walked confidently under its canopy, neglecting to share any of his ambulating roof. He was preoccupied with telling me about how important it was for a young lady to be seen in public with gentlemen of a certain class, and that I might see tonight as an opportunity to make a satisfactory appearance at a political event.

As I stepped up onto the back porch, he did pause to stare at my revealed ankle, which peeved me. Then under the communal shelter of the porch, he folded his umbrella and judged it smart to pull my wet bonnet back off my head, extracting more than one hairpin. I'm sure he thought this some sort of service to me, but again, he only managed to irritate me further as my hair came loose and strands of it fell onto my shoulders in disarray.

"Why my dear Adeline," he said. "Don't you look presentable all aglow under your red hair. I know you'll appreciate attending General Bowen's speech tonight with a gentleman."

"Certainly, if you can find me one." I snatched my bonnet back and stormed inside, leaving him on the porch to discuss tomatoes with Monsieur Carr.

Prudence followed me in. "Oh Addy, don't you see your chance? My brother is educated and successful. He is more than a provider."

"Listen, Prudence. I know you adore your brother, but what do you really know of him? How did he know where the Friend house exactly was?"

"Whatever do you mean, Addy? You led him to the claim, we had no idea where it was. I suppose Jonathan figured out where the house site had been because he's just so clever."

Clever, I thought. *Perhaps Jonathan is much cleverer than I imagined. Perhaps his blustery and braggart manners distract us from a calculating and cunning mind.*

Needless to say, I did not meet General Bowen that evening, though I could hear, late into the night, cheers and fanfare rising up from the town square. Gunshy and I preferred to snuggle up together and read ourselves to sleep.

* * *

The next morning, Wednesday, I woke up finding Gunshy

in a ball snuggled up against my head. I gave her some leftovers for breakfast before going into town in search of Mr. Brown down at the ferry. The streets were muddy and the Brownvillians could only talk of the storm. One piece of hail, it was said, was five inches in circumference. So bad, it destroyed gardens, broke windows, and killed chickens. The consensus was that the weather had been determined by that mischievous comet.

I thought of poor Monsieur Carr and all those recipes he looked forward to. I hoped for his sake that my garden had been spared.

When I found Mr. Brown, I related to him the contents of my father's letter, and I even betrayed the topic of my storyteller: *The Virtues of the Riverman*. Having gained his friendship, I inquired about the letter the sheriff had received.

"I think it good, don't you, Mr. Brown," I said as I pursued my idea for finding out about the mysterious letter, "that Mrs. Lincoln confided in the sheriff?"

"She has the marks of a decent woman, that Mrs. Lincoln."

"What, do you think, was the most important part of her letter?"

"Well, I think it speaks highly of her to declare she wanted none of her son's effects, shamed as she was to be the mother of such a villain."

"So sad, a mother who wants nothing of her departed offspring. Nothing to remember him by."

"She does have George Lincoln's journal, though," observed Mr. Brown. "She said as much in her letter. And, if I quote her aright, she said, 'and I thanks the Lord I was never taught to read or write, so I don't have to read it.' And I think she was speaking the truth about being illiterate, because she signed her letter with a big 'X'."

I believe I stuttered in asking him to affirm that it was George Lincoln's journal she held in her possession. "And what of his other effects? The things he had on him when he was arrested."

"There's not much if memory serves. But since Mother Lincoln doesn't want them, it leaves the sheriff with the responsibility of dispensing with them, at public auction."

Hearing this, I politely abandoned Mr. Brown and rushed up First Street to my office, hoping to find Teddy *in situ*. I doubted he would be going to work until the mud dried. Opening the door, I saw him spread beneath his blanket, and I thanked the comet.

"Teddy!" I called out. "Wake up. It's Wednesday and the sheriff's wife and kids go to town."

I heard a feeble "Whaa?" emanate from the blanket.

"Yes, so get yourself dressed and ready."

He responded with the same zeal he exhibited back home on the farm, when mother handed him the milk pail, opened the door for him, and then pointed him in the direction of the barn half hidden by a raging blizzard.

"Come on," I said encouragingly. "You don't want to get accustomed to sleeping in!"

He muttered a few things. Included in the verbiage were words like "sheriff?", "wife?", "kids?". Then something more structured like, "You're up to something aren't you?"

"I just need you to report a theft."

"What's stolen?" he asked. He was now on all fours, but

his forehead was still against the floor. With his bushy hair I imagined a buffalo grazing out on the plains, and this brought to mind the Pawnee, then my aunt, but I had no time for such thoughts, so I chased them away by ordering Teddy onto his feet.

Once on his hind legs, he stumbled about feeling for his jeans on the printing press. I informed him that by widening his eyelids he would find them on the table. I was proved right.

"Teddy," I asked, imitating our mother's voice. "May I inquire as to what you were doing last night?"

"Somebody made a toast to General Bowen. Then somebody else did. Then somebody else. I believe I may have toasted him too. So, the general must be in glowing good health by now."

"You took to drink?" I still employed my mother's voice, but with a stronger spirit of indignation, shock, and horror.

He faced me with his mouth agape, suddenly realizing who stood opposite him. "I...I...I...I..."

Seeing that he would not reach the second word of his sentence, I interrupted by saying, "I think the 'ayes' have it; and so have you. How could you do such a thing? You'll lose your income. People don't want to hire a drunken carpenter, unless they're building a house on a slope."

"Well," he babbled. "There are many such slopes in Brownville..."

"And when you marry, are you going to carry on like this? Your wife and seven children, what will become of them?"

"Seven? Why seven?"

"Because that's a good number, it's the divine number if I'm not mistaken. Never mind, don't get off subject. They'll be starving after you lose your situation, and then your wife will righteously upbraid you, but you'll have none of it. You'll strike her, you brute. What's she to do?"

"Is she going to be big and, you know, muscular?"

"I'm thinking of Mary, you two-timer. She deserves better. Why, when she gets wind of this, I won't be surprised if she doesn't knock you against the side of the head with a parasol and warns you off. Of course, you'll be unconscious, so it won't do much good at the moment, but I hope you'll learn your lesson."

"I'm sorry Sis, it's just with Fred Travis there, and all. It just felt like the thing to do. And General Bowen, I'm sure he appreciated the benefit of our toasts."

"Hmphf. Did you see Jonathan there?" I wanted to know the identity of the poor woman Prudence's brother would have convinced to attend with him. Not that I would have been jealous.

"No, didn't see Jonathan."

"I thought he would be in attendance at the speech."

"Oh, at the speech? He could have been there. Fred and I never made it that far. In fact..."

"Teddy, have you no shame?"

"Well," he answered, rubbing his temples. "I sure am sorry."

"Good. Now you can make amends by dressing yourself properly and paying a visit to the sheriff and reporting the theft."

"What theft?"

"That doesn't matter, the less you know, the better. Just go tell him you're on your way to see Mr. Kennedy, but that I would like to see him about a theft up here at my office."

"Mr. Kennedy? That would take the better part of my day,

and in the mud?"

"You're not actually going to see Mr. Kennedy, you're only going to pretend like you're going to see him."

"Okay." I could see Teddy blinking repeatedly, which indicated he was overcoming his morning stupor.

"Yes, now listen carefully. You tell Sheriff Coleman that I want to see him immediately about a theft. Mrs. Coleman and their kids should be in town. If they're not, they will probably leave sometime soon. When they do, you sneak into their house. I need the address of Mrs. Lincoln, the mother of the gang leader who killed the Friend family. You should be able to find either the envelope, or, more likely, a book he'll keep to record his official correspondence. You get the address and bring it to me."

CHAPTER 10

eddy told me later that he found the sheriff in his kitchen sipping on a cup of morning coffee, and it looked like he had planned on squatting there for the remainder of the day. My brother attempted to instill in the mind of our levelheaded lawman a sense of urgency by informing him that "Addy's dreadfully worked up about a theft and requests your presence immediately; she has no confidence in the marshal."

Apparently, Sheriff Coleman had better things to do, because upon hearing of my plight and panic, he just picked up the newspaper from the table and began perusing the front cover, the portion reciting congressional bills *ad nauseam*.

Teddy then tried another angle. He tried to flatter the sheriff by mentioning how much I admired him and needed him. This seemed to have a little effect because he saw the sheriff's left eye look up at him, but, on the other hand, he was pretty sure the right eye was still committed to reading about the twenty-thousand dollars of the federal budget allocated to purchasing stationary.

Then, thankfully, Mrs. Coleman came down from the loft.

She was dressed for town and sent the little Colemans out to play in the mud. Well, it doesn't seem she meant for them to play in the mud, but rather to wait for her like sentinels while she grabbed a basket; however, children can't be expected to keep clean when the path is unpaved.

In any case, Mrs. Coleman, upon learning about my request, fairly scolded our chief law enforcer, saying, "Now, you go on up there and tend to her. Nothin' worse than being a young, single woman in a frontier town. So vulnerable."

Teddy said the sheriff answered his wife by asking, "Have you met Miss Furlough?" And then without so much as politely waiting for a 'yes' or 'no,' he continued on by saying, "She doesn't need anyone defending her honor, she just needs someone to keep her out of trouble. And if you ask me, her sending her brother down here to tell me of a theft up there sounds mighty suspicious. If it were a theft, she'd be down here knocking on our bedroom window at three in the morning to let me know I'd better round up a posse before she gets agitated!"

"Oh, no," Teddy objected in my defense. "Addy's afraid somethin' else might go missing if she leaves the shop. And you're the only one she's got confidence in."

The sheriff now looked up at Teddy with both eyes, warily. Mrs. Coleman could stand it no longer and told the master that if he expected dinner to be served on time, he'd better rouse himself, because she wasn't going on her errands until he'd removed himself from the kitchen.

* * *

Sheriff Coleman appeared at my shop as scheduled. He

stood in front of the press, arms crossed, and asked me about the theft.

I thought I'd better save that topic for later so as to give Teddy more time to rummage through the sheriff's paperwork.

"Well, I'm sure you've dealt with many thefts as sheriff. What's most often stolen?"

"Money," he said curtly. I suppose his response would have been monosyllabic if it had been possible.

"Money," I repeated. "I suppose that is the easiest thing to get away with. If anyone finds you with it, you can just claim it was your own all along. Now if you take a horse, well, for one it's hard to conceal, and even if you hide it in your house, you can't keep it there for long. Think of what would become of the parlor. And then each horse is unique, so someone's liable to recognize..."

"Miss Furlough, what's missing?"

"What's missing?" I repeated. It was a good question. I don't know if you've ever been in a spelling bee and are anxious for your turn because you know all the words on the list you were given to study. It's so exciting. Then, you get up in front of the whole class and the teacher says, "Addy, how do you spell "expelled." Suddenly you feel the blood drain out of your head and into all ten of your toes. "Expelled," you repeat. "E" you say, then "x," and then the word "spell" occupies that void in your head. Somehow, you know it's not "exspelled" but that's all you've got in the noggin, and so you must forge ahead. That's how I felt standing in front of schoolmaster Coleman.

"What's missing?" he said again.

Now, I knew I had taken something from the printing

press and put it in the stove, but I couldn't think of what. "The printing press," I said slowly, my voice rising at the word 'press' as if I'd formulated a question rather than a statement.

The sheriff turned around. "Looks like they didn't get too far with it."

"No, they only took part of it."

"Which part."

"Well," I said honestly, "I can't see it now."

The sheriff looked at me over his shoulder. "I don't know what game you're playing at, but I'll leave you to play alone."

As he moved toward the door he unmasked the printing press and I saw what was missing, if that can be said. "The handle!" I cried out. "It's the handle. It was there last time I was in here and now it's gone."

He went to the printing press and examined it. "Whoever stole the handle took the bother to unbolt it, then put the bolt back in so that they could reattach it later on."

"You mean they're coming back for the whole thing?" I asked.

He glanced around the room, opened Teddy's trunk, shuffled around his belongings, and then shut it. Then he marched into the kitchen, and in no more time than it takes to say 'kitchen stove,' reappeared with handle in hand.

"Oh," I said. "I suppose someone pulled a prank on me."

I think his eyes had a scowling in them as he slowly walked past me, glaring steadily at me. I grabbed his arm and said, "I knew you could solve the mystery." I said this as sweetly as I could.

He looked down at my hand on his arm and said, "Miss Furlough, I'm a married man."

I was shocked and embarrassed that he would say such a thing, even flummoxed, though I could see in his demeanor that he meant it as a joke. Normally, I would have brushed the comment aside with a laugh and a joke of my own, except Prudence had entered the office.

Removing my hand quickly, I said, "Of course you are, Sheriff. And don't forget it."

He looked at Prudence seriously and then back at me with the word mischievous written all over his forehead, cheeks, and chin, and said, "Oh, I'm reminded of it every day. It's you I'm worried about." Upon this comment, he bid good day to Prudence and left.

Prudence stood as a statue, but not like Aphrodite with cupid on a shoulder, but rather as the matronly Hera bringing judgment. "I'm sure your father shan't approve of your suspicious behavior, Addy." Having said this, she too exited.

* * *

I sat alone in my office awaiting Teddy and brooding over Prudence. She was such a pest, but I figured I could outsmart her. I hadn't yet come to a conclusion as to how, when Teddy came bounding into the office.

"Whew," he exclaimed. "That was close! I don't think the sheriff saw me but he was coming back when I was coming back. That means we would have met face to face and he would have caught me red-handed with this," he said, landing a small wooden box on the table and dropping on it a leather ledger.

I put the ledger to the side and lifted the lid to the box. Full of letters. "Teddy, you were just to bring back one address, not his lifetime collection of correspondence. And his ledger! You think he's not going to miss this?"

"I had a lot to atone for, considering the amount of my winnings," he answered.

The two of us sifted through the letters and found Mrs. Lincoln's, Mrs. Martha Lincoln's to be precise. The contents I already knew, just as Mr. Brown had indicated. The address I did not, and I copied it down in my notebook.

Mrs. Lincoln lived in Saint Joseph, far but not too far down river. It would take, considering stops along the way, roughly three days to travel down there, see her, and return upstream.

I sat back in the chair imagining my story. George Lincoln had a caring mother…a woman with an intelligent skull, we'd say, but he made his own choice to ignore the goodly role she played before him. He shunned honest work and fair dealings. He, 'hurling defiance toward the vault of heaven,' as Milton would have it, boycotted the church door, so that his conscience could harden to his increasingly evil deeds. He embraced the Deluder, who heightened poor George's thirst for more evil by placing a bottle of whiskey before him. He dreamed dark dreams, he swallowed dark whiskey, and went into the night to the Friend cabin.

On the other hand, I imagined good old Peter Cartwright, a thorough ruffian who answered the call to Christ at age sixteen. An example of virtue, a man of God who brought back many a soul from the brink of perdition.

I could see the words floating into my gazette and taking shape before the eyes of my readers.

"Sis, Sis," Teddy called me out of my reverie. "I know you've got a plan, but what is it?"

"A plan?"

"Yes, to get the good sheriff's things back to him, 'cause I don't know who he's gonna call on to report a theft."

I sat up. "Yes, you're right Teddy. Let me take care of that. Just put my basket on the table while I go in the kitchen."

When we met back in the main room, I dropped the ledger and box in my basket and then placed the cherry pie on top of them.

My actions were mechanical, and my brother noted my distraction; so, I told him of the incident with Sheriff Coleman and Prudence's reaction. He assured me Father would think nothing of Prudence's gibberish and that he, as a true brother, would defend my honor.

I feigned to be at peace on the topic and changed the subject by announcing, "I think the sheriff and his family deserves a cherry pie out of gratitude for having found the handle to my press."

Teddy glanced at the press and saw the handle laying on top of it.

"Yes," I said. "You'll need to screw it back in, and I'll tell Mrs. Coleman that you're the last one I had seen with it. She may well infer that you played a prank on me by hiding it in the woodstove, but I see no reason to disabuse her of this."

Teddy attempted to object to taking the blame, but I reminded him of his need of atonement and he acquiesced.

* * *

I knew Teddy wanted to hear how I planned on getting the

purloined box and ledger back on the sheriff's desk, so I let him know that unleashing a cherry pie in a house full of kids would cause all sorts of confusion that Mrs. Coleman would have to attend to, allowing me to slip over to his desk and deposit the missing items.

He still thought the sheriff might take his eyes off the pie long enough to see my sleight of hand, but I reassured him that our lawman would, by late afternoon, be with Mr. Brown and other notables attending the Brownville Hotel Company meeting.

Approaching the Coleman household after the hotel meeting had commenced, I found several little Colemans outside. Of course, they asked what I had in the basket and I uncovered the treasure.

"I'm sure mother would love you to have some," I said, knowing full well that mother would prefer they eat it after their meal.

The children formed an enthusiastic train marching behind me. I felt like Cicero on campaign, soliciting votes with an army of devoted clients following him about the streets of ancient Rome.

When I arrived in the Coleman's villa, I discovered they had yet to section off the home into rooms, and I realized now how palatial my collection of Cincinnati homes must appear to the average Brownvillian. The so-called kitchen was on one end of the room, a stove sat in the middle with a desk next to it, which was followed by a series of mattresses against a wall, the children's dormitory. The parental chamber could only be up in the loft.

Mrs. Coleman thanked me for the pie, whereupon the children immediately assailed her for a piece. Like the good citizen that I am, I had ample opportunity to return Sheriff Coleman's property.

I made it home in time to catch Prudence writing a letter. I suspected it to be her missive to my father because she covered its contents with her left hand as soon as I walked into the bedroom.

"Writing to your beau?" I asked.

She sat up straight and cast an indignant eye upon me. I thought I heard the front door open, but Prudence would not be distracted. "You know I have no suitor."

"And you haven't fancied any young pioneer?"

"I would certainly be cautious of anyone connected with Brownville. Their gunplay, their gambling, their carousing, their drinking, their dancing."

A solid knock rang out from the front of the house, definitely someone was there. We both jumped at the sound.

I went to answer the call, and whom should I find but Cameron.

"Well, well, my dear, I take it you're alone?"

"There is..." I began, but he cut me off with a wink.

"Yes, yes, *there is* no time like the present. Let me hold your hand, my dear, while I tell you disturbing news."

I looked at him with my sideways glance, letting him understand I knew he was up to something nefarious.

"I was just downtown with the boys, jabbering about this and that, and the conversation invariably turned to the subject of women. And, of course, I objected that discussing ladies when they are not present is ungentlemanly, but the others put me on notice that the women in question may not appreciate hearing what things we had to say about them. 'Give me an example,' I said. And do you know that a certain gentleman mentioned the name of Miss Withers? I objected again, pointing out that I understood her to be a dear friend of my beloved." Cameron paused and pointed an ear to the bedchamber and detected some movement as my guest apparently applied her own ear to the door separating the two rooms. I distinctly heard the door creak.

"Oh!" I said, playing along. "And shall I ask what was said of her? I hope they said nothing untoward, or if they did that you defended her honor."

"I surely would. Any friend of yours is as good as a blood relative to me."

"Go on," I urged.

"Well, wouldn't you know it, this certain gentleman said, and I quote, that 'the young companion of Miss Furlough possesses the keenest and purest eyes of the Territory and that they reflect a brilliance of mind only matched by her natural beauty.'"

We stood still for a moment, and I could hear breaths of air being drawn on the opposite side of the bedroom door. I whispered in his ear, "One of those boys wouldn't have been Teddy would it have? And he wouldn't have told you about my trials with a certain Miss Straightlace would he have?" I received an affirmative nod.

"And who might this young man be?" I said out loud.

"Oh, he's not old but neither is he young. He's a man of business, established, and quite unfettered. I would say, if I were a woman, a catch if ever there were one."

"Oh Cameron, keep me not in suspense," said I, feeling a bit Shakespearean.

"Why, my dear Addy, it was the druggist Mr. Whitt."

The bedroom door burst open and Miss Straightlace tumbled to the floor. "Oh," she gasped getting up. "I stumbled. I thought I heard voices. How embarrassing. You won't tell... umm. You won't tell me I'm not *maladroit*, clumsy, will you?" She straightened herself up. "I'm Miss Prudence Withers," she said, extending her hand.

Cameron, playing the part of European nobility, his heels locked against each other, his body erect and at attention, took it gently and kissed it. "I've heard but praise about you, Miss Withers."

"Ohhh," she said, turning away with flushed cheeks and downcast eyes. "I'm sure I've made no impression whatsoever."

I won't bore you with the back and forth between my gentleman and the princess, but in the end, before announcing his departure for places unknown, Cameron warmed her to the thought that she had impressed our society.

In spite of the fact that I had fallen from grace before Miss Straightlace's eyes, she seemed more upbeat and effervescent that evening. True to her nature, she warned me about being too informal with a gentleman, especially one of doubtful references. Then, oddly, she gave me sundry other bits of advice that only a woman of a romantic disposition might give.

* * *

The following morning, Thursday, June twenty-fifth, I rose

before Prudence and, after dressing in the bathroom, went out into the parlor where I, with Gunshy periodically swiping at my pen, wrote a half dozen short letters to family and friends. I wanted to have a little breakfast to start the day, but I could hear my guest perambulating about the bedroom, and I wanted to venture out on my own.

"Prudence, dear, I'm going into town to the Post Office. Here," I said before she could react, "let me take your envelopes with mine." And I gathered them up from the nightstand, and put them with mine in my basket filled with all my writing paraphernalia. "I'll meet you down at the Nebraska House, we'll have breakfast there with Kitty."

My movements were too quick for her to mount a protest. I hurried down Water Street to Mary's millinery. I knew the Post Office would not be open as yet, but I held hopes that Mary might be in. She was, though not officially open for business as of yet.

"Come on in," she welcomed me. "I've just got a few things to set out and maybe we'll have time to chat before the emigrants come rolling in."

As Mary went about her business, I opened Prudence's mail and found what I was looking for. The address indicated her parents, but included in the envelope was not only a letter to them but also a sealed note with instructions written on the outside as follows: *To the Attention of Mr. Furlough.*

I dug into my basket, extracted a fresh piece of stationary, wrote an encouraging word to my father, sealed it, and inscribed on the outside *To the Attention of Mr. Furlough.* After putting it back into its original envelope with Prudence's letter to her parents, I had a good conversation with Mary. She seemed increasingly perplexed about her relationship with Teddy, and I had to confess that if she were ill at ease, she shouldn't press the courtship. Though I didn't want to cause Teddy any heartache, I knew he was resilient, and, to be honest, I never thought their comportments perfectly matched.

As I stepped out into the street, I couldn't decide whether it had been hotter inside Mary's shop or out in the open. If there had been a breeze, perhaps the sweltering humidity would not have been so heavy. The atmosphere slowed my pace but did not slacken my determination.

I located Mr. Brown not too far off and left my post with him, then I made my way over to the hotel, where I found Prudence, dressed in yellow. Kitty served her at the table and Stewart sat opposite Prudence.

"Going picnicking today?" I asked.

"I would like to be ready if such an occasion arose."

I studied her and noticed she had put up her hair nicely, and she averted her eyes from mine. I sat down next to her.

"How's your gazette coming along?" asked Stewart to initiate conversation.

"Splendidly, I believe. I'm to have my first edition out soon, but tomorrow I hope to gather more information on the Friend murders."

"How's that?" asked Prudence.

"I'm heading down to Saint Joseph where the mother of George Lincoln lives. I hope to interview her."

Stewart passed me the plate with pancakes and I took one. Things tend to taste so much better when you don't have to make them yourself.

"Do you have someone to accompany you?" he asked. "If you could hold off for a week, I think Kitty and I could give you an escort. Saint Joseph is not Brownville, you know. I'll be back from the Big Blue River Settlement soon enough."

"Very kind, Stewart, but I'm sure I can make it on my own."

"Fiddlesticks," said Prudence. "Jonathan and I are born travelers, so you needn't worry yourself about her Mr. Winslow." She fell silent momentarily, then announced, "We'll have to pack carpet-bags. You just leave that to me, Addy. And we'll need some supplies, medicines so we won't be inconvenienced by illness. I must press on." She stood up, fluffed out her dress and straightened her hair before donning her bonnet. I thought of offering her earrings, but she exited before anyone could make any suggestions.

Stewart politely rose in deference to Prudence. Then he looked suspiciously over at the hotel desk where stood a thin man of doubtful hygiene. "That's the hostler from Nemaha City. A ne'er-do-well," he told me softly.

Stewart walked across the room and said, "Jed, is it?"

The man looked at Stewart narrowly. I sensed a certain hostility. "Jeremiah's the name," he said, slowly scrutinizing Stewart.

"Yes, yes, so it is. You're not here for more drug purchases, are you?"

The man looked uncomfortable and glanced about the room. His eyes fell on me. "Maybe, maybe not."

"Hmph," said Stewart before returning to me. He took me into his confidence and said, "There might be another story to look into. It's complicated, but I suspect he drugs other people's horses to make them ill."

"Why would he do such a thing?"

"Like I said, it's complicated. When someone sees his horse is sick, he sells it quick for fear it's caught something chronic. Jeremiah there buys the horse on the cheap and suddenly the animal is as right as rain."

"Where does he get the drugs?"

"Right here in town."

Stewart paid his bill and bid me good-day.

I sat there for a moment, looking at Jeremiah. He didn't really seem to have anything to do at the desk, and he finally exited the hotel. I discreetly left as well and found him at the corner of the building, lighting his pipe. I followed him at a distance until I saw him turn into Mr. Whitt's drugstore.

CHAPTER 11

I waited for a moment to see if the hostler reemerged quickly or if he lingered as if buying. As I had other things to do, I decided he was making purchases and then proceeded to my office in time to catch Teddy unawares.

"Teddy," I said upon entering, "I'm leaving for Saint Joseph tomorrow, and I expect to kill two birds with one stone."

"Who are they?"

"I'll be trying to get information on the Friend murders from Mrs. Lincoln in Saint Joseph while you'll be typesetting and printing the *Brownville Beacon, A Lady's Gazette*."

"I've got some carpentry to do."

"Do you think Jesus worried about that while doing his ministry for three years? I think you can leave carpentry aside for three days."

"Does this Mrs. Lincoln even know you're coming?"

"No, I don't want to give her the opportunity to decline my visit. And elderly folk don't go out much so I don't think I'm risking anything. But you never mind about her," I continued as I tapped on my papers piled up in my box, "you just concern yourself with putting these articles of mine into print. We won't make much off the first edition. We don't have enough advertisements and the ones I do have are free for the first go-around, but once the town reads my stories, I'm confident the advertisements will flow in."

* * *

Teddy and I spent the better part of the day getting things set up for printing. I went home that evening exhausted; and finding Prudence had packed everything imaginable into my carpet-bag, I skipped my supper and went straight to bed with *Hope Leslie*.

In the morning, Friday, June twenty-sixth, Prudence and I made our way down to the Nebraska House where we met up with Jonathan. He kept an eye on the hotel registry, noting where everyone came from and where they were headed. Listening to him tell emigrants about the wonders of Brownville and the better wonders of the places he had visited, which I'm sure never matched the provenance of any of the travelers, one would have mistaken him for not only a father of Brownville but a Founding Father of the country as well. "We've got two wells dug in Brownville," he informed some folks from Indiana, "but back in Ohio I've seen 'em twice as deep, and I've been to the bottom of one of 'em."

"And nobody filled it in?" I asked.

"My, my, you haven't seen the depth. There's no way someone could fill one of them."

"I might have given it a try."

"Hmph," he said looking down on me. "I doubt you could even lift a shovel, let alone one filled with dirt, but as a female, you might get someone to do it for ya."

"Jonathan," Prudence said. "You're ever so thoughtful of the weaker sex. Now you and Miss Furlough come along, the *Silver Heels* is due at the wharf and we don't want to be at the back of the pack and be left standing at the railing for the entirety of the trip."

We passed through the door in her wake and took up positions at the wharf, carpet-bags in hand.

Kitty came out as well, after a spell, and brought in her train Stewart and Mr. Whitt who were on horseback.

"Oh," said Prudence as they approached within earshot. "Don't they look gallant." To her they were knights in armor preparing to defend their ladies' honor with shield and sword.

"They're just going to the Big Blue and back," I informed her. "I imagine they'll see Judge Kinney out there. He and his daughter Beatrice will be there for the Fourth of July. He's an investor, but she's the one delivering the speech."

"I'm not going that far. I'll be back tonight." said Mr. Whitt, and I detected he said this for Miss Withers's benefit. "I'm merely going down to Nemaha City where I have a client."

"Yes," said Stewart. "As Nemaha City is in the direction of the Deroin Trail to the Big Blue, we thought we might share the road and deter the highwaymen. Strength in numbers you know, just as the Good Book says, 'where two or three are gathered, there am I.'"

After they bid us an *aurevoir* and trotted off, we awaited at the wharf, listening to Jonathan. "Shouldn't be long," he said, "the *Min-ne-ha-ha* just left, but the *Silver Heels* is usually following close behind. One hundred and thirty steamers thus far this year." Then he went on to describe the steamers of the Mississippi. How much more spacious and luxurious than any seen on the Missouri, it being an inferior river in every way.

By late afternoon, the Withers and I boarded the *Silver Heels*, while the stevedores loaded a winter's worth of firewood to fuel the ship's engine. As this was a downriver boat, which gathers fewer passengers than when laboring upriver, we easily situated ourselves. Prudence began to discuss the behavior of the men and women she'd observed in Brownville. This gossip soon took to wing and reached the level of a sermon. She then unearthed from her carpet-bag a book on manners and handed it to me.

"No, no," I protested. "I wouldn't want to leave you with nothing to read."

It's not that I don't appreciate such literature, it serves an important purpose in protecting members of society from one another. No, rather, I knew that if I took it, she would want to discuss it with me, and there's little story to a book of manners, and one can only talk of where to place a fork on a table for so long.

"It's no problem at all," she assured me. "Take it. I'll get another book in Saint Joseph."

"I know a perfectly full and fine bookshop there," Jonathan chimed in, as a preface to a modest oration on the virtues of the great bookstores of Saint Louis and beyond, and how they overshadowed the one he knew of in Saint Jo. This discussion of theirs faded into the background as I rather rudely dug out *Hope Leslie* from my own carpet-bag. I much preferred Sedgwick's conversation.

Nevertheless, something about Prudence and Jonathan's conversation echoed in the recesses of my mind and provoked in me a queer uneasiness. I contemplated this sentiment, and wondered if Prudence didn't match Esther in *Hope Leslie*. A perfect young lady, always following the letter of the law, and yet ever repressed in her feelings. And then there was Jonathan, who represented him? My uneasiness increased. He couldn't be the dashing hero, Everell Fletcher. That wouldn't do. Then he could only be Philip Gardiner, the phony Puritan, who dissimulated his carnal appetites and set a trap for the heroine. And who was I, if not *Hope Leslie*!

* * *

We arrived in Saint Joseph on June 27th, a Saturday, and, as evening descended upon us, we proceeded to a hotel located not far from J.B. Jennings's store, where is sold everything from kanawha salt from the Appalachians to window glass.

On Sunday, we attended church. Following Prudence's lead, I put on a very simple and somber dress. I didn't want to look the part of the wealthy daughter in Saint Joseph. The minister invited us to an afternoon picnic, which suited Prudence well because it justified her changing back into her yellow dress. Afterwards, the three of us strolled through Saint Jo. It felt odd being in a real town after the few months I'd been on the frontier. The streets were filled with immigrants from Germany and Ireland taking their Sunday stroll. Stores being closed on the Sabbath, we moved from window to window with the crowd, looking at advertised wares.

I thought I might make a Sunday call on Mrs. Lincoln, but I needed to be alone; unfortunately, I failed to separate myself from my steadfast companions. The first time I feigned to wander off slowly, absentmindedly. In my second attempt, I scampered off, rabbit like, through a forest of people, but Miss Straightlace tracked me down. "Goodness, Addy," she said, "you really have to pay attention to your surroundings. Jonathan and I had no notion you'd moved on to another storefront."

We looked about us and failed to locate Jonathan.

Much time was wasted trying to discover the whereabouts of this unwanted chaperon.

"I'm sure he's fine, Prudence. We'll meet back up with him at the hotel."

"No, we need to keep searching. I need to keep him..." she hesitated, then said, "in my sight."

She truly looked distraught, working up worried wrinkles on her forehead as she scanned the Sunday crowd. I couldn't help but notice a dew drop forming in the corner of her eye. She brought a handkerchief from her reticule and held it in her clasped hands at her bosom. "You...you do think him good, do you not, dear Addy? He's such a lamb."

"I can't say I have seen him do anything evil."

"Oh, but Addy, you are so wonderful for him, even if you have trials of your own. But don't we all. It's such a struggle inside."

I really had no idea where she was going with all these exclamations, but I didn't like the tone. The result was that I too was in earnest to find the lost sheep.

We found him in front of tobacco store. Though the business was closed, the door was open and Jonathan, as was his custom, was delivering some sort of oration to the shopkeeper. When we approached, Prudence called out Jonathan's name as if she hadn't had any news from him since he left for the Crimean War four years ago.

This drew a fraternal glance, and the shopkeeper took the opportunity to efface himself and close the door with a turn of the key. Either he didn't want to be seen with Jonathan, or he had other affairs to attend to.

Jonathan, carrying a wrapped packet tied with string, came toward us.

"Whatever have you purchased?" asked Prudence.

He looked a little surprised until he realized Prudence eyed his package. "Well," he said holding it up to view, "a box of cigars."

I did make one more attempt to escape, but Prudence did not lose track of me. I asked her if she had any Pawnee blood in her veins. She didn't think she did, but knew she had some great-grandparents of Mohawk-Dutch descent. Obviously, it didn't take much Indian blood to be gifted in the hunt.

* * *

I regrouped in the evening and held council with myself. Tomorrow afternoon, I concluded after considering several stratagems, I'd feign to be indisposed in a womanly way and tell Prudence I planned on taking it easy until evening. If I felt better, I would call on Mrs. Lincoln then. In the meantime, if Prudence would be so kind as to buy me a novel.

I thought that would occupy her long enough for me to make my way over to Mrs. Lincoln's alone. Just to be certain, I asked for her to make sure the novel was in French.

I executed the plan on Monday after lunch, and it went

smoothly. As soon as I heard the Withers's combined footsteps disappear down the staircase of the hotel, I jumped out of bed as if the last trumpet had sounded, grabbed a paper from my reticule and jotted down, as if dictating to a telegraph operator: "Feeling better. Went out. Back in evening. Addy."

Upon escaping my chamber, I grabbed *Hope Leslie* and stuffed her into my reticule. She made a tight fit, but I could imagine myself on Mrs. Lincoln's doorstep with nothing to do while awaiting her return from shopping. Besides, we'd reached the dénouement of the story, and if I had any chance at all to satisfy my curiosity, it simply had to be done.

As I pushed my way down the boardwalk, I felt a tug at my reticule and turned around in time to see a little scamp dodge away from me and back into the crowd. I felt my anger rise to my cheeks, and this little incident made me nervous. I kept my reticule under my elbow and continued at a quickened pace.

When I reached the alleyway where Mrs. Lincoln lived, I opened my reticule to get the precise address. I was shocked to discover that my note, with her address written upon it, was nowhere to be found. I now walked slowly down the shady alley, studying each door and number, and humming "Oft in the Stilly Night"--whose last verse Cameron had imperfectly recited to me on our promenade along the bank of the Missouri--to mask the odd sounds, perhaps generated by rodents, that give unpleasant life to narrow lonely streets. The words of the tune soon presented themselves to my mind: *When I remember all the friends, so link'd together, I've seen around me fall, like leaves in wintry weather; I feel like one who treads alone.* Without Cameron's amendment, I found something disturbingly prophetic in their meter.

Finally, I took courage and knocked at a door. An elderly man with a scraggly beard no more than a week old answered. He smelled of tobacco, grease, perspiration, and wine. It was hard to guess which element smelt the worst. He started off by telling me Mrs. Lincoln didn't live far down the alley, but then distracted himself by recalling how she reminded him of his poor departed. I learned quite a bit about the Leonard family, the three sons, their wives and children, three of whom died of dysentery last year. And once we'd reached the death of his missus, we had done full circle and come back to Mrs. Lincoln who lived two doors down.

The building she lived in occupied a corner lot. I doubted she owned it, but then I wondered how she paid the rent if she had no husband. Perhaps she was a charwoman or seamstress or something along those lines. Standing at her door, I was rather proud of myself, having finally eluded my companions. I couldn't have Jonathan with me for the interview. He'd dominate it and tell the impoverished woman how much better apartments for paupers were in Saint Louis or Paris or wherever it was he decided he'd just returned from. As for Prudence, she would faint if she heard me claim to have been George Lincoln's beloved. Which is what I had to do to reach my objective: Getting the journal into my possession. I was convinced it would include the names of his accomplices and probably the name of the man who engineered the murders from afar. No, I couldn't have Jonathan rubbing the old woman the wrong way and Prudence fainting, and then running to my father to tell him I had been the mistress of a murderer. That wouldn't do. So, I looked over my plain dress with satisfaction before knocking timidly upon the door.

It opened only a fraction, and I could see two dark eyes staring down on me. "Whatcha need, Miss?"

"Are you Mrs. Martha Lincoln?" I said meekly.

"Could be."

"I'm so sorry I hadn't come sooner, but my heart was so oppressed and it seemed no one would understand."

Neither the door nor the eyes moved. There was a stillness. "Whatcha talkin' about?"

"I'm Genevieve, Mrs. Lincoln." I said this as if she should recognize the name.

"Genevieve?"

"Yes, Ma'am. Your son and I were very close."

"You a prostitute?"

"What?" I exclaimed, and I believe my normal voice had taken over at this point. "No, I was George's beloved. We planned to marry."

"News to me."

"It would have been good news if he hadn't been taken in by that foul, smug man who thought he knew it all."

"His father's been dead since he was thirteen."

If I'd been Prudence, I would have remarked that thirteen was very young to be a father. "Yes," I said. "I think George missed his guidance."

"I think he followed in his footsteps pretty close. Neither one was good for much, but one were a murderer and the other weren't."

"Oh, my, Mrs. Lincoln, there was a side to George you didn't know."

She stared at me for a full minute, then opened up the door. "You've got my curiosity up. Don't know what you want to see me about, but come on in nonetheless. But I'll tell you right now, I ain't got no money, and George didn't leave any behind either."

The front room was tiny, not much better than that of a squatter's cabin. We sat down on two wooden chairs facing each other with a low table between us.

"I haven't come for money," I explained. "Money means little to me now. George was so adamant about having enough, so that we might marry, and yet I'm afraid that's what led him to listen to that smug man. You know the man he spoke of, don't you?"

"Can't say I do or did."

"Yes, well, it's of little account now; but, I thought after George died, a year of mourning would salve the heart, but I fear it hasn't. And I haven't a letter left of his to remember him by; they took everything. I was wondering if you might not have our correspondence, or if not, do you have some memento of his, anything written of his that your heart might spare and that I might cherish?"

"You're awfully well spoken to be his sweetheart, but then again, he had the gift of gab and could fool anyone except his mother."

"Not as a child, I'm sure."

She shook her head slowly and for the first time I saw the trace of a smile uplift her wrinkled cheeks. "They's angels, children. Probably best that most of 'em die before they reach adulthood." Having said this, she looked up from where she sat at the mantel piece. "He was the only grandson on either side. Neither his Pa nor I had any brothers or sisters, at least none as made it past the five-year mark. But he was a curse."

"I know he said he'd done some bad things in his life," I nearly whispered, "and that he regretted them, but I couldn't help but think others had pushed him to it."

She lifted her eyes to the ceiling as if reminding God what had happened, whilst saying, "He thought he was in a good cause, going into Kansas to whip some of them Yankees. It's there that he killed one and took the poor man's five dollars. He was braggin' about the deed as if it were some noble act. I asked him if that were what the good Lord wanted of him; if that's the way he loved his enemies by clobberin' 'em over the head."

She lowered her gaze and looked me in the eyes. "You know what he told me? He said he weren't responsible for any misdeeds 'cause that's the way he was got up by his Creator. He knew better than that. At least he hadn't been raised by me to think that way."

Mrs. Lincoln rose from her chair and walked over to a pine buffet, dented here and there as soft wood is, and marked with notches along its edge where the bread had been habitually cut. She left behind on her chair a string of beads betraying a Catholic faith. I saw her slide open a drawer and retrieve a leather-bound journal. "He kept his thoughts in here, I believe." She shut the drawer slowly and held the journal in her hand as if weighing it. "It's no good to me. I can't read and I don't want none reading it to me."

As she began to step toward me there came a knock upon

the door.

"Mercy," she said. "I ain't had a caller in two months and now I gets two in one afternoon."

She opened the door and I heard her say, "I don't suppose your another of George's long-lost friends?"

"No Ma'am, but I've come to find a friend."

I turned quickly in my chair and to my horror saw Miss Straightlace entering the room. "What a surprise," I exclaimed. "However did you know to find me?"

"Oh my, you are addled. You left me this note with the address on the back of it; so I thought, why would we wait for your return, when we could meet up with you and enjoy an evening together."

"You two know each other?" Mrs. Lincoln asked as she walked back across the room to face me.

"We're old friends, childhood acquaintances," said Prudence. "And my brother has been an admirer of hers as well."

"Hasn't he been, though," I answered, as I saw him slip away from the door and down into the street. "But that was long before, you know….before last year. Because last year I was befriended by another."

"Whatever do you mean?" asked Prudence. "You were at Oberlin with me, Addy."

"Addy?" queried Mrs. Lincoln. "I thought you was Genevieve, affianced to my George."

"No, no, Ma'am," explained Prudence, as if coming to my rescue. "You've mistaken Miss Furlough for another. Miss Furlough is an Oberlin graduate and is owner and editor of a Nebraska gazette."

Chapter 12

here was a moment of silence reigning in Mrs. Lincoln's home after Prudence's announcement. Not unlike that experienced in a salon, when a virtuoso strikes the last note on the piano to end his exceptional performance. Of course, in the case of a virtuoso, one expects, after the quiet interlude, an explosive applause. Surprisingly, nothing of the sort occurred in Mrs. Lincoln's salon. Rather, there was a slow turning of the hostess in my direction, and the casting down of her eyes upon me, followed by a low-pitched sound, almost as deep as that of a well-respected guard dog, emanating from her lips. Albeit in this case, the growl formed the words, "Is she now?"

There was another moment of silence, and then indeed came the explosion. "You should be ashamed for working up a sorrowful mother's feelings! You're lucky George isn't here, 'cause he'd teach you a lesson sure enough. Maybe one of his acquaintances will. You both find your own way out."

As she opened the door to the kitchen to exit, she held the journal above her head and declared, "And you'll never lay your lying little hands on this, Miss Furlough, 'cause I aim to give it back to my son by committing it to the flames of hell."

"Well isn't she unpleasant," remarked Prudence. "No wonder her son went astray."

Mrs. Lincoln scowled at Prudence, gave a theatrical "Humph," which communicated very little, and slammed the door behind her. I believe I heard her turn the bolt.

I rose from my chair and stood there a few minutes. Odd that she would leave us alone in her parlor, although there wasn't anything of value to steal, even if we'd had had the mind of her departed son. I half expected Mrs. Lincoln to return to the stage. My mother used to walk out on my father in a huff in the middle of a hotly contested debate, announcing to one and all, as she exited, "I will say no more on the topic, Mr. Furlough." He would quietly try to count to twenty but never quite made it before her return, like a conquering general, dishing out declarative statements very much on the topic.

Well, after counting to twenty, I concluded Mrs. Lincoln was having a dashed awful time coming up with a response to Prudence's remark.

I took the opportunity to study the little room, and I walked over to the mantelpiece to see what had attracted Mrs. Lincoln's attention. I saw two pictures. One was a rough painting of a middle-aged man and the other a daguerreotype of two little girls. The three votive candles next to the pictures indicated they were all three deceased. If any likeness of George Lincoln had graced the mantelpiece, it had been removed. It then dawned on me that Mrs. Lincoln's disappointment with her son could have only come about because she had so trusted him as a youth. His surroundings were no worse than another's. He chose to embrace evil.

"Where's Jonathan?" I asked, noticing for the first time his absence.

"Not far. He wanted to smoke a cigar, but he'll be here soon. Don't you think him handsome?"

"I suspect a familial consensus on the subject," I replied vaguely.

Prudence lifted up her chin, obviously irritated that I just didn't come out and openly admit that Jonathan struck my fancy.

Gathering up my things rather brusquely I told her it was time to leave.

She stepped sideways to let me pass through the door, reminding me of a matador, and I half expected to be lanced by a pica. I wasn't all wrong. As I descended the steps, I caught sight of a dark figure in the shadows at the edge of the building across the street. Then a blast with smoke veiled him, as if he were a disappearing magician. Immediately I felt myself falling backwards. My matador had yet to step up to the door to catch me, so I landed on my back. A nightly darkness closed in on me, as if I were looking through a tunnel that got smaller and smaller.

I forced my eyes open, and looking up I noticed Prudence's face leaning over mine. "What's happened? What was that noise?" she asked.

I sat up, winded and dazed. My thoughts turned to my childhood sweetheart, Zachariah Thrumbrill. He must have felt something of the sort when I punched him in the stomach for yanking on my braids.

Prudence, with little respect for my reminiscences, repeated her question.

"I don't know," I said mechanically. "I saw a flash and smoke, and then I was on my back."

Looking at my reticule, I noticed a hole in it. Sitting up and opening it, I found poor *Hope Leslie* pierced as well, with the bullet lodged in her. I glanced across the street, but the figure had disappeared.

Standing up with Prudence's help, my mind reeled, and I steadied myself against the doorpost, looking left and right down the alleyway. I saw no one.

A faintness seemed to enrobe me. I must have hit my head hard when I fell over. I forced myself to stay upright. Suddenly, I saw a man emerge from behind the building across the street. He was running toward us. I had the impression I was dreaming but I wasn't. It was Jonathan.

"What was that noise?" he asked. "It sounded like a gun!" He looked at me strangely. "Why are you staggering about?"

"Someone shot at her!" exclaimed Prudence. "Oh, my, you haven't been wounded have you Addy?" I told her I had not.

She continued to fuss, saying, "Oh my, we mustn't stay here. Let's get her back to the hotel."

I had the oddest feeling come over me, as if my mind hadn't kept pace with events and that it was now catching up with what had just happened. I tottered this way and that, then moved back into the parlor. Mrs. Lincoln was nowhere to be found. Apparently, she had either not heard the noise, or she chose to disregard it.

Prudence turned me around and guided me out into the alley. Little by little the world around me fell back into place.

Who would want to kill me and why?

* * *

We returned to the hotel straightaway. I was dazed and Prudence thought I ought to report what had happened. She sent Jonathan out to round up the constable and she obliged me to lay down. Meanwhile, to change my thoughts, she brought a package over to me and asked me open it. She stood there, hands folded before her, awaiting my response. I untied and unwrapped the paper and found a book, in French. I'd never heard of it. *Madame Bovary*.

For the first time since she had arrived, I felt goodly about Prudence. She so wanted to please. The only problem was that she was one of those women who believe that pleasing another means directing that person's life.

I sincerely thanked her and gave her a peck on the cheek.

"Now you read this book right now. Don't you think at all about that horrible shooting. It'll drive you to madness if all you think about is someone trying to kill you."

She was right. There's something strange about being shot at. I mean, I suspect soldiers at war take a bullet in stride, but when you're simply stepping out of an old widow's residence and catch a ball of lead in your reticule, it's unsettling.

I immediately grew very fond of my hotel accommodations and didn't see the need to leave them. Jonathan returned to tell us a policeman was on his way. He seemed rather dismissive of the whole affair and related to me the time he was shot at in Saint Louis and simply continued on about his business as if nothing had happened. For once I believed him, because I could easily imagine someone wanting to shoot him.

While I was pondering this, a knock came upon the door. Prudence answered it and in came our policeman, Mr. O'Reilly. He was tall and lanky, in his twenties, seemingly new on the job, and nearly impossible to understand with his Irish brogue.

"All right, Miss," he said. "Recount if you might your wee incident." This directive that he gave me I understood after his third attempt.

"Well, all I saw was a flash, smoke, and I heard a loud bang."

"And the bullet, it knocked ya down did it?" Again, I had him repeat himself thrice, but it didn't seem to irritate him.

"I can't say that. It might have just been the surprise that made me step backward and trip over the doorsill."

"Ya mind if I have a wee look at where ya were hit?"

I understood this question perfectly. "Yes, I do mind, and partly because there's nothing to see and partly because there's too much to see. You understand I wasn't hit directly. In fact, I don't believe I felt much at all except a thump maybe."

He told me it wasn't much to worry about in his opinion, but that I might want to stay away from that side of town and confine myself to the thoroughfares.

"I wouldn't stay long in yer room," he added. "You'll become a recluse. It's best to face the world right away after such an incident."

Prudence agreed with the policeman's therapy and cajoled me enough to where I ventured out the next day.

* * *

With the shops being open on the morrow, I revived. I

could have spent the whole day in the fabric store, though I couldn't bring myself to buy anything without feeling disloyal to Mary. We moved on to a store of general merchandise, run by a man aptly named Mr. Tool. He was originally from Ohio and so we entered into conversation as one does. Being a good salesman, he eventually brought up the subject of products dear to a woman's heart: a delightful bonnet with a soft crown of periwinkle blue, the cutest patent leather gloves, and porcelain of various design.

He accompanied me over to the window arrayed with Queensware, rather bland for me but solid fare for the quotidian, and gold rimmed China, too formal for my taste, and finally some Cyprus in Davenport ironstone. The latter would have been beautiful in blue, but its dark grey looked rather funereal.

Then something caught my eye on the other side of the street, I think it was the door of the land agent's office as it closed. But between the land agent's and the jeweler's shop next to it, I saw something disturbing. I shuddered. There stood, not twenty paces away, Mr. Whitt, lighting a cigar. It had to be him. And as I withdrew from the window his eyes seemed to look my way, his face expressionless. He blew out his match and then slowly walked away. I approached the window carefully, leaning forward to see where he went. He went by the jeweler's, paused, and then continued on. I stretched forward until I heard a clatter and crash of dishes.

"Oh my!" exclaimed Prudence. "Have you fainted again? Are you shot? I didn't hear a shot."

I looked down and saw three ugly and broken Cyprus plates looking up at me. Suddenly my Ohio connection to the owner counted for very little. He wanted payment before I left the store. I thought about explaining to him that the dishes in question were better out of the window than in it, but he didn't look like a man who listened to logic, so I paid him.

I exited the shop with Prudence at my side. "Tell, me, Addy, are you sure you haven't a case of nerves?"

"No," I said, striding into the street. I had just one purpose in mind: Either find Mr. Whitt or find out what he had been up to.

I stood in the middle of traffic looking up and down and saw nothing of his smart tailored suit. Prudence, of course, was curious, but I wasn't about to let her in on my investigation. For one thing, Jonathan made me uneasy, and for another her lack of common sense might lead her to divulge information best kept secret. I put her off by saying that I wanted to see about a necklace.

"Really, Addy, is not a necklace going too far? The Apostle would have 'that women adorn themselves in modest apparel, with decency and propriety; not with braided hair, or gold, or pearls, or costly array.'"

"Obviously he was not a woman, but more importantly, if one is modest, decent, and proper, jewelry is worn for the pleasure of others to enjoy. As the lover praises his beloved in the *Song of Songs*, 'Thy cheeks are comely with rows of jewels, thy neck with chains of gold.'"

"I fear your reason leads you away, dear Addy."

"We'll see about that in a moment," I said upon entering the jeweler's store.

Herr Dwanst had a thick German accent, noticed

immediately in his "Guten tag meine damen." Without saying his name, I described Mr. Whitt and asked if Herr Dwanst had seen anyone of that description.

"Unt vye do you vant to know?"

I explained, much to Prudence's consternation, that I was looking for my husband and thought he may have come in to make a purchase on my behalf.

"Like ein vedding ring?" He asked skeptically, looking down at my finger.

Prudence attempted to come to my rescue. "Oh, she's not married. She was shot at. Someone's trying to kill her."

Without Prudence observing, I rolled my eyes to indicate to Herr Dwanst that my companion was a little daft. "Yes, Prudence," I said taking her by the elbow, "we must be wary of assassins."

"Nein, I haven't seen diss mahn," he said, understandingly.

"Thank you, sir, and come along Prudence, we must go now."

We exited the jeweler's and went next door to the land agent's office. On the door hung a notice: "Closed for the afternoon, will be back tomorrow, Mr. Beach."

Chapter 13

In the evening, we made our way down to the wharf and awaited our steamer. It came in due time and was flooded with emigrants. We spent much of our time at the railing, observing the tree-lined landscape slowly pass by. Gazing upon it thoughtlessly, one might find it monotonous; but picking out the individual shapes of cottonwoods and hackberries and the fortuitous evidences of wildlife, whether birds calling from a perch, a startled deer, or the occasional raccoon ambulating about, revealed an endless and living tapestry. I could almost understand why my Pawnee relations withdrew from the idea of clearing the Missouri's banks, overturning the soil, carving out roads, and establishing farms and erecting cities. Why spoil paradise?

But if we hadn't taken to heart God's commandment to cultivate the land, which work brings forth first farms, then cities and civilization, from whence would have come our Bunyans, our Miltons, our Shakespeares? I think something would have been lost if *Much Ado About Nothing* had been born of our red brothers' sign language. Perhaps parts of *Hamlet*? But how would one "Be or not to be" in sign language?

I must have muttered this last concern aloud, as I heard Prudence comment that I ought to be more self-conscious and mindful of my behavior if I were to win the affections of someone gallant and true.

"I beg your pardon, Prudence. I've told you Mr. Davenport and I are very close, and I can think of none better."

"Oh!" She uttered the expression as a hiccup. "I dare say your Mr. Davenport is a mysterious man, and, though I don't wish to offend, mysterious men hide nothing good. They can't be trusted. And to think he made a spectacle of you, and at a dance! I'm sure you resisted, but still, it impinges upon your reputation, and not in a good way. You shall see, someday, dear friend. You may not be left at the altar, but you may well be left."

"Prudence," I said. "Why did you come out west, and to Saint Joseph?"

She looked away and ignored my question. "I just thought of something," she said. "This is the first Wednesday of the month, the day our first edition comes out. I can't wait to see my words in print. You've done such a wonder."

"Prudence," I repeated. "Why did you come out west?"

"Well," she said as if repeating a catechism lesson, "to see you, to deliver your stipend, and then to render your father a first-hand account of your life on the frontier."

"And your brother? He seems to wander off. Where is he now?"

"I imagine he's strolling about the boat, smoking a cigar. What's wrong in that?"

"I thought he was chaperoning us, that's all."

"We're not going to be any danger on a boat, unless we hit

a snag."

"But in Saint Jo he didn't seem concerned that you were entering the house of an unknown. He wasn't even standing at the door when Mrs. Lincoln opened it to you."

"He would have heard me had I called out, just like he heard the blast of the gun."

"It's not the first time he's been to Saint Jo is it?"

"He has traveled a lot in his business ventures."

I looked back out at the passing landscape. She seemed to have an answer for everything, but I did observe that noticeable lip of hers quiver when I criticized Jonathan. And then, I wondered, how did he know of a bookstore in Saint Jo? Something wasn't quite right. Did Jonathan know the Lincolns? That would explain why he wouldn't come inside with Prudence. Following this line of reasoning, other things about Jonathan now struck me. Why did he so easily go out to the Friend farm with Mr. Whitt and me? And what's more to the point, how did he go directly to where the cabin had once stood? Is he somehow mixed up in all this? Why did he want to escort his sister out west to Brownville in the first place, if he had business to attend to? Had he heard I planned on investigating the Friend murders? All of a sudden, I felt like I didn't know Prudence's brother at all. He became foreign to me in an instant.

* * *

In the afternoon, after many stops along the way, including places like Stephen's Landing and Nemaha City, where we just treaded water long enough to let people climb aboard from row boats, we finally attached ourselves to the wharf of Brownville.

For the first time, I really felt like the frontier was not an exotic wilderness, it was home.

We went directly to the Nebraska House to find Kitty to tell her of our adventure. While waiting at the desk for Kitty, whom the clerk had gone to fetch upstairs, I looked over the newspapers, hoping to see my gazette. Not finding it, I opened up the *Nebraska Advertiser* and was pleased to see that the Republicans carried the Constitutional Convention in Minnesota by a vote of 61 to 47.

While reading I heard a familiar voice outside in the distance. "Get your copy of Brownville's latest! *The Brownville Beacon*, it's a lady's gazette, but good reading for all!"

I dropped the *Advertiser* on the counter and hurried outside. "Teddy!" I called. "Bring that over here!"

Teddy trotted over from the wharf where he had been selling copies to the emigrants. He still had a number of papers under his arm. "Good to see you Sis, you made it. Hey," he said excitedly, "I found some advertisers and believe it or not I think we'll turn a profit!"

I couldn't help myself. I kissed my little brother on a cheek that immediately turned crimson. "Ah, shucks," he said. "I was just doin' what I expected I ought to be doin'."

The two of us went arm in arm into the hotel amidst a throng of emigrants and found a place to sit down at the end of a long table. Kitty soon joined us and Prudence, who was desperate to tell Kitty all about the incident at Mrs. Lincoln's.

I heard the story more than once that afternoon, because when Stewart arrived a quarter of an hour later, she had another go at it, and I must say the second version was an improvement.

In this second rendition, Prudence had seen the shooter and had attempted to maneuver around me, to shield me, but the shot had been fired and I had fallen before her, at which moment she leaned over to protect me from further assaults. Jonathan's role improved as well. The blast had come from a rifle he deduced, because he had a long experience in firearms and could recognize the make and model of not an insignificant number simply by listening to the report. He too had come flying in my direction, looking left and right for the assailant, but seeing no one, thought it best to come to the succor of the women folk.

"What kind of rifle was it then?" I asked.

"Well, what would you imagine, Stewart?" he asked in return.

"I would have no idea."

"Teddy, you familiar with rifles?"

"Pa had a type of Kentucky rifle. I've hunted with a few others, and keep a shotgun."

Jonathan looked at the faces around the table, moving from one to the other in a slow sweeping fashion. The mannerism seemed familiar to me. Zach Thrumbrill had employed it once when he wanted to tell the class about a locomotive. Looking everyone in the eye to make sure no one had ever seen one, he gave a rather detailed description, to include the two paddle wheels on either side propelled it. When I repeated the description to my father, who worked on the new rail lines, he suggested Mr. Thrumbrill patent his idea.

As Jonathan finished studying our faces, he announced, "It was a Mississippi rifle."

"Shoots water, does it?" I asked. "No wonder it created such a cloud."

"Trust me," he said, "I've handled Kentucky, Remington, you name it. But that was a Mississippi rifle."

"Goodness," replied Stewart. "If you think this person was trying to shoot you, and from what you say, he aimed to, then you need some protection. I've heard about you and the parasol, but you're going to need something with more punch. Let me buy you a lady's pistol, Adeline, you never know."

"You really think Addy's in that kind of danger?" asked Kitty.

"Ahrg!" I growled. "No!"

Everyone looked at me as if I'd lost my mind, which was not far off the mark.

I panted breathlessly, looking across the room. I felt like I'd fallen backwards and landed on my back again. There, seated across from me was the most elegant lady, perusing Brownville's one and only lady's gazette. On the back page, which she couldn't see, but in bold enough letters for me to read from across the room were the letters spelling "LIQUOR FOR SALE."

* * *

"Teddy!" I exclaimed. "You put into my temperance promoting gazette an advertisement for liquor!"

He gave me that big-eyed owl look, then shifting his head atop his neck one direction and then another, he spotted the incriminating evidence. "Oh, uh, well, umm, it's Mr. Davis's grocery. They sell lots of things, and among them the occasional bottle of spirits."

"Exactly, it's his bottles of spirits that causes mayhem in town and family. You take a man who's merely disagreeable, open his mouth, and insert one of those bottles and he becomes a swearing, violent, abusive husband and father."

"So, if he's not married..."

"Don't you start with your rationalizations. You've set me up for ridicule. I'll never hear the end of it. I can hear it now as I walk down Main Street, 'Here she is boys, let's all lift a glass in honor of the temperance lady. Courtesy of Mr. Davis.'"

"Now I don't see it that way, Addy. I figured that if you put an advertisement for alcohol in the paper, people like Fred, or at least the ones who can both drink and read, will buy a copy. And then they'll read your temperance articles and come into full knowledge of the errors of their ways."

Teddy, having finished his rationalization, observed me carefully, like a fattened penguin might look into the eyes of a lean polar bear. I was standing with my arms crossed and my right foot tapping faster than a feisty cotillion. "Okay," I said, trying to salvage what I could of an already compromised reputation. "First, you'll return Mr. Davis's money to him. Then, I want you to print up a disclaimer of sorts. An explanation stating that we hoped the advertisement, for which we took no money, might entice imbibers of alcohol to read our lines for their own reformation. Something in that style. Wait, I'll write it, and you print it, and you distribute it, and you do both those things by early tomorrow morning."

I procured paper and pen from Kitty and dedicated a full-length essay to my topic.

Meanwhile, the others round the table, other than Prudence, didn't seem as concerned as I about the tainted gazette. The conversation wandered, with Kitty giving us the latest gossip.

She told a story about a guest who exited by an upstairs window but had neglected to pay his bill. If caught he would be assigned to the sheriff's gang of men leveling Main Street.

Stewart talked of the great work being done at the Big Blue River Settlement, and how he intended to invest a modest sum in the venture. He had seen Judge Kinney pass by on the Deroin Trail, and figured if the justice considered the colony a viable enterprise, it certainly must be.

* * *

When I finished my composition, I looked up, feeling better, but then I noticed the number of guests at our table had increased by one. The new arrival sat across from me.

"Miss Furlough, seeing you haven't your parasol, I took the risk." Mr. Martin paused before proceeding. "If I may, I was wondering if, setting aside differences, we might not put our heads together for mutual benefit."

"I would think yours big enough to grapple with any problem." I said this whilst passing my essay to Teddy and giving him a curt nod in the direction of the printing press.

"Oh no, Miss Furlough, it takes all kinds in a functioning society. In spite of our little disagreements, you and I share an educated background, and you, bringing your womanly arts to a cause, can be of benefit."

"This wouldn't have anything to do with opening a school, would it?"

"It may indeed. I think we, as a team, inclusive of Mr. Whitt, could recruit a sufficient number of young scholars to both increase our income and benefit society."

I told him the population at Brownville would not sustain a high school, but Omaha City may be fertile ground for planting such an institution.

"I truly hate to differ with you on any point," he said, gently and abstractedly rubbing the back of his skull. "But think about it. It would be foolish to open a school of any sort today at the Big Blue River, but that colony today is what Brownville was but a year ago, and Omaha City is what Brownville will be in a year."

"Have you been to the Big Blue River?" interrupted Stewart. I noted a dose of skepticism in the question.

"Why yes, I just returned. I've been on the trail for a week. Just seeing if there were opportunities there and elsewhere, but the Big Blue isn't as advanced as I had hoped."

"Did you see Judge Kinney?"

"Who?" asked Mr. Martin. "Can't say I did, can't say I didn't. He's unknown to me, even if he's a financier of the settlement, besides, I was moving at a fast clip. We could have crossed paths on the trail."

"I think you would have recognized him well enough. Buggies are not a common commodity, especially on the trail."

"Oh," said Mr. Martin as if he'd just returned from the Road to Damascus, "I see what you mean. Yes, yes, a buggy. Did seem strange on the trail, as rough as it is."

"So, did you talk to him?"

Mr. Martin considered the question. "No, don't believe I did, but I may have said 'Good day,' or something to that effect."

I observed Stewart more closely than Mr. Martin throughout this exchange. Kitty's fiancé had a look about him I couldn't define. He acted the part of an attorney questioning a witness, and he didn't look like he received the answers expected.

Mr. Martin abruptly rose, saying that he hadn't really come for dinner but merely wanted to discuss the high school idea with me, hearing that I had descended at the wharf. He promised to call on me at a later date.

Before he departed, however, I extracted from my reticule the pipe emblazoned with the letter J and set it on the table.

"Why that's my pipe," said Mr. Martin.

"I suspected as much, I found it in unauthorized hands."

"Unauthorized hands?"

"Yes, some young boys had it and I confiscated it. You may have it back, I have no need of it."

"Why, thank you, Miss Furlough," he said, picking up the pipe.

After Mr. Martin left, I asked Stewart, "Why did you question Mr. Martin so?"

"Just curious. I didn't know he was out at the Big Blue, but if he saw Judge Kinney in his buggy, I suppose he was there."

Kitty soon arrived with our repast, but as we said grace and partook, I couldn't help but noting to myself that Stewart had unwittingly supplied Mr. Martin with the knowledge that Judge Kinney went to the Big Blue in a buggy. What if Stewart had asked Mr. Martin to describe the man in the buggy? Could the phrenologist have identified the judge's fine physiognomy?

CHAPTER 14

n Thursday morning I rose early, before Prudence, gently moved Gunshy from my bed to hers, and then set out for the livery station where I found the owner, Sheriff Coleman. I had to trust that Teddy was out distributing my latest publication.

"Good morning, Miss," the sheriff said a little too cheerfully as I approached. He was tightening up a saddle.

"Good morning to you, Sheriff. I'm glad to have found you before Balaklava took you off to parts unknown."

He smiled. "It might have been to my advantage."

"Now Sheriff, I know you don't mean that. I suspect just now you were saddling up to come over to my place to tell me when and where you're auctioning off the effects of Mr. Lincoln and his cohort."

"Did that on Saturday," he said, visibly pleased with himself.

"No, Teddy didn't mention it."

"Not many people knew of it, except a few hawkers."

"You did that on purpose!"

"Just protecting my favorite citizen from getting herself into more trouble. Advertising alcohol. What fodder to your newspaper. Promoting the poison and then, through your captivating columns, troubling old dears about the worrisome epidemic. It's kind of a self-sustaining business you've created there, very calculating of you."

"No more than privately selling off public property to cronies so that they can make a profit and then vote for you come August first." He didn't bother to respond, so I was obligated to take up the slack in the conversation. "Shouldn't the proceeds go to the Friend family?"

"Never did find any relations that way. Mr. Friend was an immigrant, you could tell by his accent."

"And his helpmate?"

"She rattled off English as well as you or me."

"As you or I."

The sheriff put his foot into the stirrup and then hoisted himself up into the saddle. Balaklava backed up and shook his head, anxious, no doubt, to live up to his name and charge up some hill amidst a light morning shower of cannon balls.

"Who bought them?" I asked.

"The few trifles were purchased by a Nebraska City merchant with a warehouse up at Mount Vernon, a Mr. Stephen Nuckolls. There was a letter as well, but of no interest to Mr. Nuckolls."

"You still have it?"

"Nope, I passed it on to Mr. Muir. He seemed interested."

I reached out and took hold of the bridle to prevent the sheriff's escape. "Who wrote it and what was it about?"

"How persistent are you going to be?"

"You remember the lady in the Bible who kept pestering the judge until he answered her?"

"I've heard the story."

"I wouldn't doubt but she's a relation of mine."

"Okay, just let go of the reins so Balaklava doesn't get any more nervy than he is. The letter was addressed to 'Dearest Daughter.' That's all it said in the way of a greeting, and it was just signed 'Your loving Father.' It was about a bounty deed and the father said he'd leave the recipient the bounty, if I remember correctly, and I usually do, 'upon my demise, which seems to be around the next corner.' I told Mr. Muir he might want to track down that bounty if 'Loving Father' hasn't rounded that corner yet."

"I suppose Mr. Lincoln picked up that letter from the Friend family."

"What makes you say that?"

"I doubt George Lincoln's father would have addressed him as 'Dearest Daughter.'"

"Could have been to a sister of his. Maybe he kept it for her."

"I doubt his father would have penned a letter to his daughter."

"Oh?"

"Number one because his father died years ago, and number two because his sisters aren't any more alive than their father."

"How in the world would you know such things?"

"Well, I plan on knowing a lot more things by the time I'm done."

"Well you're not going to find them out from me!"

I think he meant this to be his departing statement, given the fact he dug his heels into Balaklava's flanks as he delivered it. However the animal seemed to enjoy our conversation and refused to move out. With a subsequent jab to the sides, the steed reared up and shook its head as it came back down hard on its front hooves, but the beast hadn't advanced the length of a horseshoe. There ensued a variety of words issuing from the voice of the law, all intended to encourage the horse to move forward, but to no avail.

I indicated to Sheriff Coleman that I would help send him on his way, which caused him to look back over his left shoulder at me with the same owl eyes I had exhibited atop Hezekiah. What generated this unusual expression, of course, was the sight of my hand slapping Balaklava on the hindquarters. If I had been Teddy, I would have placed all my money on Balaklava, because that horse reached top speed way before Hezekiah could have.

* * *

After checking up on Teddy and having a meal with Kitty and Stewart at the hotel, I headed home to find a copy of the *Nebraska Advertiser* on the kitchen table. Prudence told me the gardener had laid it there, which made sense since he sometimes serves as a pressman for Mr. Furnas.

I picked up the paper and noted that bids were being taken for building a suitable schoolhouse in town. I imagined that's what generated Mr. Martin's interest in teaching. The paper also announced bids open for a fine brick hotel.

While reading, I could distinctly hear Monsieur Carr whistling in the garden.

I stepped out onto the porch and asked, "What's the joy?"

He stopped hoeing and propped his chin upon the top of the hoe handle and said in his charming French accent, which

I'll attempt to imitate here, just to give you a sense as to what it was like to talk to him in English, "Deed you not read zee good news in zee newspaper? Someone attempted to assassinate zee emperor. It gives one, how you say, *espoir*."

"Hope?"

"Yes."

"I doubt murder solves a problem."

"Ah, Mademoiselle, when one murders a murderer, he murders no one. Otherwise, we would have no guillotine. Besides, murder of this particular man, this Bonaparte, does solve a problem, because it makes other things possible. Like a republic."

"Which reminds me, John, could you cut me off a head of lettuce for tonight?"

"Oui, Mademoiselle."

I stepped back inside and rolled his words over in my mind: How a murder can solve a problem by making other things possible. *What was George Lincoln trying to make possible? It had to be tied to that bounty. Was he trying to get land for himself?*

* * *

When I awoke Friday morning, July third, the first thing I thought of was Monsieur Carr's words. Emerging from the bedroom, I found Prudence making breakfast, and she pointed at the table for me to sit down. As she served me, she ran through all the things I needed to get done today in preparation for the Fourth of July celebration.

My first order of business, according to my quartermaster, was to go down to Davis's market and purchase ingredients for pies. There were other items that could be got at Mr. Whitt's drug store, but she could see to that. I also needed to make arrangements for transportation with Coleman's livery station, as the fete was to be held in Nemaha City. We couldn't be carrying pies in our reticules, she remarked.

I told her how her insightfulness, and her aptitude for making decisions, made of her a useful friend. She blushed at the compliment. I followed this up by asking her when she might be obliged to be back in Ohio. On this particular item, however, she uncharacteristically became fuzzy and noncommittal. I did remind her that my father would like a report as soon as possible, but this didn't prompt her toward any quick resolution. Apparently, I had so much need of her, she just couldn't fathom leaving me without assistance.

Well, I concluded to myself, a day of shopping would be better than a day at home with my insightful friend. I was right. In the early afternoon, I took my leisure, stopping even at Finney's confectionary on Second Street to have a soday and ice cream. Sitting in this sensual heaven, that, from what I can tell, compared evenly with the Mohammadan Paradise, minus the maidens, I meditated on the fate of the Friend family. So sad, I thought, to have no relations. I mean, consider Aunt Adeline, lost among the recesses of the Great American Desert, but we're looking for her. If something were to happen to me, why I could imagine Jerome running to the rescue, even if, after finding me, he were to pull some sort of prank on me. And if I were to die in as horrible a circumstance as Mrs. Friend, well the whole family would make the effort to put my relics to rest. But the Friend family. No one.

If there's no one, it's a set up for a perfect murder. Like in that song Oft in the Stilly Night: "When I remember all the friends, I've seen around me fall; I feel like one, who treads alone." That's what made the tune so eerie to me in that alleyway: The Friend family treaded alone.

"Ready for the Fourth?" came a voice from behind the counter.

"The Fourth?"

"Yes," smiled Mr. Finney. "You do remember you're to entertain us with your thoughts."

"Oh, my! You're perfectly right." I paid my bill and made my way over to the office.

Along the way, not far from Finney's, I noticed two young men sharing a bottle and propping themselves up against the wall of the bank, each with one foot on the ground and one heel against the wall. Some boys, at that awkward age between childhood and manhood, were soliciting them, either begging for a swig or a plug of tobacco.

The men paid them no attention, because they unfortunately spotted me in the street. Their confused tongue and inappropriate vocabulary, which were meant no doubt to compliment me in some way, betrayed the nature of their drink.

One of them called out, "Hey, lil bal...gal. Hot day ain't it. Ya look firstly...thirsty. Come on o'er here.'"

I quickened my pace.

"Come on, Miss, it's a flormal invitation."

I stopped, turned around, and obliged them, at least the part about presenting myself to them. "Listen," I said, with but a pace between us, and in a tone usually reserved for Teddy, "you're a disgrace to yourselves and the town. Nevertheless, I'll give you an invitation in return: Be at church on Sunday at 11 AM."

The taller of the two, who hadn't spoken up to this moment, made a good observation. "Ain't seen no church steeple in this town. We take communion at the saloon."

"The church meeting is held in the same structure as the school, though I doubt you'd recognize a schoolhouse either."

The shorter one made an attempt to straighten himself up to his friend's height. "I'll take up your offer, Miss, and meet you at the altar."

The boys giggled and his friend guffawed.

"If it were a pagan temple, I might think you serious, although," I added, glancing at their bottle, "I don't think you'll have anything left for your libations."

He looked at me confusedly, as if I'd been the one drinking.

"Good day, sirs," I said as I left their presence.

They recovered soon enough and called after me, interspersing their banter with the occasional whistle. I could feel my cheeks redden to the color of my hair. I believe I had an untoward thought in regards to Stewart at that moment, for not having given me a pistol.

When I reached my office, I seated myself at my desk and fumed. I was energized and ready to draft a speech. Oh, I thought, it must be something to motivate us to improve our condition, to drive us forward and upward to become enlightened architects of civilization. The thoughts flowed through my pen and onto the paper. Lifting my final rendition from the table, I stood and then paced the room, reading it aloud to the chair facing me. Hearing no criticism, I was well satisfied with my work. I put the speech in the bottom of my basket and hurried out to execute Prudence's errands.

I spent the late afternoon and evening with Prudence cooking up pies, but as she noted when I got the count wrong in measures of this or that, my mind was elsewhere. For one thing, I was irritated that Miss Straightlace kept me bound to the kitchen. I would have liked to have taken the ferry to Rock Port and enjoyed the ball at the Forest City Hotel, but I just didn't want to purloin, peruse, and purge another of her letters to my father, an essay about how I had abandoned my duty to the community for a frolicking night of fiddle and dance. For another thing, the Friend murders weighed heavily on my mind. *Maybe Mrs. Friend did have a relation,* I thought. *It might be deciphered through that letter somehow. Then an idea fell upon me: Why would Mr. Muir want the letter if there were no name in it? Nothing to help him track down the bounty? He wouldn't.* There had to be something helpful in that letter, and I had to get my hands on it.

CHAPTER 15

n the morning of July fourth, a string of pedestrians, mounted folk, farm wagons, and carriages stretched a thin line along the trail blazed through our rolling hills toward Nemaha City. The heat of summer had not yet risen and the string of patriots was knotted, here and there, by small groups of friends and neighbors enjoying the leisurely promenade and pleasant conversation. I was so glad that Prudence and I, with Jonathan as chauffeur, had rented one of Coleman's buggies for the pies.

When at last we reached the top of our final ascent, we could see waving down below, atop a pole of no less than one-hundred feet in height, our splendid banner. What pride we felt as pioneers to fulfill the divine mandate by overspreading this wilderness with farm and town, with school and church. And yet, how also humbled were we that God would choose us for such a glorious task.

Once in Nemaha City, a nascent village with but a handful of entrepreneurs, we attended to the rites and rituals to solemnize this sacred day. At eleven a.m., the procession marched its way from the south end of Kansas Avenue and Park to Nebraska

Avenue and First Street.

We assembled in Mr. Hiatt's hotel, where the choir sang and a prayer was said, and all this as a preamble to the reading of our dear Declaration of Independence by Mr. Kirk, a lawyer. Following this, a grand oration was given by Mr. Frederick Holmes, originally a Connecticut man, who spoke of the great changes that had visited Nebraska over these past three years when the Territory first opened its gates to us.

"We can't help but reflect--be astonished, and half inclined to doubt the reality," Mr. Holmes declaimed in a clear crisp tone. "Where but so recently glided the 'swift canoe' of the red man, now daily—yea, almost hourly—plows the rushing steamers, loaded to the guards with supplies for the thousands who have driven the copper colored inhabitant, the deer and wolf, from their long cherished retreats, and instead opened farms, villages and cities. The whoop and howl have given place to the song of the plough boy, the mechanic's clatter and the busy hum of machinery." He continued on in this vein until he finished with a thankful word for the benignity of Providence for presiding over our efforts.

Upon his conclusion, the master of the ceremonies called me forth from the crowd, and I mounted the makeshift stage forged of cottonwood planks to deliver my own oration. The crowd cheered exuberantly, as if I were Daniel Boone about to reveal the path to the Cumberland Gap. I saw not a few bottles of dubious content shifting from lip to lip. So happy they were in their liberty to turn a profit out of sod and build log-hewn castles to reign over their domains.

Retrieving my speech from my basket, I began to read aloud as I had been taught at Oberlin College with a voice piercing the atmosphere and an emotion that gave soul to each word:

"With each passing month," I called out, "we of Brownville," my fellow Brownvillians let out a cheer at this, "as you of Nemaha City," which comment was followed by a cheer from our hosts, "increase the number of private residences and shops." Both groups now cheered in unison, and I think a few unveiled their flasks and lifted them to toast our accomplishments. "But man owes a duty," I pointed out, "to society as well as to himself." Having said this, I noticed a mild sobering effect upon my supporters. I carried on nonetheless: "There is a society to be built up here. How is it to be done?

"We must have churches and schools. To be sure, we do have preaching occasionally, but half the people do not know when nor where it is, and thus many are deprived of hearing the word of God dispensed. Nor will it be otherwise until there is some regular place of meeting." Having made this clear, I noticed a few in the front had lowered their flasks and now held them behind their backs.

"A school house too, is very much needed. There are children enough to fill two rooms and employ teachers." And looking down upon Messieurs Whitt and Martin, I added, without forgetting myself, "Three teachers! We need them. Our youthful population is running wild. Little girls are seen romping through the streets and climbing the bluffs; while the boys are 'down town' contracting indolent habits, learning to smoke, swear and drink; and in short unfitting themselves for ever becoming good and influential men." Now I observed mothers looking about for children and motioning them with sweeping hands to come close to them and behave.

"But we cannot blame boys for swearing and drinking, when men furnish them with every day examples of it on our streets." I looked hard at Fred, who stood wavering before me with his flask. Seeing no other option, he conceded the argument and nodded in agreement with me.

"A lady cannot walk out in broad day-light," I continued, "without being shocked and insulted with the language and oaths of drunken men. Nor can we sit in our own door yards of an evening without having our ears constantly saluted with oaths." A few men, very few, nodded in approval; but these were jerky, half-hearted nods, executed for the benefit of their nearby better halves.

I noticed the remainder of the superior sex refrained from making eye contact with me, and silence pervaded, with only the distant flapping of our approving flag flying high outside. I took breath anew: "If men will make brutes of themselves by drinking, can there not be some place provided where they may be locked up, and not be permitted to pollute our streets with their foul presence?" Now, no one would look me in the eye, because any public construction would demand a tax on the part of all.

I sensed I had put a damper on our festivities. This hadn't been my intention. I had imagined everyone cheering me on, and Mr. Furnas and the elders of Brownville voicing their approval and circulating a sheet of paper, a petition to sign so the county's subjects might dedicate themselves to the cause. But I heard nothing, not even the rustle of a piece of paper.

What could I do? I was committed and obliged to finish what I had begun. So, I raised my voice and bullied through my final lines:

"Or, what would be better still, can there not be a law

instituted to prevent the selling of so much liquor in our place? In my opinion, he who tempts men to the alluring cup, Mr. Davis, is as bad as the one who partakes of it.

"Surely there are enough responsible men here who must see the expediency of taking hold of this matter at once! Are you with us, O women and men of Brownville and Nemaha City!"

There was a moment of silence. Then, out of the rear of the crowd I heard a singular clapping accompanied by a lone but strident voice, "Amen! Amen!"

I had the support of Miss Straightlace.

* * *

As Prudence's enthusiasm subsided, a man came up to the stage and stood beside me. He whispered something to me, as the silence permitted him this means of communication, but he didn't whisper in my ear, rather it was out the side of his mouth whilst he surveyed the crowd. He said, "I checked, and I saw neither tar nor feathers in this town, which is a good sign."

"Thank you, Cameron," I answered, in a voice nearly as low as his own.

"But just in case of an oversight, and, considering I've just heard someone took a pot shot at you down in Saint Jo, would you permit me to have a word with your supporters here?"

"Be my guest, I'd hate to be tarred and feathered alone."

"Ladies and Gentlemen! I think what Miss Furlough is suggesting, and I must admit I can only see the virtue in it, is that she wishes all you fine looking gentlemen to go easy on the spirits today so that you might benefit from your temperance tonight. Why look around you. Fred! What do you see?"

Fred looked up in amazement at our speaker, his head snapping back and his eyes squinting forward as if he'd sat upon a locust thorn.

"Go ahead, Fred, look around. What do you see?"

Fred made an effort to focus by putting himself nose to nose with Mr. Brown. And after a decisive swig from his flask, announced, "Why I believe I see Mr. Furnas."

A good deal of laughter ensued before Cameron could comment. "You see what we're driving at here don't you? Why, when I look around, I see the prettiest belles west and east of the Missouri. Why look at Miss Prudence in that fetching yellow dress. And how rosy her cheeks are becoming. Why I bet Fred here, if he could see that far, would want to land a kiss on one of 'em, or both. But it's all around us gentlemen. I tell you with the utmost sincerity that I didn't see as pretty a lot of patriotic ladies even at the inaugural ball in the City of Washington itself.

"Men of the frontier, stay the hand that would poison your lips with liquor, so that tonight you might dance straight and surefooted and enjoy the charm and dignity of our lady folk. Because I'm telling you, Miss Adeline Furlough has lined up a fiddler and a band that will be the envy of Paris!"

With only Miss Straighlace abstaining, a round of applause went up in my honor, transforming me from naysayer of the day into queen of festivities.

"The inaugural ball? You attended the inaugural ball?" I questioned Cameron as we ceded the stage.

"Well, let me put it this way, I saw neither prettier nor uglier at the inaugural ball."

"I thought as much."

"Yes, you do think a lot, and a lot of good thinking went into that powerful speech of yours. It almost inspired me to become a temperance man myself."

"That's progress."

"Oh, I'm not one to tip the bottle, but more for practical reasons than religious. It rattles the brain, and I can't afford that presently because I've been doing a lot of thinking, and thinking with you in mind."

"I wouldn't have it any other way."

"And you won't. But I note that Fred can't read and Mr. Furnas can."

"That's probably why Fred doesn't edit the newspaper."

"Exactly my point. You see you can write things concerning societal reform and print them in the paper without the least bit of worry about Fred and his esteemed colleagues because they won't read a lick of it. On the other hand, Mr. Furnas and his peers, men who hold the plow handles directing our valuable society forward, they can read and understand, and put into action your words of wisdom that the Freds of this world cannot comprehend and appreciate."

"Then I'll just have to teach them to read."

"I'd rather you dance with me after dinner."

And so we did dance, out on the green with some two-thousand others in attendance, the whole county and beyond, it seemed.

* * *

The dance was as much a success as could be imagined, though less memorable than the one I hosted earlier. There were plenty of sore feet but not a black eye in the bunch. The fiddler, however, tired after a time, and the dance necessarily came to a close.

A little winded but still full of energy, I told Cameron I needed to see Mr. Muir about the letter and he led me directly to him.

Mr. Muir did not look festive at all. He was in conversation with Stewart and the two of them seemed anxious to get homeward bound.

"Good evening," I said, extending a friendly hand.

He returned the greeting and asked me if I'd seen a leather pass book.

"Not at all."

"Blast it," he said. "I had it as I left town, but I've lost it along the way. I need to find it."

"Someone will find it, and they'll turn it over I'm sure, but perhaps without the money in it."

"I didn't have any money in it. Most of what's in it is valuable only to myself. I just wanted to show you that letter, Stewart."

That last sentence gave me a jolt. "What letter?"

"Mention of a land warrant found in Mr. George Lincoln's affairs," explained Stewart.

"Darnedest thing, if you'll forgive the expression," said Mr. Muir. "Mr. Winslow here rode by on that spirited old hack he rented from Coleman, so I giddied up mine to get up aside him with the buggy to tell him I'd like to show him a letter. Took quite a crack of the whip to catch up with him, but when I did we both stopped to talk, and that's when I discovered my pass book was no longer on the seat. It could have slipped off and onto the trail, but we retraced the wheel marks, and either the durn thing was covered up by dust or someone picked it up."

"Now," said Stewart as a thought occurred to him, "that letter might be valuable to someone. Of course, they'd have to do some digging to find out who the letter was addressed to and who's got the bounty now, if I understood you correctly."

"You're right, the bounty would be of interest if it could be had on the cheap," said Mr. Muir. "Saint Jo was the letter's origin, so I imagine the warrant might well be in the possession of Mr. Lincoln's mother. She might let it go for a fraction of its worth. You dangle five dollars in front of an old woman and she'll snatch it. When I've got other business in that city, I'll just have to call on her."

Cameron pulled me aside and said, "Do you think he's right? Do you think the letter was addressed to Mrs. Lincoln?"

"It would surprise me if she, at her age, still had a father roaming the earth."

"True enough, but in twenty years, I may not have a father roaming about the earth either. The letter may have been old."

"You have a father?"

"Does that surprise you?"

"Well, I figured you just appeared. You know, from a special creation right after an ice age, like Professor Agassiz suggests."

"Well, then be prepared for another shock. I have a mother too, but probably from another ice age; she's quite a bit younger than my father."

"Isn't he lucky to have the latest model? But I see your point about the letter."

I approached Mr. Muir again and asked him if the letter

were dated, and he said no, other than something scribbled in the upper right hand corner such as "Thursday, afternoon," or maybe it was "Tuesday, morning."

"So," I suggested, "it could have been ten years old or twenty years old."

"Could have been," he said, "but it was in good condition. Then again, if it had been in that tin the sheriff pulled it out of, it would have been fresh. What are you driving at, Miss?"

"Maybe," said Cameron, "she'll find that warrant before you do."

On the way back, Cameron joined us in the buggy as Jonathan decided to follow along behind with the pedestrians. He had a much greater and shifting audience that way, and I could hear his voice a quarter-mile distant, comparing the thin tree lines of our new homeland to the majestic groves and forests of Ohio.

* * *

We, the majority of the pilgrims, made it back to town before dark. Prudence, troubled by frivolity had by others at the dance, didn't utter a word the whole trip; but I ignored her judgmental pouting, and, in Brownville, I managed to revive our fiddler and resurrect the dance. We may have had half the enthusiasts we enjoyed at Nemaha City, but I think we had twice the enjoyment, as we danced late into the night.

I do love the long summer nights with the moon filling in for the sun. The shadows remain and yet allow for a luminescence that guides the foot, and even the hoof, as I could still hear, when the music paused, horses neighing in the distance to one another as the stragglers finished their trot along the trail.

As we sat out a dance to regain our breath, I saw my partner saunter off in the glimmering moonlight. He later appeared to be talking to Mr. Whitt and nodding in my general direction. At first, I couldn't fathom what discourse they undertook, but then I noticed their heads rotate, following someone with their gaze. I searched out the object and spotted a yellow dress fitted to a young lady with downcast eyes and moving in sorrowful solitude around the square of festive dancers. Mr. Whitt then stepped in her direction, as if propulsed by a kindly hand. Mr. Davenport had a warm-hearted but mischievous streak.

Between us a few men piled sticks to light a fire to brighten the street. I kept my eye on Prudence. She talked with Mr. Whitt briefly before withdrawing from the night's festivities.

It was well past the hour of midnight when Teddy, Mary, Cameron, and I walked leisurely to my house, to see me home, before the men escorted Mary to hers. As we said our *au revoirs*, I noticed a glow about Cameron's head. I'm afraid my countenance betrayed my wonder.

"Are you all right, Sis?" asked Teddy.

"Yes, yes, it's just strange. You're wearing a halo, Cameron."

"How can I not be, given the company I have?"

He moved forward to gallantly kiss my hand good night and I observed that the radiance left him. Teddy stepping into his spot now wore the halo.

"Just a minute," I said. "I know that can't be right, step aside Teddy."

As Teddy did, I notice the growing brightness emanated from beyond the opposite hilltop. "What in heaven's name?" I asked.

The others followed my gaze and witnessed the apparition as well. It stood there, as did we, for a long time increasing in brightness, before finally and slowly subsiding. Our sensitive noses even caught a brief whiff of smoke. Apparently, someone, somewhere, lit a distant bonfire to celebrate our nation's birth. We couldn't think who might have created such a patriotic display.

* * *

On Sunday, church attendance slipped. Prudence went for a walk, explaining that she needed time alone this Sabbath. Very odd for Miss Straightlace to not attend services, but I did not question her. Stewart and Mary, on the other hand, attended, and Cameron arrived before the concluding hymn.

"I suppose," I told Cameron as we exited, "one cannot accuse you of neglecting church altogether."

"Oh, no, my good lady, I heard every last word."

"So what were you up to whilst I listened to every word first to last?"

"I had breakfast, because one cannot sit through church on an empty stomach. Now mind you, if the Lord's Supper were veritably what it must have been back in the day, a full spread, I suppose one could come on half a stomach, but unfortunately they've reduced it to a nibble, literally but a memory of what it once was. Anyway, after I prepared myself for meeting, I directed my steps in this general direction by way of Coleman's livery, a longish route but one that affords greater reflections for this Sabbath Day."

"And by way of Nemaha City too, given the time it took?"

"I wasn't quite as pious as all that, but I did have a vision."

"Was it an apparition in a yellow dress?"

"No, but something equally illuminating."

"Illuminating? Do you mean it had something to do with the glow we saw last night?"

"Yes I do. I struck up a conversation with Coleman's hostler who was brushing down the horses. He said something spooked them in the night and the estray had worked itself up into a lather. He thought it must have been from the flames of that fire. Maybe they smelled the smoke of it. And therein lies the explanation of my brief nocturnal sainthood."

"You mean you didn't actually have a halo last night?"

"Nor any horns I would like to point out."

"Do you think the Devil has any horns? I mean, it's hard to imagine a snake with horns."

"True, that would impede slithering through holes in the ground and the like. But all the same," Cameron pointed out, "a fire, that does indeed seem to be linked."

"To the devil?"

"Yes, given the description of hell, but even more importantly, to what you're investigating."

"How so? No, let me guess." I put my brain to work. *Fire*, I thought. *How could a fire up north in 1857 be linked to the Friend murders of 1856?*

I looked up at Cameron. "I request one clue."

"Fair enough."

"Was the fire at Mount Vernon? Was it Stephen Nuckolls's warehouse?"

"That's almost two clues, but I see you are as wise as the serpent, which is peculiar in itself when you think about it. I mean the Lord telling us to be as wise as…"

"Cameron," I said excitedly, albeit impolitely breaking off his train of thought, "you're on to something! If someone set fire to Nuckoll's warehouse, he may have done it to destroy Mr. Lincoln's effects."

"That's half the story, my dear, because if someone burned down Nuckolls's warehouse, which is exactly what happened, with fifteen hundred dollars in losses, then what does that make you think of the post office fire?"

"They were hoping to burn down the Post Office and destroy Mrs. Lincoln's letter. They just failed, that's all. But how can we know for sure?"

* * *

Monday was the wedding day of George Duby and Catharine Prevencher. They are friends of Monsieur Carr as they shared a mutual tongue, though Carr being thoroughly French. Monsieur Duby is from Canada, and Catharine is of mixed heritage, her mother being of solid Indian stock. The wedding, with a Reverend Wells presiding, took place in the home of Mr. and Mrs. William Rossell, citizens of means. I feel that my present reading of the adventures of Hope Leslie, whose sister marries into the local Indian tribe, becoming a reality on the frontier. Soon there will be nothing separating humanity into competing races. We shall all be one happy family, though it may take much time to burst and cast away the bonds of slavery before this become reality.

On our way back from the ceremony, Cameron reflected that when this nasty business of slavery would be eradicated from our Christian nation, he would hope for a family of his own and a farm on the frontier.

I drew attention to the fact that the slaveholders were a hardy lot and it wouldn't surprise me if the present generation of slavers didn't reach the century mark without letting go of their so-called chattel. And unless he were as gifted as Abraham and his version of Sarah, his family would consist of but two elderly abolitionists. In the meantime, the proslavery folk would be populating the South aplenty, and by sheer number tipping the scale in their favor in terms of the vote.

"I can't see this affair being settled by a vote," he remarked.

"Are you talking of marriage or slavery?"

"Is there a difference?"

"Not in terms of being bound to another," I observed, "except one is voluntary and the other is not."

"So, the one can be settled by a vote, and one cannot."

"Yes, and I'm not one to abstain either way, I propose a vote in favor of marriage and of abolition."

"Aren't I," said Cameron, "the one to be proposing?"

"Are you?"

"Not being Pawnee, and considering the literature you read for lessons in marital bliss, I don't think I ought." Cameron then fell silent for a moment. I looked for that slight smile that sometimes makes it way up his right cheek when he's thinking of something more to say, but I couldn't find it. Finally, he said flatly, "Times are uncertain and life has become cheap for both white and black."

"And don't forget my relations."

"Yes, white, black, red. The risk is great. I wouldn't want the one I hold dear to become a widow, certainly not a widow with children."

"I don't think we hold the future in our hands either way, whether we take risks or not. Besides, a father made saint might be a better influence than a worldly patriarch. I'm not one to judge, or rather, I ought not be one to judge, but since I can't help it, I would say that Thomas Cranmer, martyred for the faith, left a greater inspiration to his children than would Fred to his."

"Did Cranmer have children?"

"That's not the point, the point is that he would have been a greater inspiration to godliness for any child he would have had than would be Fred to his."

"Does Fred have children?"

"I have no idea, and I doubt he does either. In any case, you cannot use the uncertain future as a guide for the present, which is certain."

"I thought the Apostle said it better not to marry, given the times he lived in."

"He also said Peter traipsed about the Holy Land with his wife in tow, and Peter is to Paul as gold is to silver, you can use either as currency."

"Well, you're right, there is certainty in the present, and I know what it is."

"Do explain."

"The certainty is that you got your money's worth for your lessons in rhetoric and debate at Oberlin College. And it won't be lost on the gentleman approaching us down the street."

I looked down Main Street and saw the unmistakable skull of Mr. Martin progressing toward us bobbing up and down like an apple dropped in a bucket of water. He spotted me from afar, hailed me, and presented himself.

"Miss Furlough," he said after greetings, "I must let you know, in spite of our differences, that I admire your pluck and the words to the wise you pronounced at the festivities on the Fourth. Good fodder for the education of our future generation, and as I was just talking to Mr. Whitt about the idea, we communally agreed that a medical school would not be out of place on the frontier, where maladies and injuries plague our populations more so than those in civilized parts. May I shake your hand again?"

"I don't see why not; it's apparently not given to anyone else at the moment."

"You do understand my proposal, don't you?"

"Better than any other. Or am I mistaken, Mr. Davenport?"

"Oh, if you prefer a proposal from Mr. Martin, I would understand. He's got a good head on his shoulders, just ask him."

Mr. Martin looked at Cameron with eyes half asquint. "Are you interested, Mr. Davenport, in a teaching position?"

"I'm afraid not," my Cameron demurred.

"He's afraid of commitment," I suggested.

"Rather, I'm a much better student than teacher," he objected. "On the other hand, Miss Furlough is excellent in getting a point across. You should hear her opinion on matrimony, as we've been recently inspired to speak of it on account of attending the Duby and Prevencher nuptials."

"Yes," said Mr. Martin. "I do think Miss Furlough well spoken, but it is hard to countenance such a thing, tying a knot between a Christian and a half-breed. Although, I admit from a professional point of view, it would be of interest to see the generational progression of the demeanor and intellect in the children."

I suddenly felt very naked without my parasol. I think he read my face well, as any phrenologist worth his salt ought to be able to do, and he backed up half a pace. "I mean no disrespect," he said. "It's just that Indians, you know, are hardly to be trusted under every circumstance."

"Mr. Martin," I pointed out, "they can be as trusted as any other. I doubt Miss Prevencher is the one who lit the fire at the Post Office, or the one at Mount Vernon. And seeing that there are but palefaces roaming about, I wouldn't be surprised to find it were some of your fine white skulls that got it into their heads to put the buildings to the torch."

"Oh, yes, there are men about town who would be good candidates as incendiaries. You know I have helped in crime solving back east, and if the sheriff would but let me examine a few heads, I would let him know which ones capable and how; but first, I would take a close look at the fire itself."

"Why is that?" I asked.

"Well, you must first understand the fires and how they began. This will tell you two things. For one it will reveal whether you're dealing with one or two incendiaries. If both fires were started in the same way, you're most likely dealing with one incendiary. Second, the sophistication used in starting the fire will tell you what type of brain is behind the arson, and that's when phrenology becomes most useful, as it can narrow down the list of suspects through precise skull measurements."

I stood there for a moment reflecting. He may have been

mad with his obsession about skulls and measurements, but otherwise he did seem to possess a modicum of common sense.

"I propose..." said Cameron.

"Yes?" I answered.

"I propose to pick you up, Miss Furlough, with a Coleman buggy, tomorrow morning, for a leisurely drive to Mount Vernon."

"Cameron must have the exact same measurements as I," I told Mr. Martin, "because we share the same idea."

And with that said, Cameron held out his arm, which I took, and we set off down the street.

* * *

We were able to get on the Mount Vernon trail early the next morning. Prudence did give me a sermonette about the dangers of traveling alone in the wilderness with a man, and explained she would come along to chaperon except that she suffered from headache and needed to visit the druggist. Perhaps Kitty or Mary would oblige, she suggested, just to prevent scandalous gossip if nothing else. Kitty and Mary, however, had work to do, so I took the risk and traveled alone with my beau. It was lovely.

The warehouse at Mount Vernon, which had once stood by the humble cabin serving as Mr. Nuckoll's residence while away from Nebraska City, was reduced to rubble, with the furniture turned into charred sticks of wood or ashes. Tin ware, porcelain, and iron lay about in piles according to specie. Sizeable blackened timbers, fallen from the roof, lay upon the whole mess in ranks. A number of plates and saucers that survived the flames had been salvaged and stacked on a table outside the perimeter of the disaster. Cameron and I walked about the whole methodically, not quite sure what we were looking for.

In time, Mr. Nuckolls arrived in a wagon with a young Negro man, whom he later addressed as Shack, driving the horses. In true pioneer spirit, the pair had been down at a sawmill buying a load of lumber to begin reconstruction.

"Can I help you?" Mr. Nuckolls asked as he approached. His voice cracked slightly, like a cat who doesn't know whether to meow or purr. Perhaps he thought we had sifted his ashes and transferred some of his porcelain to our buggy.

"I think you might," said Cameron.

"Yes," I joined in, "I was hoping to know if you had the effects of Mr. George Lincoln in your possession, but, looking at your warehouse, I doubt that's the case."

"Funny thing is," said Mr. Nuckolls as Shack unloaded lumber, "the contents of that tin box of Lincoln's is about all I have left. You see I hadn't yet put it into the warehouse, so it's in the cabin. Give me a moment and I'll let you have a peek."

While Shack finished emptying his wagon, Mr. Nuckolls disappeared and reappeared from the cabin in a near instant, presenting me with a tin. Opening it revealed a man's pocket watch laying upon a cloth that covered a neckless, playing cards, an empty leather pouch, and dice. "The watch keeps time real well," said Mr. Nuckolls. "And it's got real gold in it, that's what makes it shimmer yellow."

Cameron lifted it out of the box and studied it.

I picked up the cloth. It was a piece of embroidery, something you do as a young girl to show you've mastered the art. The embroidery featured floral artwork around the edges and a square two-story house with a gable in the middle. Underneath the artist had embroidered the following: *Greta Weber, 1826, Aged 10.*

"What's this?" I asked.

Mr. Nuckolls took it up in his hand. "According to the sheriff, Mr. Lincoln said this belonged to an aunt of his, but he also said that of the watch."

"I'll buy it," I said.

"Now that's mighty fine cloth, Miss."

"No it's not, and I'll give you a nickel for it because I'm of a generous nature and you've obviously fallen on hard times." We closed the deal on the sampler.

For his part, Cameron concluded he didn't want to know what time it was, so he returned the watch.

I asked about the fire and Mr. Nuckolls said his new warehouse burst into flames of a sudden. He was in his bed, not quite asleep, when he saw a light flash up in the window. He ran outside and swore he heard someone riding off into the night. He tried beating down the flames with a blanket but they just kept climbing the walls and into the rafters until the whole edifice was ablaze.

"Where did it start exactly?" I asked.

He took me to the far corner of the debris, the corner farthest away from his cabin.

Cameron looked at the ground around where the fire had started and then walked slowly out into the trees. "Do you ever cut through the timber with your horse to get to the road?" he asked.

"No, but there is a deer trail through there as you can see."

Mr. Nuckolls said he had to leave us as his two-year old boy had a fever and dysentery. He and his wife, Lucinda, would be taking the child up to a doctor in Nebraska City. Indeed, Mrs. Nuckolls, attended by a Negro maid, came forth carrying a limp little angel and got up into the wagon with him.

I wished them well, and said I'd pray for their precious child, and the four of them trundled off leaving Shack to continue rescuing what could be saved from the ashes.

After they disappeared from sight, I stepped away from the warehouse to work my way through the shrubs within twenty feet of the corner, zig-zagging to cover every square inch of ground. Finally, I discovered a whiskey bottle, and putting it to my nose, I recognized the odor of turpentine.

Shack came up beside me and scratched his head. "It ain't mine, nor do it belong to anybody abouts here." I pondered the bottle for a bit while Shack went to the cabin for I don't know what purpose.

I saw Cameron following the narrow trail deeper into the timber that logically led to a junction with the path to Brownville. He paused when forty or so paces out and got down on his knees. I made my way over to him and showed him my bottle. He pointed to some soft ground with his index to show me the perfect imprint of a hoofmark. "I'll have to double check, but I think I've seen that hoof-print before."

CHAPTER 16

ameron wouldn't divulge the name of our horse. He said he didn't want to tell me because he might be wrong and he didn't want me jumping to conclusions and pounding some innocent man over the head with a parasol.

Seems everyone had heard of the parasol incident. Amazing how trifling happenings of no importance or interest should travel as quickly as a wire from the telegraph. I did have to ask if the horseman was a phrenologist and Cameron assured me it was not. This narrowed the list down, but when I made another attempt by suggesting Mr. Whitt, Cameron caught on to my stratagem and became abruptly silent, though smiling and eyeing me all the while.

Our ride back into town took less time than our leisurely trip out, but mainly because our hack sensed it was headed home and was anxious to get out of the traces. However, the bumpy trail didn't prevent us from discussing our respective findings. I wondered who might sell turpentine and I remembered reading in the *Advertiser* that John Maun's drugstore sold *"chalk, paint brushes, tooth brushes, soap, almonds, and turpentine: cash exclusively."*

It seemed hard to imagine that a happily married man with a darling little one-year old daughter that he dotes on would slaughter a family, infant included.

"Do you think," I asked Cameron, "that Mr. Whitt might be the culprit?"

"Well, I do think he holds a flame for your good friend Miss Straightlace, but that hardly qualifies him as an incendiary."

"You've got a point; a criminal would hardly want to tie the knot with someone who's going to be looking over his shoulder every minute to make sure he never walks astray."

"You're awfully optimistic about Mr. Whitt's intentions, but I hope for the best as well."

"You know, you're right," I said, reconsidering. "He does seem to be a slippery one." Then an idea popped up in my brain, eliciting a smile of satisfaction.

Noticing the transformation of my countenance, Cameron nodded knowingly. "But none too slippery for you I see."

After leaving the buggy with Coleman's hostler, Cameron and I went our separate ways.

I ventured downtown, where I found a crowd listening to Colonel B.P. Rankin, candidate for Nebraska's delegate to the City of Washington, haranguing one and all about squatters' rights. "Let the farmers have the land! Not the speculators! Give us two more years before payment, when the price of grain will have surpassed the greed of the bankers and land sharks. And as for moving our territorial capital out of Omaha or not, let that be decided by Nebraskans and not the U.S. Congress. Let Congress preoccupy itself with national and interstate matters, let the Washington government grant lands to the railroads south of the Platte River so that we can receive and ship goods hither and thither amongst our sister states, or at least build a road from the mouth of the Platte through our counties and on down through Kansas and then east into Missouri. And while they've got their shovels, axes, and hammers in hand, they can bridge the Platte River into Omaha and thereby link that city and us to Saint Jo."

The politicking went late into the night and my tired eyes and ears forced me to retire before the good Colonel ever got to the subject dear to my heart. Our impending land settlement with the Pawnee.

Teddy accompanied me home and I discussed the fires with him and the problems I was dealing with in unraveling the mystery of the Friend murders. It was a healthy discussion, as such heart to hearts are with siblings, who know you best and always have your interests foremost.

* * *

The morning of July eighth, a Wednesday, was auspicious, with the sun illuminating the rooftops and warming the timbered knolls that were astir with wildlife. The carpenters, pounding with their hammers, competed with the raucous chirping of the insect and the cheerful song of the bird. Walking down Water Street, viewing Nature's brush strokes in its painted sky and verdant flowing landscapes, broken only by newborn homes and businesses, I saw a beautiful future for my little city as it stretched its arms into the countryside. Workers were even then afoot, cutting a road through the hills in the direction of Fort Kearny. To receive our visitors from afar, those coming to reside among us as well as those passing through toward either the rising or setting suns, Messieurs Clark and Chastain promised to put down the stone and lay the brick for a hotel worthy of our promise. The woodworking and painting fell to our talented and farsighted architect Cyrus Wheeler. But what of material gifts, if the town have not purity of soul? The town fathers were not to neglect my call to arms, for as a gift to the gentler sex, they now considered laws to mend morals and secure domestic tranquility.

The one flaw in this bright morning that otherwise inspired my hopes was my encounter with a Mr. Paris Prouts, Esquire and editor of the *Saint Joseph Gazette*, and his companion, whose name happily remains unremembered by me. Cameron warned me of the editor's arrival and enlisted me as a spy to keep him informed as to the intruders' continual whereabouts. For some reason, my beau felt it his duty to remain unseen by either of the two. "Bad for business," he told me rather cryptically.

Mr. Prouts, Esquire, was, as I found out in my brief conversation with him, a sterling democrat immune to the suffering of the Negro. According to his associate, the only qualification to consider when comparing candidates for office, whether in Nebraska or Missouri or anywhere else for that matter, was the number of slaves the man owned. The more he owned, the more qualified he would be to represent us. Of course I let him know that such a man would not be representing me.

I did have my parasol in hand, but Mr. Martin's untimely arrival obstructed my good intentions, as the phrenologist guided the unfortunate editor, and his second, into less interesting conversations with other Brownvillians.

What made the morning still joyful was the idea brewing in my head, the idea only Teddy was privy to in any detail. It was in discussing my grand scheme the night before, and a problem accompanying it, that Teddy gave me a key to solving the problem.

I couldn't wait for nightfall, because that's when I could execute my plan and solve the mystery of the arsonist.

* * *

I waited an eternity...all day, that is, until the hills grew silent, except for the buzz of insects and the occasional yelping of the coyote, when a solemn greyness, reflecting the full moon, fell upon the town like a fog, before I issued forth in my black mourning dress to slip among the buildings, holding ever so closely to their walls. In such a manner I stole my way to Mr. Whitt's drugstore.

I don't know if you, as a child, ever snuck downstairs and into the kitchen to partake of a fortifying midnight snack consisting principally of cookies. You know the type: ginger cookies flavored with molasses. The kind mothers intend to donate to a church potluck, where they'll be wasted on overfed neighbors who have brought rye bread in exchange. You have that elation, that nervous hope that you shall succeed, and yet you remember your last such venture, when you discovered a note, in the otherwise vacant tin, reading, "Sorry Addy, better luck next time, Love, Mother."

This time, however, there was no question of Mother intervening, and pure excitement fed my pounding heart as I produced from my purse the key Teddy had given me, entrusted to him by the druggist, so that Teddy might work on his shelves when the shop was closed.

I still wasn't totally sure Teddy hadn't given me the key to Mr. Whitt's house instead of the shop, as he had a key to each, so I held my breath while inserting the key, then I pursed my lips just right before turning, and the door opened.

I looked over the shelves for a bottle resembling the two of whiskey I had found. Then it hit me, and I don't know why I didn't think about this earlier, but the two bottles, the one at the Post Office and the one at Mount Vernon, they both resembled another...the one lone whiskey bottle seen near the ashes of the Friend house! Whoever started these latest fires had also seen to the scorching of the Friend house, had also engineered the murder of seven people. The mastermind of murder and conflagration was definitely among us, and he was after me.

The darkness made it impossible to read labels, but I could see and feel the shapes of the bottles, and nothing matched what I was looking for. I moved behind the counter and searched in the shadows underneath the till. My hand fell upon an oddly shaped object, and by force of curiosity I held it up to the moonlight. A pistol. I felt of its barrel and fit my index finger into it. After studying it from every angle, I put it back in its place as nearly as I could guess. And then it happened, the back of my forearm brushed against a bottle.

I went to my knees and carefully lifted up the bottle. The exact shape. Its cork stood tall, as if it had been opened and then recorked. Filled with turpentine no doubt. Who next would be the victim?

I stood up and grasped the cork firmly in hand and twisted.

The front door swung open and in the frame of it appeared the silhouette of a man, motionless. I don't know what makes stillness eerie in the night, but I rather think it has something to do with death and the indiscernible, the dark unknown. Whoever heard of a ghost ringing the door-bell at high noon to pay you a visit. I can see no purpose to it, I doubt a man of flesh and bone would even flinch at a daylight apparition. The phantom might extract a "Oh, my, what are you doing here at this hour?" but that's hardly satisfactory for any self-respecting spook. With the specter at hand in the doorway of Mr. Whitt's shop at midnight, the spirit got the full package. I let out a scream so forceful in nature that it moved both me and the apparition a full step backwards.

A crack of a match illuminated the intruder's face, and as he raised it high to get a picture of me, his brow cast a foreboding shadow across his eyes. He then lowered the flame ever so slowly to light a candle. Calmly blowing out the match, he took two paces toward me.

There I stood, a whiskey bottle in one hand and its cork in the other and Mr. Whitt facing me.

"Lookie what we have here," he said, with an ominous amusement bound up in his rather monotone voice.

As he cleared the doorway, another figure emerged, Miss Straightlace. "Whatever are you doing, Addy?"

Sniffing the bottle, I was disappointed. I had enough experience to know that Jerome would have gladly consumed its contents. It definitely was not turpentine.

I looked up at Miss Straightlace and said, "You can't guess? O, innocent, naive, and helpless Prudence. Have you no conscience to consort with such a villain? There are four gallons of liquor to every man, woman, and child in the country, and you, Mr. Whitt," I said in turning to the druggist, "are the source!"

I then took the bottle by the neck and shattered it on the counter, asperging with whiskey everything within a three-foot radius, including my mourning clothes. "Shall I destroy the rest?" I threatened. "No, I shall leave them to your conscience Mr. Whitt. And as for you Prudence, how is it that you walk the streets at night in the company of such a man and enter into this room to fulfill who knows what evil intentions he might have toward you?"

"Addy!" she protested. "You've very much the wrong impression. I have a fretful nervous condition and Jonathan took me to rouse Mr. Whitt from bed to attend to me. Isn't that right Jonathan?" she asked.

Jonathan immediately came through the entrance. "Yes, yes," he confirmed. "Lucky there was a full moon, otherwise I don't know if we would have found his house in this darkness. Should we have been in Baltimore we would have had street lamps lighting our way. They've had public illumination for decades now. This is supposed to be 1857 *anno domini*, but here it's like you're living in 1857 B.C.."

"If it were 1857 B.C. my dear Jonathan, you'd be telling us how much better it is in the wilderness where people have Moses and a pillar of light to guide them. In any case, Prudence, I wouldn't tolerate a man who holds a bottle of whiskey under his counter. And when you get home with your medicinal elixir that he is sure to concoct with some admixture of rum, remember to lock the door."

Having said this, I pushed my way through the threesome.

Mr. Whitt, though, let fly a parting remark. "Miss Furlough, you think you're so holy, I suppose you walk on water."

"Indeed, come January," I told him, "and on skates."

CHAPTER 17

he next day, Thursday, I found Prudence to be rather cool toward me. I tried to explain to her that Mr. Whitt could not be trusted.

She got defensive. "He's a bona fide druggist and a conscientious citizen."

"Did you know he kept whiskey and a gun under his desk?"

"I asked him about it. He showed me where he kept it, and I did see the pistol too. He explained to me the whiskey was for medicinal purposes only. And as for the pistol, he keeps it in his store unless he's traveling, in case of robbers. If there's anyone to be concerned about, it would be the man you frequent. I would keep him at arm's length, I'm sure."

"And well *you* should!"

Needless to say, Prudence did not accompany me into town.

Later in the day, Cameron stopped by the office of the *Brownville Beacon* to let me know he had business up at Nebraska City and then down in Saint Jo. I told him of my adventure the night previous, and about the three whiskey bottles.

"You know," he observed, "I'd hate to become a widower before I get married."

"Do I now hear a proposal?"

"I've been thinking about what you've said, and I think you're right. We can't let the future rule our present. So, when I get back from Saint Jo I'd like to discuss the subject with you."

I'm afraid Prudence would have accused me of losing my dignity, because I flung my arms around Cameron and looked up into his face. In spite of his stoic calm, I could see his blue eyes brimming with emotion. Discretion forbids me to relate our intimate conversation, but the world about us seemed itself to tremble with our excitement.

As he stepped toward the door, he said, "In Saint Jo I hope to find a token of my commitment at the jeweler's."

"That's so sweet of you, Cameron. But," I said, thinking of the name of Weber embroidered into the sampler I'd purchased from Mr. Nuckolls, "if you could also render a service for me in Saint Jo it would be equally kind."

Cameron knitted his eyebrows at the request. "You wouldn't be stirring up more trouble, would you? Making enemies in Saint Jo as well as here?"

"No, whatever would give you the notion?"

"Perhaps that tone of voice. I've heard you use it before with your brother, usually when you're asking him to do something no man would want to be caught doing in broad daylight."

"I have no idea what you're talking about, besides, I see myself as one who solves problems rather than as one who stirs up trouble."

"You do know that Mr. Coleman has declined to present himself anew for sheriff in the August election."

"And you think that's because of me?"

"You do keep him busy."

"As well I ought, seeing how he needed me to discover an arsonist burned the shed in Brownville and the warehouse at Mount Vernon."

"Now you do see how that causes trouble. Without there being an incendiary, Mr. Coleman could sit back and relax, but now he's obliged to hunt down a criminal, at least until August."

I was about to reply when we heard harsh words outside. Stepping into the street we found two men arguing for a bit and then thrashing each other about.

"What's this?" I asked Cameron.

"You're the expert on stirring up trouble, you tell me."

"I bet it's over either a woman or a piece of land."

"There's also politics and religion."

"You see," I observed. "I'm not the only source of trouble around here."

"Certainly not, but I'm glad to see you own up to your role, even if it's a minor one. So, while I'm away, take care of yourself... for me."

"That I will do," I said, returning to my interest in the sampler, "if you'll see if a Mr. Weber owned a house in Saint Jo. It's a needle in the haystack, but if we find it, I think we can start stitching together a solution to the Friend mystery."

* * *

I spent Friday and Saturday in my office reading letters from the States and sending out as many. The number of stories and miscellaneous information from back east put me in a predicament. I didn't know which ones to select for the gazette, they all seemed of interest.

Then there were my own essays I needed to polish, but I must admit I wasn't as diligent as an author ought to be as the lure of *Hope Leslie* and *Madame Bovary* undermined my well-intentioned work habit. Delving into *Hope Leslie*, time passed quickly through the hourglass. The tricky part was guessing which words had been deleted by the bullet. When I finally put the book down, *Madame Bovary* seduced me, and it, being in French, took me to a distant culture that yet seems so real and palpable. Flaubert's descriptions of landscape, of peasant life, and the small town were so beautifully wrought, as was each character's personality. He was the Rembrandt of literature, who, replacing the brush with a pen, lifted the veil from a face to reveal its soul.

To shake myself from my addiction, I set about working with my hands, hoping to develop skills in typesetting and presswork. I had come to the conclusion that I could not always count on Teddy to do this, because his carpentry skills were in high demand on the frontier. I could perhaps oblige Monsieur Carr to jump ship and work for me, if he wished to continue on as my well-paid gardener; but I don't know if Mr. Furnas, who currently employed him part time at the newspaper, would take kindly to such impressment.

I should say that I didn't spend those two days in complete solitude. Indeed, on Friday, in the late afternoon, Mr. Martin called at the office. I think he came to waste time with Teddy as he often did in the late afternoon. I do wish I could disentangle him from my brother as he cannot exert but a malign influence.

Not finding Teddy at his post did not deter Mr. Martin

from pulling out a chair from the kitchen to make himself comfortable. I tried explaining to him that I had work at hand in writing articles for my gazette.

"Well," he said, "I might be of assistance to you."

"I can't see how, as this is a lady's gazette, written for and by ladies."

"Why, I can bring you news of interest to the ladies. For example, do you know Congress has made it more difficult to import indecent literature? They've even banned certain daguerreotypes, and it doesn't take a thick brow to conjure up what might be their subject matter. I doubt you'll be able to read anything in French from now on, especially from the pen of that Flaubert fellow, whom, I think even the French government, lude as it is, being monarchical, has charged with immorality for that book of his celebrating the life of an adulteress. Something called *Breviary* or *Mrs. Breviary*, or a title of that sort. In any case, it may be a good idea to keep these things from the eyes of the weak willed, but as for men of solid physiognomy, I think such boycotts harmful. The governments ought to let ideas flow betwixt nations, lest we stagnate in our inbred ignorance. Now don't you think your lady readership might have an interest in that bit of news?"

"Oh?" I answered as I lifted myself up to sit on the table, fluffing out my dress to cover up my latest interest in reading. I had only begun Flaubert's novel and had not yet discovered anything untoward, and I didn't expect to, but I wouldn't want Mr. Martin spreading about town that Miss Furlough spent her time up in that office of hers reading salacious novels.

I followed up on my exclamation by stating the obvious. "I

cannot object to a boycott. Just as we would not want to import poisons for the body, nor should we wish to import poisons for the mind. Let food for both body and mind be pure, for by indulging only in the good, we all become healthier and better. So, keeping the bad from our sight can do no harm. I do wish peddlers of sin would move on. I would pay them well to do so."

"I remember a do-gooder like you doing exactly as you say, and I must admit I admired the result."

"I'm flattered."

"Yes, as I recall, this do-gooding woman, who even dressed a bit like you, paid each of the two ladies of the evening in her town a hundred dollars in gold to move, and so they did, each moving into the other's abode."

"I don't think your do-gooder resembles me in the slightest, because I would have done quite differently."

"How so?"

I examined Mr. Martin's physiognomy carefully as I said, "I would have used less than one-hundred dollars in buying a bottle of whiskey, emptying it, and then refilling it with turpentine."

He stared at me, and I could not tell whether he did so because he felt judged or because he didn't know what I was talking about.

"Do you know what I would have done," I asked him, "with my bottle of turpentine?"

"Drink it?" he said. "That would certainly end all your worries about the two women."

His frivolity did not distract me from the idea that a guilty man often resorts to flippancy when cornered.

I rose from the desk while gracefully sweeping up *Madame*

Bovary into the fold of my dress. Opening the door, I informed Mr. Martin that I had to return to my work and if he lingered, I would have to charge him a consulting fee.

He kindly left.

However, in his wake, an idea lingered in my mind. Something about his story and the shifting around of properties intrigued me. I couldn't say exactly how, but in some way, it seemed a clue to the unraveling the Friend mystery.

Chapter 18

n Saturday, I ventured out of my office and witnessed the arrival of a cartload of books and other mobiliary items, which made its way down Main Street from the Post Office to the newly established Nemaha Land Office. I espied Mr. George Nixon, register of deeds, escorting the load. After directing the dispersal of his stock, Mr. Nixon headed up toward the levee to two lots he had purchased next to McPherson's warehouse.

I noted that the dock was throbbing with activity as McPherson's competitor, McAllister, was still moving some seventy tons of goods he'd received there last week. This was a decent ten tons more than McPherson had squeezed into his store. I heard someone comment that if McAllister hadn't extended his warehouse earlier in the year, he wouldn't have been obliged to import so many goods. I suggested that if they hadn't been Scotsmen, they wouldn't have to worry so much about making money.

Nixon's land ran up from the levee onto a hillside, where he employed a half dozen men to level it. It's there that I had an opportunity to query him about bounties and the like. He explained how bounties functioned, and how they could change hands, but he also said that if there were any warrants already processed, I would have to go to the Omaha land office to review them.

Mr. Rossell interrupted our conversation to discuss a petition for Mr. Nixon. The petition, I learned, concerned postponing land sales in Nebraska. A popular idea in these parts judging from the list of signatures. Mr. Rossell's intent was to convince Mr. Nixon to forward it to Washington City to see if it might resonate there as well.

As I headed back down the hillside, the words *bounties, shifting properties, and signatures* floated about in my brain until I concluded that I must needs make my way to Omaha, bridge over the Platte or no, if I hoped to stay the hand of my would-be assassin.

* * *

On Sunday, July twelfth, I attended church with Prudence, Jonathan, Kitty, Stewart, Teddy, and Mary. Mary made a fuss over Teddy's attire, straightening up his collar and dusting it off, a common occurrence; however, it seemed to me that this time she was more exasperated than amused.

After the service, Kitty asked to talk with me apart. We strolled off with our Sunday baskets onto a vacant lot where last year someone had buried a next of kin. The gravesite provided an open space amongst the brambles.

"Why the secrecy?" I asked.

"Because I'm not so sure as to whether I ought to do this or not. You know I'm not one to take chances like you, but for this once, and because I love you, I'm taking a risk. It's so exciting."

"What risk?"

Kitty delved into her basket and produced a pistol. "I found it in the room of the gentleman who left the hotel by a window without paying his bill. He had it under his pillow with a pouch of a dozen balls, and he forgot it in his hurry. I told Stewart about it and he told me to ask the clerk if the man left a forwarding address. That's when we discovered he hadn't. Stewart wondered if his secrecy and flight didn't have something to do with Sheriff Coleman coming into the hotel at the time. Anyway, Stewart and I had the same idea, we should let you have it, thinking of what happened to you in Saint Jo. Of course, if the gentleman comes back to pay his bill, we'll have to return it to him, but for the time being you'll have something better than a parasol to defend yourself with."

I took the pistol and instinctively put my finger in the barrel. It felt oddly familiar. I placed it and the balls in my basket and we rejoined our compatriots at the church.

There was a lively discussion in progress with one of Furnas's men, printer Thomas Fisher, discoursing on politics. He said that California expected to divide itself into two or three states. Jonathan followed this up to let us know that he personally knew three gentlemen out there, and he gave the names which now elude me, and that all three had intimated to him their intentions to be governors. I made the observation that they would only become so if two of them were slavers, as the only objective in creating three states out of one would be to have four more senators to represent the interests of slaveholding states.

My intervention in the conversation won me one of those compliments you'd just as soon gift to another.

"My, my, Miss Furlough," suggested Mr. Whitt with a wink, "if it weren't for the dress, you'd be in the Senate yourself. I'm sure plenty of senators young and old would make a declaration of sentiments in your favor."

"I believe half the senators, those from the South, haven't any sentiments at all, at least any human sentiment."

Mr. Fisher took exception to my comment. "We don't need any more people getting riled up about this slavery issue. If people would just leave it alone, it would solve itself. The way those abolitionists get fired up, they drive themselves to crime. Why think of that poor old Jimmy Lyle getting killed in Kansas by one of the Bible pounding abolitionists."

"And how many Negroes did poor old Jimmy kill?" I asked. "I suppose we don't keep a record of that."

"Don't tell me," said Mr. Fisher, "you're at one with them rabble rousers."

Before I could answer, I heard a familiar voice come to my defense. "I think she's just honest, and unlike most of us, plays her cards straight and tells us what she thinks. Besides, you don't just need abolitionism or anything much to start a raucous out here. You know that we of the territory just held a political convention up north in Bellevue, don't ya?"

"No, Mr. Davenport," I said warmly, pleased to see that he had stopped off to see me during his trip from Nebraska City to Saint Jo, "but do tell."

"Well up in Bellevue they put forth Judge Ferguson for delegate to draw votes away from Mr. Furnas's man, Colonel

Rankin. That would put Omaha's Colonel Bowen in the lead. Well, that was enough for our good gentlemen to adjust their diplomacy by pulling out pistols and bowie knives.

"So let me tell you Mr. Fisher, it's not because Miss Furlough speaks the truth that young men throw punches, it's because young men want to throw punches that they find a reason to do so. If it ain't for abolitionism, it'll be for Colonel Rankin. Like the Good Book says, we're a sinful lot. Just think of Mr. Christ. He told the truth and somebody wanted him crucified for it. Now who was wrong, Jesus or those who nailed him to the cross?"

Thomas Fisher mumbled something about being needed at home.

"*Mister* Christ?" I asked. "You refer to the Lord as *Mr.* Christ?"

"Well, I don't know that he had a professional title. Wouldn't sound right saying Doctor Christ."

"Though he did heal nearly as many men and women in three years as the average surgeon here puts in the ground in a month."

"Doctor Christ then."

"Savior might be sufficient."

"As you wish."

I felt like I needed to have a theological discussion with my beau someday. He had not attended Oberlin as I had, so I could excuse his lack of vocabulary when discussing soteriology and other commonplace subjects of a religious school, but even accounting for this, he seemed yet rough around the edges on some necessary issues, and I couldn't let them go without resolving them.

I considered this seriously as the two of us walked toward my house. If I didn't fully understand his spiritual state, there could be no marriage. I could not yoke myself to someone not equally bound to Christ. Christ is not only our hope for the afterlife, he is also a woman's only protection in this world. Indeed, if a man is not bound to Christ, he is not obligated to serve his wife as Christ serves the church. What abuses would a man, no matter how good he may seem, levy upon a wife, if he have no heavenly guidance?

In spite of these nagging misgivings, I did ask Cameron if he could do me one more service, and I was pleased to see that he accommodated me. I told him, if time allowed, I would that he meet me up in Nebraska City, on my way down from Omaha City. He inquired as to why, and I told him because I would be a damsel in distress in need of a prince charming.

"Normally a lady doesn't plan these things out in advance," he observed. "Half of the fun in getting rescued, I imagine, is the surprise."

I told him I had many things to do, which necessitated a schedule of events, and therefore I hadn't time for surprises, so he'd best get used to my rather predictable and tedious way of life.

* * *

On Monday I reported early to my office, anxious to get my essays completed in order to take the stage on the morrow.

I must admit that Jonathan provided fodder for my first essay, and I should thank him for it. The title was *Things not to Do as a Man*. I thought it well that the ladies read this and inculcate the lessons in their male children whilst they were young, so that they might not grow up into Jonathans. The gist of it said that a young man ought not take off a woman's bonnet or watch feminine ankles climb steps, and that he ought not be remiss in putting an umbrella over a woman's head or in helping her on with her cloak. Neither should he complain when sick or when the meal is ten minutes late, or wear out the carpet in front of the looking-glass.

For my second essay, Mr. Martin proved to be my muse. *Ladies,* I wrote, *The blood of a single person, and the blood of a million persons, is to be held in one estimation. Difference in physiognomy or complexion argues no difference in the susceptibility of grief or pain. Men cannot be classed into orders. If it is good for an Englishman or an American to deal justly with another, it is good for him to deal justly with all men--including Indians and Africans. The world was made for no one man or set of men. God made it, and he made it neither for angels, nor kings, nor nabobs. He made it for humanity!*

I was justly proud of my creations and went home with a full heart to pack my carpet-bag.

* * *

On Tuesday, the fourteenth of July, what Monsieur Carr joyfully referred to as Bastille Day, I found Prudence in the kitchen. She moved about mechanically making breakfast, but I could see tears streaming down her cheeks.

I know that I haven't spoken well of Prudence, but pity filled my heart. I ask her for the source of her distress and she hesitated before confiding.

"I so wanted to help you, dear Addy. I wanted to do something right and good. I find it so hard. I hoped to save you from yourself, from your waywardness, but you seem to have such joy, and I'm the one who suffers."

She put down a frying pan and fell on my shoulder, and I found myself patting her on the back to comfort her.

"There are things I appreciate, Prudence," I said diplomatically. "You are so very attentive."

"And I thought you and Jonathan would be so good for each other."

"Well, I do have Cameron, you understand."

She attempted to straighten herself and looked at me with searching eyes. "You don't understand. I fear for Jonathan. I know I say wonderful things about him, because I love him so, and deep down he is a good fellow, but he seems indifferent to things of the heart, like he keeps putting off thinking about things that really matter by going on and on about where he's been and what he has done. It's always the past and never the present."

I have to admit I was a little stunned, as I realized how perceptive Prudence really was. "Prudence," I said gravely. "I think you mean well, and that you make herculean efforts to please, but I also think that just may be the problem. Your father is a hard man, demanding, and I just fear that you're always trying to live up to his expectations, just as your brother is. Your brother does it by always claiming to be the smartest, the most accomplished. You do it by trying to follow all of the rules society has laid out for us. You both need to realize that you only need to live up to God's expectations. God made you a woman to enjoy life, to dance with David, to feast with the disciples, to converse with the guests rather than run around working all the time. You don't have to be Martha, you can be Mary. It's much easier, much more fulfilling."

"You think I ought to have danced with Mr. Whitt?"

"Maybe not with Mr. Whitt, but if the music enlivens your heart, follow it."

Prudence wrapped her arms around me and melted my own heart. I fear dew formed in my eyes too, and trickled down my cheeks. She kissed me and thanked me and said she thought it best she stay home at present. I didn't discourage her. She needed the comfort of solitude to let her new thoughts convert her emotions.

Teddy soon appeared at the house with a wagon to load me up and take me on down to Main Street to meet with the stage coming up from Nemaha City. He told me I picked the wrong day to leave because a band of minstrels would be entertaining the town tonight, but I had no regrets, considering my favorite minstrel was by now in Saint Jo.

The stage arrived in its own good time, it had stopped behind the post office where the passengers descended and the driver switched out the horses, then he went in to the post office to collect some mail and tell tall tales to Mr. Brown, who reciprocated. Eventually he brought his coach to the front of the post office, and we ascended.

Entering the coach, first, was a healthy German family, the wife of which had apparently consumed half her family's allotment of pretzels, so she wouldn't have to carry them in hand. She held one of their boys on her lap while the brother occupied that of the father's, who appeared to have consumed the remaining pretzels. The two gentlemen on the far end of the facing benches, having entered by the opposite door, made themselves as thin as possible to squeeze into their seats.

We all looked silently at one another, like children at the dinner table on Sunday afternoon.

Of course, silence by children at our dinner table, now that I reflect upon it, was justifiably instituted by Mother. I remember the very Sabbath she established the rule; it was the day when stuffy parson Totley and his self-effacing wife came to dinner. He asked us what usefulness we had accomplished before his arrival, and I told him all about Mother dropping the chamber pot on Muffin, the cat, and all my brothers and I chasing Muffin about the table to shoo him out the door without touching him. "But Muffin ended up on your chair, Reverend Totley," I said, "and we had to scoot him off with a broom. What a mess."

Seeing that it was not Sunday dinner, I broke the silence and introduced myself to my German neighbor and easily entered into conversation with her. She was good-natured and immediately began a lengthy discourse about the new high school to open up on the second floor of the bank building in Nebraska City. I wondered if she might not be an acquaintance of Mr. Martin or Mr. Whitt.

"The phrenologist, you mean?"

"The same."

"Oh, isn't he an informed person. So much knowledge and logic wrapped up into one brain."

"Yes, rather tightly isn't it?"

"It's funny you should mention him because he asked me about the high school when I was in the drugstore. He seemed most interested, as did the druggist. The phrenologist went as far as to say to the druggist that he'd come across some money that he'd like to invest in such an enterprise at Brownville, but if there were shares to be bought in the one at Nebraska City, he would be very generous in that direction as well."

"He came across some money?"

"Oh yes, a great aunt of his, an old maid as I understood it, had passed away and left him a tidy sum." She turned her head a bit, looking amused. "You know, the druggist said he might be able to help out too. He could build a drugstore in Nebraska City, and he thought they might make a good pair of professors. Seems he must have money too."

Her husband chimed in. "With the Territorial government licensing all these empty banks to print up money with nothing to back it, it's no wonder everybody's got money nowadays."

Opposite me in the coach sat a Mr. Emmor Lash, a pioneer accompanied by a sizeable wooden box. It had taken all of his teeth gritted together to hoist the box into the coach. I asked him why he didn't just toss it on our roof rather than burdening his leg space. I questioned him partly to bring him into our conversation and partly because I did wonder as to why he'd put such a thing in the tight coach.

Mr. Lash just looked at me kindly and nodded. I took another tack, inquiring as to what he had in his box, and he thought about my question for a moment, then said in as few words as possible that it contained parts for a McCormick machine. Having made a little headway, I again asked him why he didn't stow it away, and he again looked at me friendly-like and said mildly, "So I know where it is."

This struck me as odd because I really don't believe anyone is going to steal mechanical parts, considering all the variety of machines. Now children might. I remembered Teddy stealing Mary's lunchbox at school, while leaving his behind. He was interested in her cakes, which she had languidly munched on in front of him the day before. The stolen lunchbox, of course, contained only blood sausage, which Teddy then and now abstains from. Mary thanked Teddy not only for returning her lunchbox to her but also for the cookies she had extracted from his. I think that was the day Mary decided Teddy needed some looking after.

As we moved across the countryside, I glanced from time to time at Mr. Lash. He was a slight man, reserved, but he exuded a certain control over his immediate environment. It was a strange blend of pleasantness and seriousness. It made me uncomfortable. I think it best to be one or the other, hot or cold. The Bible has very little good to say about someone who's lukewarm.

Another thing that bothered me about the man was his Mona Lisa eyes. Every time I glanced at him, his eyes seem to meet mine. It was as if he were keeping watch over me.

Our coach made it well past Mount Vernon before a wheel wobbled. This obliged the driver to stop at the mill on Camp Creek to mend it. He cursed freely at the situation until he remembered ladies were aboard. Then he vociferated against whoever had trafficked his axle and wheel.

"Had to have sawn through this back behind the post office," he growled. "We could have had a serious accident." Then, putting his head through the window, he said, "You'd best all get out while I do the repairs, it'll make it lighter to jack up the axle to straighten it out and band it back together."

We all descended, though Mr. Lash offered to remain near the coach to make sure our belongings were unmolested while we exercised our limbs.

This behavior made him rather more suspicious. Perhaps he was carrying a load of gold in his box. As I walked in the direction of the mill, I peeked back over my shoulder. There stood Mr. Emmor Lash, leaning against one of the rear wheels, and of course he noticed my movement. *Was he keeping an eye on me?* I really wanted to get a look inside that box of his.

* * *

A Mormon by the name of Jimmison ran the mill operation, and we found a group of pioneers awaiting their turn, but a thirteen-year old was ahead of them all, and this boy said he'd been there since dawn waiting for his grist to be ground. He thought it would have been faster to hire a squaw to grind the wheat by hand, but he hadn't seen an Indian for four days.

Mr. Jimmison, being in earshot, called out to the boy to explain that the squaw would want her wampum just like everyone else.

"I've got all the flour I need," the miller said eyeing the young man, "what I want is hard money and none of them phony bank notes." He said this while his fingers touched the side of his mouth, as if he were putting a coin between his teeth and biting down.

The young man, obviously ashamed, cast his eyes toward the ground. "If you won't take the flour, we'll get you paid in cash Mr. Jimmison, just as soon as harvest is all over and sold."

One of my stagecoach compatriots, the German lady, asked the youngster where his father was, and he said his pa had gone to Saint Jo to buy some items for a store he'd opened up near the Peru settlement, next to Mount Vernon.

That piqued my interest, as Cameron was in route for that city, so I stepped into the conversation and asked him when his father left.

"Sometime in June of last year."

There was a weighty silence as we all realized the boy's family had been abandoned.

However, the date of the man's disappearance interested me. "What's your name young man?"

"Frank."

"And your father's?"

"Al, well that's what folks called him. His real name was Alfred, like the king. Mr. Alfred Medley."

A warmth swept through me. I don't know how else to describe it, but no doubt not unlike that feeling overcoming a prophet of the Old Testament when God reveals a vision to him. Something clicked in my mind as George Lincoln's final words came back to me: "Some smug man gave me the means, and if you don't know him a medley...." Maybe the word "medley" was actually a proper noun? Maybe George Lincoln was referring to Mr. A. Medley. This would mean Frank's father knew who the "smug man" was, but he was slain while in Saint Jo, just like someone tried to kill me there.

"Did you hear of the Friend murders?" I asked.

At this point Mr. Jimmison entered into the discussion. "Did we hear of it?" he said sardonically. "Why they grabbed

Amos didn't they? Just because he knew the truth. Knew the truth about Joseph Smith and about that miscreant who egged 'em on to rob Jacob Friend. Wouldn't be no trouble at all, he told them, there being no law in the Territory, and, even if there was, no one would lift a finger against the good deed of killing the Friend family, bein' Negro-loving folk, as they was."

When I heard this, the whole affair became very personal. "And Mr. Medley knew who this evil, smug man was?"

"Oh, I wouldn't doubt it. He was terribly riled when I told him Amos got penned up. And that ain't like a Gentile to get worked up if one of us Saints gets a beating or a lynching."

"No Ma'am," chimed in Frank, "Pa didn't like to see no unfairness. He said they all ought to hang together, and if someone didn't do something about that blowhard, he would, but he never did. He just went down to Saint Jo and that was the last we saw of him. Ma figured he just found someone more likeable than herself and with less appendages."

"You know, Mr. Jimmison," I said, opening my reticule. "I'd like to pay for the grinding for Frank."

Now it was Mr. Jimmison's turn to be embarrassed. "Oh Ma'am, you don't have to do that. I'll take my portion out of his grist like usual."

"Well cap the climax!" cried young Frank looking into my reticule. "Why here we talk of Pa and you've got a gun just like his!"

CHAPTER 19

 took out the pistol and had Frank examine it closely. He insisted that it resembled his father's to a T. In case it were the exact same gun, I told him, I would indeed like to recompense him for it. Having said this, Mr. Jimmison finally accepted my coin and I rejoined the stagecoach. Mr. Lash had absented himself for a moment, no doubt a call of nature, and I, being alone inside the coach, took the opportunity to pry open his box. I espied a collection of tools--wrenches, a small hammer, and a Bowie knife--mixed in with sharp triangular metal teeth, but as I shifted through them, I saw something metallic and long and round with scratches incised in it.

"Miss Furlough," I heard as the door opened suddenly. Mr. Lash stood there like the grim reaper who'd forgotten his scythe.

"I just wanted to see if you had pieces to a mower or a reaper. Just plain curiosity."

He reached in and slammed the box shut. Then he returned to his seat eyeing me coolly, sending a shiver down my spine. I went into a lengthy discourse on the variety of machinery, remembering a most boring conversation between a group of farmers that I'd once overheard. I mentioned mowing machines engineered by Ketchum, by Allen, by Manny, and by a half a dozen other tinkerers. I also threw in the Young America by Rockafellow & Howell, a mower and reaper in one.

After a half an hour of my blather, Mr. Lash relaxed and asked me where I was headed and where I planned to stay.

Suddenly I was sorry we were once again on speaking terms. Did he want to follow me? Was he the one who had fired a shot at me? I didn't know how to extricate myself from revealing too much, so I just told him the simple truth. I intended on spending the night in Nebraska City before journeying on to the land office in Omaha. That seemed to satisfy him, as he turned toward the window and closed his eyes.

Now I took a good hard look at the man. Though his hands were rough, he was otherwise fine-featured. He didn't quite look the part of a pioneer. The roughness of his hands could have come from handling horses, which would mean he traveled a lot on his own, on horseback. But then why was he taking the stage? Oh my, it was because I was in the coach!

But why would he saw through the axle of a coach he was riding in? The answer was obvious. Because in the confusion of the stage toppling over, he would discreetly bash me over the head with his hammer, or slip a Bowie knife blade through my fifth and sixth ribs. I stared at the murderer until I reasoned that I couldn't keep vigil all evening, and furthermore, he wouldn't do me any harm inside the coach with the other passengers in attendance.

By the time the stage arrived at the environs of Nebraska City, its rocking motion had forced my own eyelids to slip half way down across my eyes. I viewed the world as a dream, with the greyness of night playing upon the shapes of the fields, or upon the occasional tree or house or business we trotted by. Every so often I sensed more than noticed, a glimmer of candlelight glowing from a cabin. Then as my mind slid from this world into that of dreams, the flame of the candle engulfed the little structure. Smoke poured forth but through its haze I witnessed men, women, and children with misshapen heads roasting in the fire. Finally, the horses instinctively brought the stage to a halt, and the alteration from a see-sawing motion to stillness awakened me completely. And there I saw Mr. Lash puffing on a cigar whose smoke lingered under our nostrils.

I shook my head while my hands felt for my reticule and carpet-bag. All was as it should be. Emmor Lash motioned for me to exit first, and I wasn't one to discourage gentlemanly acts, even in an assassin. I also allowed him to carry my carpet-bag, which I think did him good because its weight offset that of his tool box in the opposing hand, plus it made access to his stock of weapons difficult.

We made our way into the hotel lobby and I found myself thinking ill of emigrants. They were everywhere, lounging about with their soiled clothing and matted hair; but what irritated me most was that they had taken up all of the rooms.

The hotel manager was nowhere to be found, and I think he played his cards well, because no one should want to deal with tired, dirty, grumpy customers when running a hotel with no open lines in its registry. Mr. Lash, seemingly unconcerned about his own condition, insisted that the clerk find an accommodation for the young lady, and I thanked him for his concern, somewhat in the spirit of the criminal who pays his executioner.

The clerk went into a back room and after a pow-wow of some sort, he reemerged with a key. He told us that a Mr. Thomas Lipscomb had a new brick house on Nebraska Street, between Seventh and Eighth, that had two bedrooms in it and no occupant. He would be willing to rent out the two rooms at the same price as a hotel room.

"If it's not too much to ask," I said to the clerk while nodding toward the door behind him, "I'd like to reserve a room there for my return trip from Omaha as well." I believe I subconsciously thought that if I reserved a room for the future, I would somehow survive the night.

The young man disappeared and reappeared as before and agreed to the proposal upon receipt of payment, which I duly accorded him. The clerk specified, after handing Mr. Lash the house key, that each bedroom had its own key, which we would find on our respective doors. I didn't see this as any insurance against an assassin, because I imagined Mr. Lash held, within his box, tools adequate for picking any lock.

The house was a fine structure with a cellar underneath equal to the length and breadth of the ground floor. Here below were located on the west side the kitchen and a dining area, complete with a table and enough chairs to outfit a family of ten. The room on the east side was for storing produce and wine. Upstairs, at ground level, were an east and west room, one obviously designed to be a parlor and the other a living room or bedroom, but for the present each had been arranged as a bedroom. The high ceiling dissipated very little of July's heat and I would have gladly slept in the cool cellar except for the humidity that is ever so anxious to infect us with consumption.

After touring the house, I took the east bedroom which featured a grand fireplace, which is of little use in July. After bidding Mr. Lash a good night, I closed the door and laid down on the bed, listening to the sounds of insects outside. But their calling was interrupted by a thud next door. I rose and went to my door and pressed my ear against it. I could hear a metallic clanking sound. Mr. Lash had opened his box and was emptying its contents on the floor.

Suddenly, I realized that the long object I saw in the box was the barrel of a pistol. Its scratch marks indicated the number of victims he had assassinated. Noticing the key on the door, I turned it sharply and it clicked home. Mr. Lash stopped whatever he was doing. I don't think he had planned on me locking the door so soon.

I could hear him moving about again, and I realized my room had a south exit door opening onto the path to the privy. It too had a key in it. I ran across the room and locked it. I then went to my reticule and drew out my pistol, and thus armed, I laid back once again on the bed.

The window, I thought: he could simply break the window and shoot me. I closed my eyes and sent up a prayer. If God would preserve me, I would be ever so dutiful in the future. Did this mean I would have to confront Cameron about his faith? I struck a deal with God, I would ask Cameron about his faith, eventually, if I were to survive the night, or, if that didn't please God, I was willing to join my Lord in heaven... right after I solved the Friend murder. I mean, how can God expect a woman to die before satisfying her curiosity. He didn't even demand this of Eve.

Then I tried to look at my situation optimistically, hoping to build up some earthly courage. Why would Mr. Lash kill me? He would be the first suspect, being the only other person in the house.

Of course optimism at night can only last a matter of seconds. I had to look at the situation rationally. In this frame of mind, I quickly questioned if the man's name really was Mr. Lash. Afterall, who knew he was Mr. Lash? He simply told everyone that that was his name. His real name may be "Smug Man" for all I knew. And he, being a horseman, he would simply steal a mount after dispatching me, and ride off into the night to join the Sioux, mortal enemies of my Pawnee relations.

There was only one thing to do, and I did it. I ripped off the blanket from the bed, leaving the sheet, then I stuffed the pillow and carpet-bag under the sheet in such a way that it would appear that I were fast asleep. I stood in front of the window looking back upon this bedroom landscape and was satisfied. The greyness made it really look like someone lay in the bed.

Then, I took the blanket with me, removed the key from the back door, stepped outside and locked it. I went around to the east side of the house, found a soft spot upon the grass and rolled myself, fully clothed, into the blanket, with pistol in hand. Now I awaited my prey. When alias Mr. Lash would attempt to pick the lock to the door or smash one of the front windows, I would hear him, approach him from the rear, jab the pistol into his back and escort him to the sheriff.

It then crossed my mind that I didn't know where the sheriff resided in Nebraska City. Oh well, I would march him up to the hotel clerk and he would find the sheriff. It's always good to have a backup plan.

Laying there in wait, I discovered I was not alone. Not less than one-hundred thousand mosquitoes had decided to hide out with me. The buzzing was infernal, but shooting them one by one was pointless, so I tucked my head under the blanket.

I must not have kept vigil for long. It's true the coach ride had taken all the wakefulness out of me, so I feel no shame for having fallen asleep within minutes.

The next thing I remember, after tucking my head under the blanket, was a feeling of shaking. I dreamed I was back in the coach and a wild driver by the name of Wrangler was running the horses at top speed over a trail filled with gullies, rocks, and logs.

"Miss Furlough! Miss Furlough!" I heard.

I opened my eyes to discover that at some point during the night the mosquitoes had lifted the blanket off of my face and settled down to a feast on my cheeks, forehead, ears, chin, and neck. I was aflame.

But this surprise was nothing next to what my eyes beheld in the blinding morning sunlight. It was my assassin, Mr. Lash, with a metal rod in his hand. I looked at the rod. It had scratch marks on it.

"It's not a revolver?" I asked

"What?" he asked in return. Then he looked at what he held in his hand. "This? It's a shaft for my mower. It's broken, and I was headed to town to see if I could find a replacement."

"But the scratches, they're not for dead people?"

"Are you alright? Do you have measles?"

I felt of my face. There were little welts all over it. "No, Mr. Lash, I often break out like this when I sleep outside with the mosquitoes."

"What are you doing out here?"

By this time three other well-meaning citizens of Nebraska City had come off the street to investigate.

"Well, I needed to go to the privy but lost the key to the house."

"With a blanket?"

"Really, Mr. Lash, you should know better than to ask indiscreet questions of a lady." Having given this rather ambiguous answer that always confounds a male audience, I made an effort to raise myself, which induced my entire retinue to gather round me and help me to my feet.

I thanked them graciously, then walked toward the privy ever so carefully until I was distant enough to exclaim, "Oh, here it is!" and reach down to retrieve the invisible key from the path and put it in my reticule with the real one.

CHAPTER 20

I had to wait until Thursday, the sixteenth of July, to catch the next stagecoach, so I had all of Wednesday to enjoy the sights of Nebraska City and its partner along the Missouri bank, Kearny City.

Like in Brownville, Nebraska City's Main Street has its source at the river, and from there, as the town heads eastward, it is crossed successively by streets creatively named First Street, then Second Street, and so on toward the western horizon. At Sixth Street I found the bank with the high school. I gathered some information about the school and the need for teachers.

I then proceeded down to Fourth Street where I found a gunsmith. I pulled from my handbag my precious bullet, which I had retrieved from *Hope Leslie* without telling anyone I possessed it, and asked him what type of gun might fit it. He held it up to the light for a moment.

"Why this thing's been fired," he said.

"Yes."

"A tad mashed, but it's still a peculiar ball. Don't know if I have something to fit it, as you put it."

Then I withdrew the pistol from my handbag. "How about

this one?"

He took out a caliper and applied it to the ball and the barrel. "Should work. Are you wanting to buy a mold?"

"No, it came with a dozen balls and I don't plan on shooting more than twelve people." As I put the pistol back in my handbag, I asked him, "You say it's a peculiar ball, which means I must have a peculiar pistol. Do you think a man who owns such a pistol would have two similar weapons?"

"If he has a second pistol, it most likely is of the same variety, but not necessarily."

"Why would it be the same?"

"So he doesn't have to have two types of ammunition."

I thanked him for his help and assured him that if ever I needed a second such pistol I would inquire of him first.

On my way back to the house, I considered what I had learned. It was probable that my would-be assassin had come and stayed at the Nebraska House. He wasn't from Brownville or he would have been recognized. He had to be a hired assassin, and a forgetful one.

Just my luck. I was being pursued by an absent-minded killer.

Why would the assassin leave behind the tool of his trade though? Suddenly it dawned on me there on Main Street in Nebraska City. The gun may not have belonged to him. Perhaps whoever hired him supplied him with it, and when he got spooked by Sheriff Coleman entering the hotel, he decided not to go through with the job and left the gun behind.

I didn't know exactly why someone wanted me dead; I hadn't any real proof of who did what for anything. In fact, I didn't even really know why anyone would have wanted to kill the Friend family. But it seemed to me it had something to do with the land warrant.

Regardless, one thing was evident: The man who wanted me dead didn't want me to reach the Omaha land office. That's why the wheel on the stagecoach had been sabotaged.

I just hoped I could get to Omaha and back before the mastermind, or one of his assassins, tracked me down.

* * *

I did survive long enough to get the stagecoach out of Nebraska City. It was a long, hard, hot ride, and when we reached the Platte River, we all had to descend and unload to take ourselves and our belongings to a nearby ferry. The boat was no longer than two Cincinnati houses, or about twelve paces. Once we walked on, the water came up to the edge of the deck, and I began to imagine what it might be like to swim in a dress.

The hull or bottom of the boat consisted of hewn cottonwood logs. The captain and his crew of one made use of ropes and poles to ply the river, but the ferry didn't have much ambition to cross and it hung itself up on a submerged sandbar to rest awhile. Shoving on their poles with all their might, the two men, joined in their efforts by two travelers impressed into service, succeeded in tipping up one side of our ship, the action of which sent the rest of us, with some of our belongings, toward the far railing. The added weight on that side fortunately gave the boat the lift needed to free it from our sandbar, but there was much talk coming from the polemen about the necessity of our returning to a more central position. In my willingness to oblige, I daresay I surpassed my fellow passengers and made it well past midship and successfully latched on to the opposite railing.

Once ashore, another stageline picked us up and took us on to Bellevue, where we stopped at the Bellevue House to take a quick dinner while the horses were switched out. We were expected and the proprietor was well stocked in macaroni, as we enjoyed a macaroni soup followed by an entree of macaroni cheese. I neglected to inquire of dessert because I feared a macaroni pie.

A hostler came in to tell us that we would have to make ourselves comfortable because we were awaiting another party, a Mr. Samuel Allis.

While digesting my macaroni, Mr. Allen, the hotel proprietor, boasted the attributes of Bellevue. He notified me that the town, as of yesterday, included a school to train the eager minds of its youth. A Mrs. Nye, finding a room above a store, now instructed boys and girls in writing, grammar, arithmetic, and geography for five dollars a term, and for only one dollar more, they would be endowed with the knowledge of French.

Decidedly schools were the thing, but in a roundabout way this talk of schooling led me to think again about the Friend murders.

I knew someone inspired George Lincoln to lead a gang to the Friend house and murder its inhabitants in order to rob the Friend family of its money. In the end, there wasn't much money, if any, to be found, but he was still obliged to burn down the house to mask the murders.

I also knew that a "smug man" put Mr. Lincoln up to the

deed, even contributing a whiskey bottle full of turpentine to set fire to the house. Why engineer such a hideous crime?

Because the Friend family possessed a land warrant Mr. Smug desired for himself.

You might think Mr. Smug told George Lincoln to get the warrant from Jacob Friend's corpse or cache and bring it to him. But George Lincoln never mentioned a warrant, and none was found on his person. This led me to the conclusion that the warrant was already in the possession of Mr. Smug, but for some reason, in order to validate it, he needed to get rid of the Friend family.

I couldn't explain how that might all work out, but I thought I was on the right track. I also thought I needed to confront the man I believed to be Mr. Smug, however I had more than one suspect. What I needed to do was to get my suspects in one place and question them both. If I exercised my skills in rhetoric properly, the answers of one would undoubtedly convict or exonerate the other.

Mention of Mrs. Nye's school gave me a grand idea for executing my plan. I wrote a note to Kitty to round up my three suspects. Of course, I wouldn't tell Kitty what I was up to. That would make her so nervous as to incite suspicions.

Dearest Kitty, I wrote. *I have been to Nebraska City and to Bellevue and have come up with a most fantastic idea that I would hope might inspire you and all those interested in joining me in a worthy enterprise. Nebraska City is proposing to open a high school in its bank building. They would be in need of teachers of science as well as English. I would wish to discuss such a project with Messieurs Whitt and Martin at Mr. Lipscomb's dwelling in Nebraska City. I am thoroughly sold on the idea and am willing to pay not only your fare but also those of Messieurs Whitt and Martin, as well as of Prudence's and Jonathan's and Teddy's. I'm certain Prudence will be interested, and I can't imagine her leaving her brother up to his own devices. Teddy, I need present to attend to some errands. I will arrange for the schoolmasters of Nebraska City to confer with us. I do think you, Kitty, would not be averse to exchanging your cleaning brushes for chalk and join in the venture with us.*

I successfully located a traveler bound for Kansas, an abolitionist I suspected, because he refused to talk of slavery in the open, and I asked him to deliver my letter to Brownville. I offered him a coin for his trouble but he declined to take it. He said it would weigh him down, and besides, from what he'd heard of the Platte River Navy, there was no guarantee that the letter would make it to the southern bank.

* * *

Finally, Mr. Allis arrived. He made an impression with his strong square jaw, outlined with a healthy and trimmed beard, and with a clean shave about a pair of firm, precise lips. Above this rather stern physiognomy, one observed two clear eyes that expressed an inviting gentility. Encouraged by the latter, I asked him about his affairs, as fellow frontier travelers do with one another when on the trail, and his answer electrified my soul.

He said he preoccupied himself with the welfare of the heathen and spoke passionately of the Pawnee, insisting it "our duty to encourage them to abandon hunting in favor of the raising of stock, of agricultural skills, and of manufacture of goods, and thereby prove to themselves that less land and labor will maintain them better than in their former mode of living."

"I'm sorry," I said, "but your solution only addresses their physical needs."

"It is but a first step in bringing them to the knowledge of repentance and divine forgiveness."

I heard a gentle cough beside me and Mr. Allen said, "Sorry to interrupt, Miss, but I'm afraid you're unacquainted with Mr. Allis. He has spent decades living among the Pawnee as a missionary of sorts and speaks their language."

My mouth dropped open and I immediately said, "Hair on Fire!"

The two men looked at each other and then back to me.

"Hair on Fire," I repeated. "Have you ever heard that name?"

Mr. Allis sat back in his chair. "Oh yes, Miss, it was given to only one squaw, and I doubt anyone named a child after her."

"That's my aunt, my Aunt Adeline. I'm searching for her."

It was Mr. Allis's turn to become electrified. His clear eyes expanded as he studied me. "Good Lord, yes! And I say not his name in vain. You are she, some twenty or more years ago!"

"Can I see her? Where is she?"

He mulled these questions over for a moment. "I can't tell you where she would be now, or even if she yet lives. But I'm assisting with the treaty negotiation with the Pawnee that should wrap up this fall."

"I've heard of this," I said.

"Well, you come to the pow-wow and I'll help you. If she's not among them, someone will know what has happened to her or where to find her. If you go looking for her now it could be a wild goose chase, or rather a wild buffalo chase."

I promised him I would be there, Lord willing.

* * *

After our conversation, we took the stage and were in Omaha by late Thursday night. I found a room at the Washington Hotel, which was actually a refitted and moored steamboat that formerly chugged up and down the Missouri under the name of *Washington City*. In spite of the exhaustion attendant to a coach ride, I slept very little as I imagined Aunt Adeline out on the plains, scraping buffalo hides. I tried to envision what expression she would display when I would approach her for the first time. Would she be like Esther in *Hope Leslie*, shorn of her native language and only at home in her beaded buckskin dress? Just before dawn I finally laid my mind to rest in sleep, but in the morning my imagined portrait of Aunt Adeline returned.

No matter how exhilarating it had been to think of my Aunt, by now, even though I yearned to find her, I was becoming somewhat nauseated by my obsession. I needed to think of something else for a bit, so I ventured out, even though it was too early to go to the land office, and perambulated about town.

Omaha City is a bustling concern, especially at the end of the week, on a Friday, and touring it did change my mind. Like other frontier cities, she hoped to become the capital of the Territory, and had already begun work on a capitol building as evidenced by elevated pillars awaiting the finishing touches.

The city had as many businesses as Brownville or Nebraska City. On Farnam Street, I successfully forced myself past the ice cream saloon and easily glided by Dr. Verdi's dentistry. I eventually reached my objective: Woolworth's bookstore, which held a copy of Mr. Kingsley's *Westward Ho!*

Whether along the street or in the bookstore, the town was abuzz with political talk. Of course, every section of the territory wanted its very own delegate to Congress, even though there was only room for one; and the list of candidates formed a veritable army: General Laramir, General Bowen, General Thayer, General Estabrook, Colonel Rankin, and other men of rank.

Their main arguments concerned a definitive location for the Territory's capital, which was undecided, in spite of Omaha's pillars, and where to place a national road through Nebraska. In regards to the former issue, one pragmatic candidate, hoping to please everyone, suggested we just put it on wheels.

I should add that candidates south of the Platte River also seemed equally interested in the construction of a bridge. They had no doubt used the same ferry I had.

But since I had my *Westward Ho!* secured, I found myself wanting to move on and satisfy my curiosity about the bounty issue, seeing that the land office now had to be open.

I presented myself at the land office, where I found the Register of Deeds, John A. Parker, at his post. I asked Mr. Parker about any bounty issued to a Mr. Weber that would have been redeemed in June of 1856 or later. He pulled out a large register where he privately kept a list of original warrant holders and the number assigned each warrant. I looked down the list and found the name Hans Weber. Mr. Parker then opened a drawer, and, after thumbing through a pile of sheets of paper, no doubt ordered numerically, retrieved a land warrant. The original owner of the warrant had indeed been a Mr. Hans Weber, but he had signed it over to a certain Stephen Nemlon. However, as if things hadn't become complicated enough, this man's name had been crossed through and the final proprietor was a certain Hamish Sinclair, who had delivered the warrant to claim a section of land down near Nebraska City.

I didn't know who Steven Nemlon was, but if he wasn't a middle man, or if he wasn't someone used by the smug man to do his dirty work, Steve Nemlon could be the smug man himself. This meant that if I could just locate Mr. Sinclair, maybe he would help me identify the smug man.

* * *

I won't bother you with the details of my return trip to Nebraska City on Saturday, July eighteenth, except to say that I procured two solid loaves of bread and boarded a Missouri steamship, a singular diet of bread is often less disturbing to the digestive system than variety when traveling. Those who fast seem to be less likely to bow to the gods of dysentery and cholera. Despite the illness often attendant with river travel, going downriver is swift enough and gentler than any stagecoach, also there's no ferry to tackle.

Once in Nebraska City, I called at Barnes and Barnum's hotel to collect any letters. I found two, one from Cameron and another from Kitty. Cameron informed me that the hoof-print found up at Mount Vernon matched that of the estray kept at Coleman's livery. He apologized for not having told me sooner, but it had slipped his mind. He also said he had not yet been able to complete my commission in Saint Jo but expected to do so on the morrow and hoped to see me soon. He couldn't promise a date. This troubled me as I had included him in my plans for exposing the mastermind for the Friend murders.

Kitty, in her usual style, apprised me of Brownville news first. Little Mary Maun, daughter of Mr. Whitt's competitor, died of lung fever, she was soon to be two years of age. Kitty even included a little poem she'd written to the intent of the dear child, and hoped I might include it in my gazette. It ended with the lines "*I would not awake thee from thy dream, it seems too bright and fair; I would not change the holy scene, for those of earthly care.*" She also told me the Nuckolls's little boy had succumbed to dysentery, and she'd like to pen a little poem in his memory as well.

Obviously, my enthusiasm for the day collapsed, and I offered up a prayer for the Maun and Nuckolls families, that they might find strength in Kitty's thoughtful words.

As concerns our little world of local politics, Kitty informed me that Mr. Kennedy, my abolitionist friend, stood for election as justice of the peace. I think Esquire would be a well-suited title for the gentleman farmer.

She even thought it important to mention there was yet another fire in Brownville, though not to worry, it was only the bank burning its money in the street. It will replace the paper dollars with new issue.

Finally, at the end of her missive, she informed me she would be, Lord willing, in Nebraska City as planned, and that they, meaning she and Stewart, would be accompanied by Messieurs Martin and Whitt as well as Prudence and Jonathan. Teddy she had not been able to locate as of yet. Decidedly, my plan to have a band of able-bodied men on hand to subdue the exposed murderer had unraveled.

Nevertheless, due to the fatigue of travel and a lack of mosquitoes inside the house, I spent a restful night at the Lipscomb residence.

The next day, being Sunday, I thought it right to attend church to prepare myself for the upcoming encounter with the murderer. It was a mistake. I found myself before a certain minister I'd had the displeasure of meeting before, one full of himself and emptied of humanity. Although one cannot criticize his creativity, because Reverend Chivington knows how to twist the Lord's message of salvation into a judgement against the Indian. He found it apt to expound upon the recent Sioux attack near Spirit Lake in Iowa, which left barns, homes, and white people in flames. Of course, he meant to bring to mind that we were all under judgement and soon to fall into the incendiary hands of Lucifer, but I couldn't help but notice that he failed to mention the friendly Indians who helped chase away those bent on harm.

Arson. It brought the Friend family murder back to mind. Chivington couldn't blame that on the Sioux, because I had a fair idea that Mr. Smug wore no feathers and was an upstanding citizen of our community.

After church I inquired as to the whereabouts of a certain Hamish Sinclair and was pleased to discover that the man actually did exist and held a claim not far from town. I employed Harry, a boy who works for Sterling Morton's newspaper at Nebraska City, to deliver a note to Mr. Sinclair with precise instructions as to when and where I hoped to see him. I not only paid the boy to run the commission for me, I also offered

Mr. Sinclair a wage to do my bidding.

In spite of a mild rise of anxiety concerning the upcoming confrontation with my assassin, at least part of my plan seemed to be falling into place.

* * *

In the evening I unlocked the Lipscomb's house, left my parasol in the entryway, and, advancing to the end of the hall, took the side door to the left to descend the stairs. The stairs spiraled back so that the bottom landing was directly beneath the front door, or nearly. Here, I turned to my left and unlatched a door leading into the kitchen. A round table stood in the middle and I assembled around it all the chairs I could find. It rather reminded me of King Arthur's table and I wondered where I should place the most likely candidate to play the part of Mordred. Wherever I put him, I wanted my Sir Galahad, if he would show, next to him in case he tried to escape or become violent.

I, taking the position of Arthur, would sit with my back to the far corner of the room so that I might face the door and place people as they entered. I assumed my travelers would be famished, as I told them to appear at eight o'clock, so I laid my remaining loaf of bread on the table with a full pitcher of water. Spartan fare, but one of them should get used to it. I loaded my pistol and put it beside my chair in my handbag, so that I might draw it out when I revealed the killer. Of course, events unfolded in their own haphazard way.

Messieurs Martin and Whitt knocked first and as I escorted them downstairs, Kitty and Stewart arrived, and as I attempted to place Mr. Martin, I found that Teddy had slipped in behind me and had selected his own seat, as did Kitty, Stewart, and Mr. Whitt. The room was soon a jumble as everyone had brought a carpet-bag and placed them pell-mell either on the floor or on the table. Jonathan I could hear upstairs, telling Prudence that a house built of soft brick wouldn't last ten years. Prudence was astounded they would use such poor-quality brick and suggested that Jonathan present himself to the city's stockholders to offer his services as an advisor.

"Well, well," announced Jonathan as he entered the kitchen. "If they had dug another three feet, they would have had a fresher and cooler room."

"I find it refreshing enough," said Mr. Whitt.

Mr. Martin agreed with the latter but wanted to get discussing the high school proposal. I needed to stall for time as my Galahad had not yet made an appearance.

"I'm sure you're all famished," I said. "I have bread to plug any hole one might have in the stomach, but I feel we ought to say grace first, no matter how meager the offering."

"Forget grace," said Mr. Martin. "For one thing I'm not an admirer of your God and for a second, we all ate at the hotel before coming your way."

"Oh, my," I uttered, sitting down rather slowly in my chair. The door had been shut and I heard no footsteps from Cameron. My only consolation was that I did manage to get my back to the far corner and my face oriented toward the door, but with no one coming through it and everyone seated...it seemed a rather hollow victory.

"We'll see about the school tomorrow," said Mr. Whitt.

"All we need to know at the moment is that if we cannot find ourselves a home here and teaching in their high school, whether or not we'll build one in Brownville."

"Fair enough," said Mr. Martin, pulling out a deck of cards from his pocket. "How about a game of whisk."

"Count us out," said Stewart. "Cards are an incentive to gambling and gambling to drink. I prefer to retire, but I thought I would escort Kitty here since she's spending the night with Miss Furlough."

Stewart rose and so did all the others. Things were falling apart quickly.

"If you don't mind, sirs," I said with a wobbly voice that evinced an evident nervousness, "I would ask you all to sit down as I have something very important to tell you."

At this Kitty shouted with glee and clapped her hands. "I knew it," she said. "It's tomorrow isn't it? I knew this was a ruse to get us all here for your grand day!"

"Oh," said Mr. Martin nodding his head. "Where is the lucky man?"

Mr. Whitt was more subdued, but not as much as I.

"Is he not shown up yet?" asked Stewart.

"No, he hasn't," I said, "and I'm afraid he's unaware of the grand day."

They all fell silent and looked at me as if I'd just returned from burying my mother.

"No, it's nothing serious...well, yes it is, but you misunderstand me." My skills of rhetoric declined with each new word.

"Please," I insisted, "take your seats."

"What is it Addy?" asked Teddy, whose attuned empathy

detected that I was troubled.

Everyone obliged me and sat down, I remained standing, like a schoolmistress. "My dear friends," I began, "I believe I have solved a mystery."

"What kind?" asked Prudence.

"The murdering kind," I said. My little group of suspects became very grim. "Yes, I have looked into the Friend murders and I am sad to say that I discovered that one of us was really responsible for the murders."

"Us?" said Stewart.

"Well, I don't want to point out anyone in particular just yet, but let me tell you what I found out."

"It was Amos who engineered it wasn't it?" said Mr. Martin. "It takes a certain head shape to become a Mormon and it's the same that..."

"No," I interrupted before he could begin his first high school lecture on phrenology. "No," I repeated with a growing strength in my confidence and voice. "It was not George Lincoln or Amos Davis or any of the others hanged for the crime."

"You mean they didn't do it?" asked our druggist.

"Oh, they did it all right, but they didn't plan it out or profit from the crime. Someone else did."

"Who did then?" nearly all asked in unison.

"Well, whoever did it had a whiskey bottle and turpentine." All eyes turned to Mr. Whitt.

"Anybody can buy turpentine," said Mr. Whitt.

"But does everybody end up owning the Friend farm?" asked Jonathan.

"Are you suggesting I would kill someone? Sounded more

like you might be a killer than me."

"What?" responded Jonathan incredulous.

"I heard the story. You were down in Saint Jo with Miss Furlough, waiting outside her house when she was shot. Sounds awfully fishy to me."

"Why would I want to hurt Addy?" Jonathan protested. "We saw you in Saint Jo, bet you didn't count on that, assassin!"

"Class!" I hollered. "I mean gentlemen, please withhold your speculations for a moment and let me explain."

They all folded their hands and turned their attention my way.

"Jonathan, you do have some explaining to do. Soon after you arrived, the little shed behind the Post Office went up in smoke."

"Addy!" exclaimed Prudence. "You can't really be accusing Jonathan of starting a fire or any other such nonsense!"

"Not if he can give me an account of himself," I said sternly. Then turning to her brother, I continued, "So, Jonathan, you arrived and soon after a conflagration broke out. I found matches near where the fire started and I suppose you use a match to light your cigar, don't you?"

"Like more and more people do today," he rejoined.

"And it is true that when Mr. Whitt took us to the Friend farm, you knew right where to go to find the ruins of Jacob's cabin. How could you know where it had been?"

"Just the power of reason, some of us have more of it than others."

"In Mr. Wither's defense," said Mr. Whitt. "He was simply walking up the trail. It made sense that the house would have been up against it."

I hadn't thought of this, but that didn't clear Jonathan on other points. "Be that as it may," I continued, "it is true that you stayed out of Mrs. Lincoln's house and were the only person present outside after someone had shot at me. And what's more, you seemed to be overly familiar with the city of Saint Jo. How did you know there was a bookshop there, and one that would carry novels in French?"

"Because a man of importance travels for his business. I noticed the bookshop because it was inferior in size and contents to one I frequent back in Saint Louis. As for being outside the house wherein you, Addy, were to interview a woman concerning matters of little importance to me, I plead guilty as charged; but let me ask the gentlemen," he said turning to Teddy and the rest, "what would you have preferred: listening to an old widow lady rattle on about her deceased family members or smoke a fine cigar?"

"He's got a point," said Teddy softly.

I had one last card to play against Jonathan and I showed it. "Let me see your box of matches."

He fumbled about in his pocket for a moment and produced the evidence. Meanwhile, I extracted the Bryant box of matches from my reticule. I held the two side by side, and without attempting humor, I must say they did not match.

"So much for your little inquiry," said Jonathan spitefully. "And that's why women are not constables."

CHAPTER 21

fter Jonathan's denigrating remark, a hush fell upon the room. I think Teddy believed he ought to retrieve my parasol from the upstairs entryway so that I might give a solid response to Prudence's brother. The parasol was totally unnecessary.

"I'm far from done," I said as I put my handbag on the table. "I do admit, Jonathan, that you are less suspicious to me now than earlier, but you did need to give an account of yourself.

"On the other hand," I continued, turning to Mr. Martin, "I have some questions for our phrenologist."

"Fire away," he said. "Unlike Mr. Withers, I'm amused by all this."

"I'm glad to hear it, but maybe it's gallows humor." Mr. Martin looked unphased as I said this, so I proceeded. "It does seem strange to me that you were here in Nebraska Territory just over one year ago when the Friend murders took place. It also seems odd that you took such an interest in the case, even claiming to have written down everything the condemned men had to say about their crime. It seems all very convenient. However, what really surprises me is your pipe. If you'd be so kind as to show it to us, I will tell the others what's singular about it."

Smirking, Mr. Martin laid his pipe on the table.

"Everyone will notice," I explained, "that this is an unusual pipe, being porcelain. It comes directly from Germany, and it has the letter "J" embossed upon it. Might not that letter indicate Jacob Friend's first name?"

"Miss Furlough," said Stewart, "I do believe that stands for Jaeger, the pipe's manufacturer."

"That's a possibility. But how about this, Stewart...Can Mr. Martin tell us who was in the buggy with Judge Kinney on the Deroin Trail?"

You may wonder why I asked this question, so I'll explain. When Stewart asked Mr. Martin, some days prior, if he'd seen Judge Kinney on the road, you may recall that Stewart had inadvertently supplied Judge Kinney's name to Mr. Martin. It was therefore easy for Mr. Martin to answer that, yes indeed, he had spotted Judge Kinney in the buggy, even if, in reality, Mr. Martin had never been on the Deroin Trail at all. Even if, I might add, as a not implausible conjecture, Mr. Martin had really been on a steamship bound for Saint Jo where he attempted to assassinate me. So, if Mr. Martin could now describe who was with the judge in the buggy, then he would prove that he had indeed seen Judge Kinney on the Deroin Trail, because only I knew what the judge's traveling companion looked like.

"Well, yes, I do remember the buggy," replied Mr. Martin, "and I rather suppose it was the gentleman you speak of driving it. And come to think of it, and this may be a bit of an embarrassment to myself, but if I didn't notice him so much, it was because I noticed a young woman beside him. Yes, a pretty young woman, could have been the judge's daughter."

"Describe her," I commanded, setting the trap.

Mr. Martin's portrait of Beatrice, however, which included details about her head shape and probable intelligence, convinced me that my phrenologist had indeed encountered the judge and his daughter on the Deroin Trail.

There reigned a silence after Mr. Martin finished his description, but it was soon broken by the voice of Mr. Whitt. "I guess you haven't come any closer to solving the crime, Miss Furlough, but I do think a game of whisk might prove distracting and pleasant."

"No," I said softly, turning on the druggist, "we haven't questioned you, have we?"

"And I don't see the point of it," he objected. "None of us had anything to do with the Friend murders."

I looked him steadily in the eye. "Why did you put a claim on the Friend property?"

"It's a good farm, has black soil. It grows walnut trees, so you know it's rich."

"I doubt that's the only reason. I found it suspicious that you led us away from the ruins of the old house, didn't you also find that strange, Jonathan?"

"I did," concurred Prudence's brother, "although Mr. Whitt may not have as sharp a mind as some."

"You mean to tell me," I insisted, maintaining my gaze upon the druggist, "that you really didn't know where the ashes of that cabin lay?"

Mr. Whitt shifted uneasily in his chair. "Well, I, uh...I

mean…I can't be expected to remember everything."

"And yet you were so adamant about the Friends having left behind a treasure. It seemed you had combed the area carefully looking for it, except that you hadn't a woman's intuition to find it, had you?"

"You see," Jonathan echoed himself, "not everyone has a sharp mind. Some even weaker in thought than a woman."

Pursuing the role of a prosecutor I declared, "You knew where the house was. You wanted to lead us away from it, didn't you?"

"By gads!" he exploded. "If there's a treasure there, it's mine. I don't want some Addy Comelately digging it up!"

"Mr. Whitt, it wasn't just about the treasure. You wanted me eliminated completely didn't you?"

"What?"

"Working out a deal with my landlord to buy my office. You don't need that shack or that land."

"We meant you no harm."

"We?" I asked.

"Yes, a couple of us businessmen got together and thought it best to discourage you. I mean, that newspaper you threatened to produce, and now this gazette. It's going to give us a bad name. We've got money invested in the town."

"You know, I might believe one of your made-up stories, but there's just such a collection of them, that I can't believe them all. But let's try. I've established that the Post Office shed and the warehouse were put to the torch to destroy evidence relative to the Friend murders. The only person who would have done such a thing, would be precisely he who set fire to the Friend cabin; and the only person who could easily produce the means to create these fires had both whiskey bottles and turpentine at hand. And who possesses these two things in quantity? A druggist, and you are a druggist."

"Every druggist in the Territory carries whiskey and turpentine. Besides," he said, lifting himself up a bit in his chair, "how would I get out to set fire to Nuckolls's warehouse when I don't own a horse to get there."

"Easily," I explained. "You used the estray at Coleman's livery. Its hoofprint was found up at the warehouse. The hostler said it was all lathered up the morning of the fire, like it had been on a run. He thought the fire spooked it, but I think the explanation much simpler. You, knowing nobody would miss the estray, rode it up and back to Mount Vernon in one night to set fire to the warehouse. Plus, I observed you in Saint Jo striking a match to light your cigar. You've got matches."

Mr. Whitt looked around the kitchen table, his eyes dancing from one person to another. "You can't believe her, she's just a woman, she can't think rationally."

"Well then, explain how this is irrational. One, you carry a pistol with you when you travel. Two, I was shot at in Saint Jo. Three, you were observed in Saint Jo."

"How would I have gotten to Saint Jo in time to shoot you when I went to Nemaha City and back the day you left?"

"That's true," observed Stewart, "he accompanied me down to Nemaha City."

"Oh, it would be easy. Mr. Whitt would just leave his horse with an accomplice, like that shifty-looking hostler from Nemaha City, and then have someone row him out to a passing steamer to catch a ride."

Mr. Whitt jumped from his chair and pulled his pistol from his pocket. Teddy and Stewart acted in unison, Teddy throwing him against the door, whilst Stewart wrenched the gun from his hand. "Let me go!" hollered Mr. Whitt. "You have nothing against me!"

"I think we do, Mr. Whitt," I said, observing him struggle. "I think we do."

Mr. Whitt finally ceased to fight back. While Stewart kept the pistol leveled on him, Teddy grabbed an apron, cut the string, and then bound Mr. Whitt's hands behind his back.

EPILOGUE

here are few things more satisfying than righting an injustice. The Friend family had been wronged, and if it had not been for the mastermind, Jacob and his own would yet walk the earth fulfilling God's commandments to multiply mankind and cultivate God's creation.

"You see, Mr. Whitt, your downfall was your pistol. That night, when I was in your shop, I handled it and felt its barrel. I knew it was roughly the size of the musket ball lodged in my book, *Hope Leslie*. The bullet fired by my would-be assassin. The local gun seller here in Nebraska City told me that gentlemen tend to buy the same caliber pistols, so that they don't have to carry two types of ammunition. That's what put me on your trail, though I must admit, I had two other paths to walk down as well. Tonight's meeting was to exonerate Mr. Martin and Jonathan, and to catch the culprit, you."

I walked over to him and took the ball out of my little purse. "You see, this is what condemned you. If it hadn't matched the size of your pistol barrel, you would have had no worries."

I placed the ball in the muzzle of the pistol in Stewart's hand. It didn't fit. I tried again. Same result. I took my pistol out of my handbag, and Stewart held it for me. The bullet fit rather nicely.

"Kitty," I said slowly.

"Yes?"

"Why did you want me to drop the newspaper idea and start a lady's gazette?"

"We just thought it would be more your style, why?"

Hmm, I thought, *that's interesting*. I'm afraid my arched eyebrows revealed that I now considered everything relating to the Friend murders in a different light.

"Well, Mr. Whitt," I said. "I'm going to give you one more chance, because it looks like this bullet may have just saved your life."

Mr. Whitt, who after ending his struggles had assumed the airs of someone digesting a cupful of laudanum, came out of his stupor, looking up at me with hopeful eyes.

I turned to the door and called out, "Enter, Mr. Hamish Sinclair!" In my instructions, I had told him to enter the house at a quarter past eight and to secrete himself in the storage room down below. I could only hope he had been punctual.

I held my breath, and everyone stared wonderingly at me for a moment before the door opened. A smallish Scottish gentleman entered the kitchen. Teddy shut the door, and I directed our newly arrived guest to the far side of the room. We turned to face our suspects. "Mr. Sinclair, I would like you to tell me if you recognize anyone before you." He eyed each face carefully, and then pursed his lips and shook his head to indicate he recognized no one.

"Mr. Whitt," I said, "would you please step aside."

As he did, Mr. Sinclair exclaimed, "Why yes, that's the man, sure as life! Hello sir, you do remember me, don't you?"

Everyone stood motionless and stared in disbelief at Stewart, who pointed my pistol in our general direction. He put down Mr. Whitt's pistol and reached into his carpet-bag to withdraw another gun. "This here," he said, "is a Smith and Wesson revolver. It is primed to deliver six bullets. A bad experience in Saint Jo inspired me to buy it to replace this one." He said this while waving my one-shot pistol at us. "That makes for a total of seven bullets, one for each of you if you don't behave. Now everybody up against that far wall."

Kitty slumped back down in her chair and said with a weak voice, "Stewart, what does this mean? What are you doing?"

"Don't you worry, my dear, you come over here with me."

"I don't understand."

"Well, Miss Furlough understands. She may have had the wrong man as her suspect, but otherwise, as to how things happened, she figured it out fairly well. And now, with that bullet not fitting into the muzzle of the pistol, she finally pegged the right man. And, I don't know if you realized it, love, but she confirmed her most recent suspicion by finding out I wanted her to publish a lady's gazette rather than a newspaper."

"What's that got to do with anything?"

"I was hoping she'd dedicate herself to subject matters peculiar to women, rather than investigating a murder case long forgotten by everyone else." He turned his attention directly on Mr. Whitt as everyone but Kitty, who sat dumbfounded, had gathered on my side of the room. "Yes, Mr. Whitt was kind enough not to mention my interest in booting you out of town,

Miss Furlough. I thank you for that, sir. Mr. Martin though, deserves no thanks, telling you to see if all the fires had been started in the same way. If he hadn't done that, I'm not sure Miss Furlough would have made all the connections. By the way, I'm pleased my beloved didn't divulge to you my use of Bryant matches."

"I, I thought..." said Kitty hesitatingly, "they were common. I never imagined...."

"And that's what keeps us together," he said softly. "We trust each other. You'll have to trust me now."

I was too curious to point out a little idiosyncrasy in his logic. I wanted my deductions confirmed before he went about placing a bullet in each of our hearts. "So, Stewart," I said, "I would be right in saying you caught the steamer at Nemaha City, and that the hostler we saw at the hotel, the one you pointed out as shifty, was actually your accomplice who kept the horse for you while you were supposed to be on the Deroin Trail."

He said nothing, and, as Monsieur Carr would put it, "Qui ne dit mot, consent," or "He who says not a word, consents." So, I continued, by asking, "You never did travel down the Deroin Trail, did you?" After a pause, I answered the rhetorical question myself: "No, you never even saw Judge Kinney, you just knew he went to the Big Blue Settlement because I told you he would. I bet if we asked Judge Kinney if he ever saw you on the trail, he'd say no. And as for the mysterious man who left the gun under his pillow, that too was an invention of yours, right?"

Stewart still said nothing, though he smiled, and I think he enjoyed hearing me explain everything. It made the smug man look smart. I obliged. "When you heard a man had fled the hotel without paying, you were pretty sure he would not have left a forwarding address, and you checked the hotel register which confirmed your suspicion. Then you went to his room, which would have been open for cleaning, and you stealthily deposited the pistol and bullets. Finally, you encouraged Kitty to give me the pistol, so it would look like you wanted to protect me, when in reality you wanted to kill me. Am I not too far off target?"

"You know, Addy," he finally remarked, "you were even right about how a man, who didn't own a horse, could get to Mount Vernon and back within a night. That estray really should be included in Teddy's horse races."

"And Mr. Muir's leather pass book. He said you were making good speed on Coleman's old hack. That means you probably trotted past him, and as you did, you leaned over and stole the pass book from the buggy seat."

"He didn't see a thing."

Kitty stared blankly at the top of the table and mumbled, "My fiancé is an assassin."

"No, no, my dear. Charles Lincoln and his mercenaries did in the Friend family. I just needed the land warrant to get a little seed money to invest in Brownville lots. I thank Mr. Sinclair for his contribution."

"And A. Medley, Stewart?" I asked.

"Well that was man-to-man. He threatened to turn me over to the law, and I got the best of him, and his pistol."

"Who's Steven Nemlon?" Teddy asked.

"Why that was just very bad penmanship on my part."

"Well they probably won't hire you at the high school then."

"I don't think I'll need to worry about that, and neither will the rest of you. Come on Kitty."

"Never," she said as she rose to sidle up against Teddy, who put his arm protectively around her.

"On the contrary, Kitty," I said, "you should go with Stewart. He's got a bullet for each of us, but he doesn't have one for you. However, I would fix the wedding date for April, 1917. A spring wedding is always more inspiring and picturesque."

"1917?" she asked.

"Yes, hopefully by that time your tottering old suitor won't have the strength to pull a trigger. The only reason he's pursuing you is because he's in love with your grandfather's money. Once gramps is dead and you're married, there'll be no more reason to keep you around."

"That's not so," said Stewart so stridently that it was evident he lied. He stepped back toward the door and raised his revolver squarely in the direction of my bosom.

"'If there ain't no witnesses, there ain't no criminals,'" said Mr. Whitt softly, as if resigning himself to the inevitable.

"That's always been my motto, Mr. Whitt."

Blam! The door burst open with the force of a locomotive hitting it, slamming into the back of Stewart's head. He fell straight to the floor with the pistol going off and its bullet missing my ear by an inch.

Stewart twisted to get up but a fist came down hard on his jaw and his eyes rolled back into his head as he went limp. Teddy had the revolver now, but Cameron stood astride over the killer.

My beau looked up at me with his clear blue eyes, his blond

hair glimmering in the lamplight, or was it a halo? He said in his deep voice, "Sorry to barge in like this, Miss Furlough, but I had a delivery to make." He reached into his pocket and produced a small little package.

"You weren't eavesdropping, were you?"

"That would be impolite, I was just observing you through the keyhole."

Unwrapping the package, he revealed a small box. My heart sank to my feet. I could guess what might be inside and I wasn't ready. If he were to propose, even in front of all these witnesses, I couldn't say yes. I knew he was caring; I knew he was ever so handsome, but we could not be yoked together unless we shared exactly the same faith. How would we resolve differences if the Bible were not our arbiter, God our counsellor? Who would judge between us? We would be left to sort it out with our own selfish selves, each his own prosecutor, defender, and judge. Endless rankling. It's not that Cameron rejected Christ, it's that he had never made it conclusive to me that he embraced him wholeheartedly. He was ever the mysterious man, even to me. I needed clarity. I could not do otherwise.

"I carried out a couple of errands with you in mind, Miss Furlough, while I was in Saint Jo. Firstly to a land agent, and yes, the Weber house was briefly in the name of Stewart Winslow, but it takes a pair of spectacles to decipher the name on the title. My guess is that the aged and ailing Mr. Weber, when he learned his daughter and grandchildren had all died, agreed to sell Mr. Winslow his house and the land warrant on the cheap, if Mr. Winslow would take care of his final expenses. And I will give credit to Stewart, he saw to it that Mr. Weber had a fine funeral when the day came. The undertaker affirmed it."

"What an evil man," observed Mr. Martin looking down upon the unconscious Mr. Winslow. "And to think he wears a skull like that. Who would have guessed?"

"Well, Mr. Martin," Cameron said, "we all have choices to make, no matter what we look like. And Miss Furlough here, beautiful as she is, also needs to make one." He opened the box and in it gleamed a sparkling ring. "Would you be mine, so that I could be yours? Will you marry me?"

"Oh, yes!"

AUTHOR'S NOTE

Many of the names, events, essays, and speeches found in this story are taken from the pages of Brownville's *Nebraska Advertiser* and a few other sources dating to the year 1857. Addy's Fourth of July speech, for example, is taken from a woman's open letter to the *Nebraska Advertiser*; Addy's article decrying racism comes from an article found in an 1857 edition of the *Ladies Repository*. However, I want to point out that the Friend murders, although they did occur in 1856, did not take place near Brownville, but rather four miles south of Saint Joseph, Missouri. Originally, I did think they happened in Brownville, and I found several posts on the internet that referred to them as a Brownville tragedy. Even Marion Marsh Brown's *The Story of Brownville*, a history of the town, places the incident at Brownville. Why the confusion? Because the 1856 *Nebraska Advertiser* article states that the murders happened "a few miles below this city." What the *Advertiser's* editor did, of course, was to simply copy the *Saint Joseph Gazette's* story verbatim onto the page of his own newspaper. A summary report of the affair and the outcome of the trial can be found in the *History of Buchanan County and St. Joseph, Missouri*. I decided to remain faithful to the story of Brownville and keep the murders in Nebraska Territory. After all, it's historical fiction and authors have license to do such things. Also, I'd already written much of my story before I found out, and I was too lazy to start over. Finally, I think I wanted to see justice for the Friend family. In Saint Joseph, the culprits got off scot-free. Not in Brownville, by golly.

www.prestonshires.com